Pacific Paradox

Kev Richardson

A Wings ePress, Inc.
Historical Adventure Novel

Wings ePress, Inc.

Edited by: Karen Babcock
Copy Edited by: Joan Powell
Senior Editor: Pat Evans
Executive Editor: Marilyn Kapp
Cover Artist: Trisha FitzGerald

All rights reserved

Wings ePress Books
www.wingsepress.com

Copyright © 2012 by Kevin Richardson
ISBN 978-1-61309-947-6

Published In the United States Of America

Wings ePress Inc.
3000 N. Rock Road
Newton, KS 67114

gave up thought of more. He simply decried his luck in having chanced on a master first up.

And yesterday, his birthday passed unnoticed, at least until dinner, when he acquainted Siegfried with the fact. Those at his table toasted him, yet most were German, and he couldn't but help feel that all except Siegfried seemed somehow reticent about fraternising with anybody from England.

The war's been over twenty years, for God's sake. Can't they yet put behind them that they got beaten? And wasn't Father absolutely furious at Chamberlain for having agreed that Germany should have its way with the Sudetenland! But shouldn't the fact that we did it illustrate that we are at one with them?

But I don't really care. Who needs them? Hitler's going to be satisfied with Continental Europe, so why be upset with us? And I've always been taught that when there's one in a small crowd who doesn't speak the common language, they're given consideration. Yet other than Siegfried, none has considered it.

So he didn't particularly enjoy mealtimes either, except that he found many of the unfamiliar tastes in German cooking delightfully exotic—from soups to desserts. He would like to have discussed these with those at his table, yet when raising the subject, there was little response. Siegfried then explained how English names for ingredients would be unknown by people with only a little English language.

"Even me," he had summed up.

So he read every single piece of printed material Ego had advised him to pack.

The young cabin steward who made their beds each morning and supervised the middle-aged *hausfrau* who vacuumed and dusted one day brought three English-language novels from the First Class library, should Beresford want to read them; two he did indeed retain—one a murder mystery, the other an epic tale of Kitchener in the Sudan.

"*Ich heisse Karl,*" the steward introduced himself.

Beresford chose not to extend his own name, nor offer a hand.

"*Danke sehr,*" he responded, exhausting nearly all his knowledge of German.

Karl did a little shuffle, almost of embarrassment, it seemed. He then smiled and took the unwanted novel away.

Beresford felt chuffed.

That's what I do call service.

He suddenly felt more pleased with himself—someone had, at last, noticed him.

Even if only a fellow of servant class, yet it was jolly decent of him.

~ * ~

Panama Canal was an eye-opener.

Beresford had his sea legs by then and found he could walk confidently, almost anyway—at least without consciously having to be careful of each step. Every morning he would 'test out' the state of the ocean as his feet hit the floor—which 'gait' was called for, that for calm sea, or medium, or rough? How he must tense his body to react to his gait? And he no longer, in calm to medium conditions, needed to grasp the rail along the passageways or even on the stairs.

And he was bemused by the fact that, having been sailing from east to west all the way to Colon, once entering the canal, the direction to Panama and the Pacific, was in fact west to east...

...Or if one should be asked to be more specific, then sou-east by south.

The man-made lengths of canal were, he felt, surprisingly narrow. The *Konig* wasn't a big ship, yet even the pilot who had come aboard needed exacting concentration to keep her from bumping the loch-sides. He could only imagine how tense every soul aboard must be on the largest of ships. All were clinging to rails as it was, every now and again leaving the port side to follow progress on the starboard. And he found the lochs they must be bound in when changing levels even more exciting. And there were many huge lakes within the isthmus.

And at Panama he farewelled Siegfried.

"For your friendship, thank you," he told Beresford. "I am sure you will much learn as you the islands travel."

Beresford tried reading what was behind the smile on the German's face yet couldn't grasp it.

"And thank you too, Siegfried. And good luck with your bridge."

For the rest of the journey, he was to have the cabin to himself. The only Second Class passengers coming aboard were doubles. Yet they discharged much cargo there, and took on other—all of which took a week.

The changes in the dining room seating arrangements with the fewer number of passengers worked well for Beresford Branson. His table now comprised, apart from himself, only two of the Germans he had shared with—the elderly diplomat Dieter and his Frau, along with three French schoolteachers returning to their assignment after holidaying in the Caribbean. And as Beresford could at least converse with the French—two fellows in their twenties and the woman he assessed around the thirty mark—and the Germans being also comfortable with it, French became the mealtime language. For the rest of the journey, it enabled Beresford to quickly realise that, even including the Germans, he had at last found friends.

"You teach where?" he asked the Frenchies, and all were in Papeete on three-year contracts.

"And we have options to extend our tenures if we wish," they explained.

"I am in my fourth year," declared Francoise. "I teach high school English."

"I have just signed on for my second term," said Gaston. "I teach fourth and fifth grade English and German."

"And I have just finished my first year teaching second and third grade English," said Pascal.

So Beresford had three friends with whom he could converse in either language, so was highly delighted. And they included him in their interests.

"Language is always a problem when one runs across words in the vernacular," Francoise told him. "I do hope you will call me to task if I should fall into that without thinking," she added once he'd nodded.

"And you do the same for me, please," he replied.

"What brings you all the way from Britain to Tahiti?" the boys asked.

"My father believes I need to broaden my horizons. I've three years in which to see and learn what I can before beginning a career. He decided that finding my way among third-world islands would be good for me. I feel I've been sentenced to serving a penance."

"Good heavens, no," exclaimed Gaston. "You should see it as opportunity. That is why I am here. I applied for this post so I could broaden my horizons. Being exposed to other cultures is a marvellous opportunity. I will return to France a far more worldly man."

"And me too," declared Pascal. "Except that I don't want to return. I have no family and want to see the world. If I can better my English by trying to teach it, that more than doubles the horizons I have available. Does that make sense?"

Beresford had never been in a situation of having to even ponder such things.

"In one way it does. Yet isn't teaching a rather limited career?"

That left Pascal pondering.

"Not at all. Teaching doubles my opportunities. I can teach French to English-speaking children, or the other way about. I have learned that the vast number of islanders speak only their own dialects. Tahitians speak French only to Frenchmen. In British islands they speak English only to Britons. That's the way it works all over the world."

Beresford was amazed. If he had ever given it thought, he would have imagined that every third-world native was eager to learn English. He had never at all given thought that any language but English could even be in anyone's mind.

"Good heavens!" he eventually said.

Three

Karl again brought books for Beresford, who began to notice that he did so every day after having taken away one already read. He always brought at least two so there was a choice. And he always had ready smiles, which not many of the Germans aboard gave him.

He was a handsome young man who wore his uniform proudly.

"I do appreciate this, Karl," Berry told him.

And the boy faltered... *"Ach, Entschuldigung! Ich spricht die Englisch nicht."* And he simply stood there, smiling, as if waiting for a response.

Berry was conscious of the *hausfrau* pausing her vacuum cleaner, glaring up at the fellow with icicle eyes.

"Zuschliessen!" she snapped in a half whisper.

The comments of both were lost on the Englishman, yet he noted how Karl suddenly turned away to open the wardrobe and begin tidying Berry's clothes.

When she had finished her cleaning, Karl finished his tidying, again fluffed up Beresford's pillow before picking up the unwanted library book to smile sweetly before leading the *hausfrau* into the corridor.

Huh. These Germans sure are strange people.

~ * ~

Crossing the equator was a great bit of fun.

When the Frenchies, over breakfast one morning, explained the ritual, Beresford was astounded. As he had become conscious of the heat increasing, also the glare of sunlight off the waves increasing day-by-day, he had been reducing his clothing until even borrowing shorts from Gaston, who was his build, and shirts with short sleeves. Never in his life had he been seen, beyond the privacy of his room, except occasionally with brother Thomas sharing a bathroom at *Folly Drift*, with bare legs or bare arms showing. In northeast England's July he would go so far outdoors as to sometimes drape his blazer over his shoulder rather than wear it, yet the thought of appearing in public with bare knees and elbows was abhorrent.

However even in winter approaching the equator, he was glad of the loan of 'tropical' wear.

"Will I be able to buy such in Papeete," he asked, which reduced all the Frenchies to raucous laughter.

"It is standard street wear," they explained.

"Even in the schoolroom?"

"For much of the year, for us younger ones, yes."

All his dining companions had previously crossed the equator and experienced the initiation ceremony.

"You need not fear it," they explained. "At first it feels embarrassing, but as you see others being initiated, you begin enjoying it as well as everybody else."

And they explained it to him.

"I simply will not be in it," he declared. "I shall politely decline."

Which brought more laughter. "You have no option. If you try to hide, they will search until they find you. Then it will be the worse for you if you don't submit."

"It is a time funny," Frau Dieter explained. "I, it already do. And my Zetan *hier*."

Zetan Dieter acknowledged that with a hearty laugh.

For three days before the event, arrangements could not go unnoticed. The decks were swabbed to even more gleaming, spaces were cleared and many signs in German began appearing in all public places.

Beresford could understand little of it, but as he spent most of his time with the Frenchies, Gaston translated.

"They ask you to be punctual on deck tomorrow, Beresford. However, if you stay with us after breakfast, for we 'cross the line' just after ten, it seems, we will explain it to help you enjoy it."

"Please call me Berry, Gaston. All my close friends do."

He had taken quite a shine to Gaston in particular.

The more I see of the fellow, the jollier a bloke he seems—the sort of chap I would feel confident of having around once arriving in these antipodes.

"Then I am honoured, 'old chap'." And they shook hands on it.

"Do you enjoy the company of Francoise, Berry?"

A strange question. I wonder what's coming?

"Indeed yes. And I'm inclined to feel she is feeling somewhat lonely on this vessel."

"I am glad you see that, for it is the point of my question. She is indeed feeling rather left out of things. Even when booking, she was averse to travelling on a German ship, yet already we will be late getting home. So is it all right with you if we include her in our talks and chats? Pascal and I think that is the way friendship should be. Do you agree?"

"Oh, yes. Rather, dear chap."

Yet having given the right answer, Berry then thought on it... *Is that how some people see friendship? That they go out of their way to make the odd-man-out feel wanted?*

He'd never bothered to think about a third person.

Surely every soul is responsible for finding his or her own pleasures without being pandered to. Haven't I promised myself to simply go along with what I meet in this outside world while getting a measure of the differences? And Francoise is indeed a pleasant woman. And who knows, that when in Papeete, she may be of some help to me?

And the morrow indeed proved a wonderful day.

He had heard of the 'crossing the line' tradition, yet had ever cast it aside.

That's only for really intrepid travellers. I've no need to give it a second thought.

Yet he was now to experience what some could describe as embarrassing torture in the name of fun. Yet he had been prepared. Thanks to at least sometimes listening to advice when a Boy Scout when it came to things like hiking and camping, he now decided to undergo whatever they might want him to do, rather than lose face.

So he did it.

And indeed found it fun. He was stripped to only under-shorts, adorned with a wig of coarse rope, chucked into a net that was lifted by the ship's crane, to be given a five-second dunk in the briny.

He came up spitting and spluttering, yet by the time he had regained his breath, he was ready to laugh with the rest—whether a forced or natural laugh was left for all the 'been-there-done-that' passengers to ponder.

~ * ~

In the lounge that evening, a broadband radio programme was airing for whoever wanted to listen. Every German present was eagerly listening, for it was 'Berlin calling'. And as the Frenchies were also lending an ear, Beresford joined them, Gaston whispering snippets in his ear at every opportunity.

"Germany has invaded Czechoslovakia. Troops, tanks and batteries of artillery are streaming across the border," Gaston whispered. "It is war!"

Bloody hell! It's barely a year since Britain and Italy signed an agreement with Hitler, giving him the Sudetenland. And Chamberlain comes home waving documents in the air, assuring us all that it will be "Peace in Our Time"—that Germany is now satisfied and has no more annexation intentions. What a bastard of a man, telling such lies! He already has the Saar. And Austria. And the Sudetenland. Yet now wants more. When will he bloody stop?

Francoise beckoned her three male escorts. "Let's move out," she whispered. And every German in the room was indeed conscious of the French and English departing.

And might it seem significant too, that we are departing together?

He felt a little shiver run up his spine.

The four returned to Gaston and Pascal's cabin, Francoise buying a bottle of wine as they passed the bar.

"There is no doubt it will be war," she insisted. She poured Riesling for all while telling what was foremost in her mind.

"I was a child during the Great War, in the little town of Guise on the Oise. For three years we lived under German occupation, and every stem or branch of food we grew was taken for the German war effort. If we refused to donate the food our farmers grew, we were shot—men, women and children, old or young. And we were tortured if they thought we might know something of French or British troop movements—there was much to-ing and fro-ing of trench-lines in those days. The German soldiers were bestial. They showed no mercy, and I have great fears that all Europe is going to now be swamped by German greed. Including Britain, Beresford."

"But, Francoise, Britain last year came to Germany's aid. Our people were not happy about it, but Chamberlain gave his nod to Hitler to take the Sudetenland off Czechoslovakia. Surely that illustrates we are not his enemies."

"Dictators are never satisfied, *mon ami*. They are power-hungry ogres. Look at Spain—not only did Hitler send his Luftwaffe to bomb Spanish cities but supplied Franco most of his munitions. So as recently as last month, Europe has another dictator—and a neighbour of France at that! And Stalin is rattling sabres against both Poland and Finland. There is no way that Europe can avoid another great conflict, and my heart bleeds for all its people."

She began to weep.

"And those kraut bastards up there in the lounge are all smirking inside," declared Gaston as he wrapped an arm around his friend's shoulders. "They'd have noticed us walk out, all right. And at breakfast they will look at us as if we are already their pawns."

Berry was indeed, now, struggling to understand some of the French idiom, yet he was left in no doubt of the message each was giving.

A week later, when within days of reaching Papeete, the evening broadband from Berlin reported Germany and Russia signing a Pact of Friendship.

The four were indeed now feeling bonded in a bloc, glad that they were soon to be quit of the atmosphere engulfing *SS Konig Wolfgang*.

Four

Beresford was invited to move into Gaston and Pascal's apartment in downtown Papeete, which he was both relieved and anxious to do.

"We won't ask you to share rent," they explained, "but would appreciate if we split three ways on food? We eat out three or four nights a week, but you will find things a lot cheaper than England. Polynesian food is both cheap and exciting, with plenty of seafood, chicken and pork. But beef steak is expensive. Does this sound all right to you?"

He didn't have to think about it. It would be far better to be with them than having to struggle in a strange place when he couldn't afford rent of any kind. He would 'play things by ear' for a week or two—see how big a hole eating with them would make in his hundred pounds. Half of his mother's twenty pounds had already gone in beer and wine aboard ship and ashore in Panama, and buying clothes for the sub-tropics would eat up the rest.

"We each have mopeds," they explained. "Gasoline is expensive, and there is really nowhere to go that is not easily accessible by bike."

Once ashore he could see what they meant. Traffic drove on the right, of course, and whilst there were hundreds of mopeds scuttling through it, there were very few motorcars or even pick-ups—those there were, mostly old and rusted. Taxis were pedal-bikes, and big, buxom Polynesian women pedalled tandems with a baby's cradle strapped to the rear seat.

Papeete seemed the sort of town in which one could find all sorts of facilities within walking distance. There were no large buildings, indeed few of even three stories. On the streets, old motorbuses belched black smoke as if trying to out-do the rusted vehicles. And the sun was mercilessly hot. He even wore his pith helmet off the ship. The four rented three pairs of pedal-bike-rickshaws to take them to their apartments, no more than a half mile from dockside. Gaston and Beresford rode in one, Francoise in the second with half the luggage and Pascal in the third with the other half.

They rode in line to the boys' apartment, taking their luggage and dismissing two of the rickshaws, leaving Francoise to carry on only another street to her own.

The boys' apartment was small but delightful. It was on the upper floor of a tenement, on the corner of its building, with an indoors and outdoors. Inside was but two rooms, seeming small only because the ceilings were so high. The bedroom had two single beds, a wardrobe and commode, with a cubicle-sized bathroom off it. The living room had a four-seat dining table, two comfortable divans with lots of pillows, a coffee table and bookshelves, and tucked into a tiny corner was the kitchenette. Both rooms had an outsize ceiling fan. The whole, Beresford couldn't help but compare, was but fractionally larger than his bedroom at *Folly Drift*.

Yet as well as colourful, it was light and airy. An entire wall of sliding glass graced one side, and windows backed the dining area on another. Outside was an L-shaped terrace larger than the entire inside, with glorious views to lusciously green mountains. The balcony 'railing' was all a broad ledge with potted plants of exotic bougainvillea in an array of colours. The balcony was furnished with a cane lounge, and two hammocks were slung in shaded areas. Jardinières of bougainvillea were scattered around the terrace floor. In a sheltered corner stood a gramophone and cupboards, with a dartboard on the wall, a punching bag suspended from the ceiling and an exercise pedal-bike.

"Ah," the Englishman exclaimed. "How delightful."

"We spend most of our time out here. Weather permitting, we do our work here. You would be surprised how much homework teachers must do, even doubled around exam time. And we exercise here when the streets are too wet or too hot for walking. We often eat here and sometimes sleep here."

Pascal pointed to a ceramic contrivance including a metal grill with considerable ash piled under it. "That is a Polynesian griller. We use small chunks of coal, which can be bought cheaply, and oil to set a fire for grilling meats and fish and brewing coffee. As you see, it gets lots of use."

They had arrived on a Friday, and school term was to begin come Tuesday.

"Schools have a strange timetable here," Pascal explained. "We have an extremely long holiday at this time of year—long enough for business people to sail to Europe for Christmas and back again, then only one other break in the rest of the year. Easter sometimes falls in our southern summer break, sometimes not. And we have two weeks in July for Bastille and culture celebrations."

"We start school Tuesday," Gaston added, "so this gives us three days to help you acclimatise—to see that you can cope once we disappear for eight or nine hours each day."

Beresford laughed. "It's going to take all that time, I fear, for me to get my thoughts around just using your money. Mentally converting pounds, shillings and pence into decimals is not easy."

"Another serious difference for you, my friend, is stepping off a pavement. You instinctively look first to your right. If you do that here as you move into the road, you can find yourself fatally flattened by a bus driving into your back."

So there were many differences for him to get used to, right down to listening to the radio over breakfast, when it was already 4 p.m. in Durham and 5 p.m. in Europe, where daily news was nearly all on Nazi Germany, or occasionally on how far Japan had progressed since invading China. And he was feeling the humidity; he could see why so many locals wore short trousers and short-sleeved shirts.

"We are already through our wet season of high summer, Berry," said Gaston. "The 'wet' officially ends with the arrival of March, although it and April can still have showers every day. So, yes, it is still humid. Another month is the regular start of glorious weather. It will be mild, fine and dry for May through November.

"Tomorrow we need to shop for food, also help you buy clothes for the sub-tropics. Already you have seen most of the men outside are in short sleeves."

Pascal looked at his watch. "We have to report in, Gaston."

"Ah, yes." They needed to phone the school to confirm being home and that they would be in on time come Tuesday.

"There is a pay-phone in the landlord's apartment downstairs for local calls, Berry. But if you wish to call overseas, you must go to the post office. They will raise your number and time your call from the moment it answers."

So he was left alone for several minutes to rue the fact that he could not afford to call home. The "no reverse-charge calls" threat still rang in his ears.

I shall write, to tell them I arrived safely.

Just the thought of home had him a little homesick.

Oh how I need to tell them of the magic of the endless oceans, the sun playing tricks on the eyes as it glistens on the restless water. I shan't tell them I was seasick but can make a big thing of crossing the line. Mater will enjoy that. And I'll ask at the post office if they freely hold mail until I call for it, so I can give them that as my address.

The boys were a long time. Berry waited on the terrace, gazing at the mountain, watching the clouds wisping around the green peaks. He was used to mountaintops being rocky crags, yet here they were smothered in greenery so thick that one couldn't see spots of colour where flowering trees must surely bloom. It was getting towards mid-afternoon, and the clouds certainly didn't seem to know that this was still part of the rainy season. All were white cumulus, lazily rolling and sensually twisting into each other.

He was sitting poring over a magazine when the boys arrived carrying éclairs, three bottles of beer, fish to barbeque for dinner and croissants for breakfast.

"We decided on eating in tonight, Berry. Is that all right with you?"

"Jolly good," he answered.

They talked on the food expenses, agreeing that whoever paid when they went shopping for things that were shared got reimbursed once home.

"When friends or family visit," Gaston explained, "we do that. I am usually exchequer, paying all, then once home, agree the sharing. Yet if one is the sole buyer, like you shopping for clothes, for instance, you pay. Pascal and I work that way even between ourselves."

Beresford could find no argument.

"What do I owe you for the food you just bought?"

"The beer is on us, just to welcome you," said Gaston. "The food was two-twenty, so your share is seventy sou. And we were given free ice with the beer because the shopkeeper's daughter has an eye for Pascal."

For which quip Gaston got a punch in the shoulder from his friend.

Beresford almost grudgingly paid his seventy sous—ungrudgingly realising it was fair, yet begrudging the sight of it disappearing out of his pocket into somebody else's.

They managed to squeeze the fish into the icebox but decided on drinking the beer there and then as aperitif to dinner—and while the ice lasted.

So after a hectic day, what with arrival, getting through customs and settling in at home, all agreed on an early dinner and retirement.

One of the sunbathing beds on the terrace doubled as a guest bed, and cushions from the lounge doubled as pillows. A spare mosquito net could be hung from strategically placed hooks in the ceilings, subject to whether the visitor wanted to sleep on the terrace or in the living-room—yet on the terrace, one could stretch out.

The terrace and the delightful aroma of jasmine that climbed from its jardinière up one of the roof pillars had considerable appeal to Beresford.

"Have your mosquitoes been tamed?" he asked.

"Day and night, if not using the net, rub citronella over all flesh not covered by clothing or pyjamas. And yes, all are tame, but young ones might be tempted to try the blood of Englishmen."

"Top marks for humour," the grinning Englishman told Gaston.

He slept outside, using the net, yet had the problem of readjusting to not rolling with the ocean's swells.

~ * ~

If the Frenchies wondered at their visitor not offering to help lay out the breakfast things or even ask if he could help in any way, they said nothing, simply raised eyebrows on noticing him sit with a magazine, waiting to be served.

Same as with the barbecue last night, flashed through Gaston's mind.

Same as with the dishwashing last night, flashed through Pascal's.

There wasn't much to serving breakfast, of course, traditional French breakfasts being extremely light—croissants and jam with a huge bowl of coffee, whereas for Englanders, it was often the biggest meal of the day...a couple of eggs boiled, scrambled, poached or fried, with two or three bacon rashers and two or three sausages and several cups of tea.

The Frenchies rose on finishing, Beresford picking up a magazine to await the next course. He was still reading when the dishwashing was done and the lads were making out their shopping list.

"Can you pile up your used garments, Berry? If we drop it off at the laundry on our way to the market, it will be ready to pick up tomorrow morning."

The Englishman looked up in surprise. His eyes roved the breakfast dishes in the strainer, including his own, then the room where all the divan cushions that had been left higgledy-piggledy last night were by now tidied, and his eyes caught, as they scanned the room, the open door to the boys' bedroom to note that their beds were tidily made whilst his own on the terrace remained in its dishabille.

It suddenly flashed through his mind that maybe he was expected to do his own.

And I guess that's probably reasonable in the situation. I just never thought of it.

"Laundry? Oh, that had not entered my mind. But I shall be buying clothes today, so what is soiled can wait."

Gaston smiled.

"What is soiled, there, Berry, are not your clothes, but mine. Otherwise, by mid-week I shall have to go to school naked."

Berry smiled. "By Jove. That would be a lark, wouldn't it?"

He brought his luggage into the room and extracted a great pile of things that he had never thought to send to the laundry whilst aboard. Then he noticed he'd inadvertently packed one of the *Konig's* novels that he hadn't yet read. He put it aside.

That will give me something to do whilst these fellows are at school all next week.

Pascal dropped a ball of twine on the divan.

"Here, Berry, bundle up your things. You'll find scissors in the kitchen drawer. Write your name on some notepaper and push it under the string. That way she can keep it separate for you."

Oh, looks like I'm expected to pay for Gaston's clothes too. Yet on reflection, I guess that's fair enough. It was good of him to lend them to me.

On the way to the market, it being two blocks, and having deposited their three separate parcels at the laundry, the sights for Beresford's eyes were all wonders. Polynesians outnumbered white people twenty to one, and the women wore the most brightly coloured cotton prints, none shapely, all seeming dropped over their fat bodies like artist smocks, in either bare feet or crude sandals. They jabbered away with friends in their own language and laughed uninhibitedly as if unaware of anybody around them. And traffic was crazy—motorised vehicles, bicycles, pedal rickshaws and honking buses seemingly vied for clear passage as if they thought such unalike conveyances could all keep at the same steady pace.

They stopped at the local *quincaillerie* to have a key cut for Beresford, and it was nothing like ironmongeries in England where they were like any other store—a counter where one ordered your pound of nails, stick of paraffin wax or pint of kerosene. Here was a walk-in workshop with a smith's anvil at the back by a roaring fire, dirty shelves stacked with poorly packaged tools and hardware items if packaged at all. All was a great jumble. Yet the key was ordered, and they were told it would be ready in thirty minutes.

The market proved another eye-opener. Market days in English villages were organised affairs—fresh meats and seafood in a separate hall, greengroceries in a section all their own, cakes and pastries in another—yet here it was chaos. It seemed market gardeners had arrived with their wares and claimed whatever spot was vacant. Meat was laid out on one table, and right next to it were cakes and pastries. Store attendants seemed not too fussed that flies might eat too much before somebody bought whatever. Lemonade and other drink stalls were set up alongside native clothing, and next to it was a table of bibles.

Oh, what a shambles, he thought.

Yet the boys knew their way around. They had their lists and seemed to know where to go buy what they wanted. Beresford had all he could do to keep up with either one.

"We try to get here early each Saturday, before the crowds arrive. Polynesians love their beds, and they seldom shop before mid-day, so the entire afternoons are chaotic. Also, early means a better choice of vegetables and meat. You wallowed in your éclair last night, I noticed, so do you want to leave these desserts and we call at a *pâtisserie?*"

"Oh, yes, Gaston. Cream-cakes are my dream food. 'Plenty of cream means plenty of health,' my mother insists."

"My mother too, although my father claims dairy products are not good for us."

"What? Milk, butter and cheese? Surely these are what builds up our strength."

"Ah! That's what we forgot—cheese." And he began to dart off, before turning back. "What cheese do you like? Do you have a favourite?"

"I like *Camembert.*"

"Me too. So I won't ask Pascal—he has a different favourite. Oh, and I'll get some *pâté foie.*"

He dove off again.

Meanwhile Pascal returned, pushing his way through people. "I hope you like cheese. I just bought some *Roquefort.* It is my favourite."

"Oh that sounds nice."

Not too laden yet with food to last them a week with some evenings out sampling Polynesian food, they called to pick up the key. Beresford wondered why, the key having been put in his hands, that his friends and the ironmonger, a Tahitian as robust as was likely his wife, all stood watching him—as if waiting.

"He waits to be paid, Beresford," said an amused Gaston. Berry suddenly realised this was a cost specifically for him, and he should pay direct, so he turned to the fellow.

Behind him, Pascal gave a thumbs up to Gaston.

Berry shoved his hand into his pocket for the second time since cashing in pounds for Polynesian francs at the customs office, conscious of so soon having to part with several more sous out of his limited funds.

Yes, of course. I must get into the habit of thinking about such things when a guest in their home.

He resolved not to fall into the same trap come afternoon when they would shop for his clothes. Which thought reminded him that they also had to pick up laundry tomorrow morning.

Then I shall pay for all of my bundle including Gaston's clothes. That would be a nice gesture.

~ * ~

That afternoon, rather than wait until Sunday, Gaston took Beresford shopping for sensible clothes while Pascal cleaned house. Once returned they found him cooking a chocolate dessert for when arriving home after a Polynesian dinner out.

Before bed, Beresford wrote his second letter home.

Dearest Mater and Pater,

How can I describe my good fortune in meeting up with two French lads on the ship out of Panama (did you get my letter from there?). They are both jolly fine fellows. It was a most pleasant voyage the rest of the way, and I am accommodated with them. You will be surely pleased to hear that I am paying my way. Last night was an incredible experience. They introduced me to a Polynesian restaurant where even the poor Polynesians eat, apart from tourists. I experienced food like octopus cooked in coconut milk. Also a side dish for which I forget its name, yet it is pawpaw and banana mashed in a yam starch, then dipped in coconut cream; chicken braised in palm-tree oil and pineapple, served with rice cooked in coconut juice rather than water; and what they call Polynesian fried rice with chilli peppers and baby pork, scrambled with wild swamp-turtle eggs and bacon. You simply cannot imagine the exotic tastes. My one third share of the dinner was an expensive fourteen and seven-pence, which of course I cannot indulge in every night—yet the experience was something I shall ever cherish. And with this sort of food throughout the entire South Pacific, I look forward with excitement to the one thousand and fifty-one days still to serve of my confinement.

Your loving son...

Five

Come Sunday, using both mopeds, he was taken to the beach.

He had yesterday declined to purchase the patterned cotton shirts that were even cheaper than plain colours. He bought the more formal plain in three different 'quiet' shades. And knee-length shorts to match, and knee-high socks that were worn with them. And sandals.

"These shirts and shorts can be worn in 'mix-and match' style," it was explained.

No one made jokes about his lily-white skin any more, because two weeks in shorts aboard had fixed that problem. He had gone happily through the lobster stage and was quite chuffed when finding the pink turning to a light tan.

He was advised to buy what to him seemed a 'daring' cut of swimming shorts—body tight and brief, with still a belt buckle.

"All French men wear these," he was told. "Of all ages. And they are still more formal than Polynesians wear. Theirs are far too revealing for my liking."

Most Tahitian beaches were black sand, he was informed at breakfast.

"Papeete's beaches fall into that category, so Beachcomber Hotel imports white sand from south of the island and spreads over the black, so this is where most Europeans go to swim. It suits the hotel, which also has a pool, so even folk who prefer pools to salt water come here—especially on Sundays. Right next door is the naval base, so ratings also use it. A condition is that visitors cannot bring their own food, but the poolside food is not too expensive. We hire a security locker, and we use the guest tables and chairs and rubber beds poolside. The entire site is delightfully shaded by palm-trees."

And so it proved. It was indeed welcoming, even for one living on non-renewable funds.

On the way home, they picked up their laundry.

"There are surely free beaches on the island?" Beresford tossed off as a question rather than statement. "I could rent a bicycle, to go surfing during the week?"

Both friends frowned. "Yes," replied Pascal, "there are many beaches nearby, yet with the naval base west of town and docks and ship-building east along the coast, the shoreline is spoiled by oil and grease. You must go a long way to find what the tourist brochures promise. This is why Beachcomber Hotel is so popular."

~ * ~

So there was much to learn, and it was quickly obvious that absolutely everything he touched cost pounds, shillings and pence.

He had, by now, worked out that his British pound in Polynesian parlance was a franc-twenty. Or a Polynesian franc was sixteen shillings and eight-pence. Every sou was tuppence.

Being worth tuppence each, makes the sou an easy conversion, but a franc at 16/8 is simply something too difficult to cope with.

He tore a page from his notebook and made a list beginning with one franc equalling sixteen shilling and eight-pence, down to ten francs being eight pounds six and eight-pence. He tucked it into his wallet. And he trusted his new friends enough that, when they told him to be careful of pickpockets and muggers, he had them secrete in

What They Are Saying About

Pacific Paradox

5 Star!

It is a sensitive story of a naïve young man growing into his manhood.

Multi-published historical writer, ***Kev Richardson's*** latest release: ***PACIFIC PARADOX,*** reveals WWII from an English man's perspective. We see the war through the eyes of worldly naive character, ***Beresford***, the aristocratic son of Baronet Sir Thomas Branson, who has been sent out into the every-day world to earn his own worldly experiences. From his lucky adventures, to his incredible misadventures, he discovers a whole new attitude towards life. He becomes involved in the war effort in the Pacific Islands. Kev's accurate historical research is prominent in this telling. This is a wonderful adventure tale as Berry finally becomes the man his father can respect.

JoEllen
Conger Book Reviews, USA

One

Christmas 1938 passed quietly at *Folly Drift*.

Sir Thomas was, despite the young age of his sons, ageing, and continued to insist that the family had been in residence since *Dun Cow*.

Dun Cow was local idiom. Rural English lore had local idiom aplenty, and this particular tenet was founded on St. Cuthbert's bier. When in transit not too far from where *Folly Drift* was to be founded, the bier had become stuck in mud. It could not be shifted further, so camp was struck. And that very saint on that very night appeared in a dream to the monk Eadmer, advising that, should it be made known the casket was being taken to DunHolm, it would be freed of its stricture. However no one had ever heard of DunHolm. Next morn, Eadmer came across a milkmaid wandering the foothills of Mount Joy, looking for her dun cow. He followed her, finding the cow by the River Wear. So the bier miraculously freed itself from the mud and was brought to where a small church was erected to house it. That was how DunHolm, or Durham as the name became over time, was founded—and *Dun Cow* was remembered in the district. And oft quoted by Sir Thomas.

Young Thomas, in line to inherit the title, well remembered his grandfather whispering that the wider family doubted their roots could be traced back a thousand years.

"The family Bible dates back only three hundred since Cromwell's Puritan scoundrels burned every old Bible they could find," he had said, "at the terrible risk of folk having their head on a pike in the town square. And with baptism and marriage recorded in Durham only a hundred years prior, how can anyone, with surety, trace the line further?"

Yet young Thomas didn't try to dissuade his father.

Let the old boy enjoy the halo he believes hovers over his head. I will certainly not try convincing my son, in turn, of it. I'll leave the hand-notes in the family Bible be the judge.

Younger son Beresford, however, was of a different ilk from brother Thomas.

Beresford saw his future one of good fortune. With inherent responsibility on his brother's shoulders, he saw family money ensuring the younger son a comfortable life. At nineteen years of age, he had no desire to even finish his degree at Durham University—he would rather enjoy life partying and charging around the hedge-row lanes of England's northeast in his MG.

"What the pup needs, Mother," Sir Thomas told his wife, the long-suffering Lady Alis, who persistently asked him to desist calling her *mother*, "is a stretch of discovering what life beyond the protection of our cultured garden is really like. The wilds of Africa, for instance, or the cannibal islands in the South Pacific."

"I doubt, dear husband, that our lad is ready to cope with such dangers. Even visiting London, and even then under his brother's steadying hand, he found himself in dire straights."

"Yes, and a pretty penny it cost me getting him out of them. Getting drunk in a pub dining room is one thing, but getting to the men's room by jumping from table to table upsetting everybody's food, wine and ale is another. He needs blooding in common sense, that's what he bloody needs. And he will only learn it by having to get out of scrapes using his own bloody resources. What he lacks, Mother, is Forward Vision."

~ * ~

Spennymoor had suffered severely, not only because of the great economic depression of the early thirties, but since the decline of the coal mining industry and its ironworks in general. The district's gentry had the benefits of the area's deer-shooting bounties of both coin in the pocket and game on their tables, yet the less fortunate were only now beginning to find low-paying jobs and sustainable food, even if spare food was not yet stacked on larder shelves.

Sir Thomas and Lady Alis spent considerable time and energy supporting the newly found Spennymoor Settlement, an arts community founded to encourage budding artists as well as other interests. It was part of keeping up community spirit, which they both saw as important. It helped locals increase awareness of new projects and inspired interest in current affairs and job opportunities. It established a library that brought people together. It encouraged a number of new 'cottage' industries—home-cooked take-out meals and house cleaning for expectant mothers and such. And each enterprise created other 'scratch-my-back' opportunities. *Folly Drift* often opened its doors and gardens for community fetes and musical recitals.

Whilst young Thomas threw his inspirations and time into helping the project, Beresford would have none of it. He was too engrossed in plotting how he would meet the challengers thrown at him by his father.

"Get out," he'd been told, "and don't come back for three years."

He'd been challenged to take no more from the house than his own clothing and possessions he felt worth physically carrying, to start finding his way in life with no more than the hundred pounds his father would give him.

And my personal bank account has never held more than four or five pounds.

Several 'round-table' family dinners brought forth suggestions for him to ponder. All the family, and even the staff, contributed ideas. The South Pacific Island nations, of which he knew absolutely nowt, was agreed for his challenge, as was that his second-class fare would be found, including food, to Tahiti. That island group was chosen because it was closest, despite lying in the absolute antipodes. Sir Thomas chose it because, with Beresford's excellent command of the French language and Papeete having one of the most advanced infrastructures of the island nations, it should prove the most gentle introduction.

"Being French, however, young man, means it is likely they won't let you work there without a permit. Your status will be entirely that of 'foreigner'. The colonies of Samoa, Tonga and Fiji, however, are British dependencies. And maybe the Solomon Islands, although I've a feel it may fall under Australian administration like Nauru and Papua—not sure on that, lad—maybe you should check it."

"How do I do that?"

"I suggest you make that your first target in considering your new future, lad."

So Beresford realised that all the help he could expect from family had been given.

Seems I have to begin right now, listing what I should take with me. And that means deserting everything left behind. Girlfriends, for instance. I must forsake them all? Oh dear! How many should I ask to please wait for me? I should make it a few, else it leaves me quite insecure about life once returned. Nor can I take any hope of Pater helping out with a few pounds should I be in a desperate plight— he's already made that quite clear. He won't even accept reply paid telephone calls! And even insists he will pay hospitals direct, only if my admittance was, in their opinion, a life-threatening one.

And he won't even contribute to my fare home!

Nor accept letters from me if there is excess stamp-tax due on them!

So 'hope' was the main thing he would be leaving without—except only hope for a safe return once he could prove to his father that he was reformed and a son to then be proud of.

It all sounds like they're telling me I'm not, now, a son to be proud of.

And that only reduced him to further depths of self-incrimination, which put him into an immediate sad mood.

Leaving from Liverpool in only three days' time is certainly too soon for letting myself be drawn into a sad mood. I've too little time left to overcome it. There is too much to be done, like milking all the love and affection—and help, of course—that I can garner.

Or is that mean of me?

Three days? The MG? Bloody hell—what does one have to do about mothballing a car for three years? He scratched his head. He couldn't even sell it, for it was registered in his father's name.

Murdoch should be back from dropping Pater at the station. Why have a chauffeur if he can't take care of something like that? I'll go see him—let him put it on blocks or whatever has to be done.

Three years? What sort of work am I going to find, for God's sake, in snake-infested islands, enough to feed me and also pay for a steamer home?

And that cast his quick snatch at a positive straw right back into depths.

He was starting to realise that he must concentrate, quite often, on Forward Vision.

I wonder what it feels like, to be hungry?

Two

February 1939

The family gave him sensible *bon voyage* gifts.

His father handed him the hundred pounds in small notes; his mama a declared gift of a pith helmet with mosquito gauze veil, also leather gaiters and high-ankle boots. She also quietly slipped him an envelope containing four five-pound notes. Thomas presented him with a leather satchel on a shoulder-strap containing vials of quinine against malaria, citronella to ward off mosquitos, a skin balm for sunburn and various tablets to take at the first sign of sea-sickness, smallpox, cholera, diarrhoea, scurvy, typhus or yellow fever.

All very practical of course. And Thomas was a dear, accompanying me all the way to Liverpool to help with luggage and to wave me off...

...Or could that also have been to ensure I departed?

He ended up having only one large suitcase, a leather strap over his left shoulder with his travel documents along with books and magazines, Thomas' satchel of medications over his right shoulder and his pith helmet on his head minus, at this stage, its veil.

SS Konig Wolfgang was no liner. She was a six-thousand-ton single-screw freighter-passenger vessel out of Hamburg, calling at Liverpool and Panama en-route to Tahiti.

"That's unless we get a radio call to pick up cargo at Puerto Rico or Jamaica," the master told him.

He shared a cabin as far as Panama with a German engineer on his way to Costa Rica, where his company was building a bridge. Beresford had been laid low with sea-sickness. He'd felt fine gliding down the Irish Sea, thrilled with the promise of adventure, not only crossing the Atlantic Ocean but to then venture as far again into the great Pacific. Yet on rounding the Irish Coast and Fastnet Rock into the teeth of where the infamous Gulf Stream became the North Atlantic Drift, and with winter's low-pressure gales sweeping out of the west, the ocean became a rage of rolling corrugations.

Thomas's seasick tablets he used sparingly, yet for two days he felt he wanted to die.

Already he believed it well on the cards that he would be lucky to even reach Tahiti, let alone ever get home.

"Will it be like this all the way to Panama?" he asked Siegfried, who was only slightly stricken. He had travelled much of the world, so his system was somewhat acclimatised.

"No, *mein* friend," he replied in his very Germanic English. "Dis for you maybe one day or two days. Den mit me, you can again to dinner come."

Beresford spewed again. Even the mention of food was enough to turn his stomach into what felt like revolutions. Certainly eruptions. He kept telling himself that every meal he couldn't eat was something that had already been paid for, so was proving of no benefit to him on his now tight budget. It was utter waste, and he was conscious of his need to consider every little thing an item of value.

Oh! No longer can I ignore feeling I am getting something for nothing. Everything now has value of some sort, and this illness is robbing me of taking advantage of it.

"So, Berry," he told himself, "get well quickly."

He began calling on every thread of will power in quelling the churning in his belly. The young steward had also, now, brought him some tablets.

Oh, if only I can keep them down until they've done their work on my poor innards.

And he now regretted having taken the tablets Thomas gave him.

If only the steward had brought his supply earlier, I could have saved something out of the little I could bring with me!

Yet he survived. After three days, and with the weather improving, he was suddenly hungry. He would accompany Siegfried to dinner.

"If me you, friend Beresford," the German said as they sat, "I d'a small dinner haf. D'stomach—it need come slow back."

Beresford smiled. "Not tonight, Siegfried. I am famished. I could eat a horse."

Siegfried shrugged his shoulders and reached for a menu.

"Please, mit fish, you me join—how you say? D'steam?"

"Steamed is the word. You go ahead, but I'm having steak."

Beresford ordered a salmon starter, and... "What is this, Siegfried? er.. *Rostbraten gegrillt*? It sounds good."

"Rump steak, d'grill. Big meal for d'stomach. You d'fish haf, eh?"

Beresford completed his order. "*Rostbraten gegrillt*, very rare, with baked potatoes and greens, and for dessert..."

He looked again at the menu. "...and apple-strudel."

He picked at crackers and cheese until the salmon arrived.

"I'll go easy on the drink, however, my friend," he then said, and during the meal he drank only water yet ate every skerrick of his steak and vegetables and *Apfelstrudel*.

He was thankful it was the starboard rail he was leaning on only thirty minutes later, still talking with Siegfried, when his stomach reacted. It was so quick. The wind was still blowing strongly and still from the southwest, a fortunate situation that saved all bystanders from disaster. Had it been at the port rail, it would have proved most unpleasant.

He was back in bed two more days with the most dreadful stomach cramps.

"They should have told me," he complained to Siegfried, who was more than a little taken aback.

I wonder who are 'dey'? D'doctor? D'nurse? Should I suggest that in d'future he listen to dose mit experience more? No—is my place not. I dink he man who always listen not.

~ * ~

The ship's master had not been able to give Beresford an estimated time of arrival so that he could start working on a daily budget.

"Four thousand miles yet to Panama, M'nHerr, and we not yet half so far. Then to Tahiti, three thousand more, we have. Much can happen when so far. Other side of d'world it is, M'nHerr. But radio say good weather with us stay."

Ah. Panama, Tahiti. What exotic names. But with several weeks in front of us, with only Panama to break the monotony of shipboard life, I must find something to do. And Siegfried, although the perfect gentleman, seems somehow remote. I think he likes me okay, but just wants to be alone.

Beresford was not into active sports. He preferred watching. Tennis attracted him somewhat, yet only when visitors at home were using the court and needed a partner. Or opponent. Billiards was more his line. He played a reasonable hand of snooker yet preferred billiards. Easing the same two balls around a table excited him. He would set himself the challenge of simply keeping his opponent from even getting to the table.

Just keep those two balls on the gentle roll and one can not only build a healthy score, but keep the other fellow frustrated longer.

A billiard table was the last thing one would find on a ship, of course. But he found a chess club. He would check it out.

"What was that, Ego?"

In his mind, he invariably had altercations with his alter ego. All too frequently throughout life, it had questioned decisions he had arrived after what he considered adequate judgement. When he was small, Ego had invariably taken his parents' side, most often ignored, only to be realised later that Ego had been right and Beresford wrong.

But then he would, on those occasions, justify his action by deciding there were always two ways of looking at things and that Ego couldn't expect to be always right.

Just lucky on that point, you were, old boy. Just give me a little more credit next time, will you, please?

On this occasion, Ego had urged that maybe he should be using his ample free time not on billiards or chess, but concentrating on plans once arrived.

Plenty of time ahead for that, old boy, he insisted. *Meanwhile just let me enjoy the opportunity of finding adventure in the journey.*

What Ego had also persisted in hinting was that every soul Beresford came across during his new future would be different from anyone he knew in England—that they would have different ways of looking at things, entirely different attitudes to facing problems either personal, social or business. And on what sort of jobs might be available.

These too he tossed aside until later.

Jobs? Different personalities? Different attitudes? No problem. They'll still be people, and I've always been able to get along—at school, at uni, with girls. When I get there will be time for that. Then just line'em up and let me look'em over, is what I say. It's still weeks away, and I'm looking for something right now. Something real.

He was on the lee side of the ship, and the sun was delightful. He stripped off his shirt, lay back, pulled the shirt over his face and fell asleep.

~ * ~

By the time another week had gone, he was wretchedly lonely. Only amongst the crew were there fellows his age. And certainly no girls in Second Class who weren't carefully chaperoned by mothers. And most his age, anyway, spoke little or no English. The rise of the Nazi party in Germany had seen English, in educational institutions, banished in favour of continental languages...

Russian in particular, I read somewhere.

In his first game at the chess club, he was thoroughly beaten, so he their wall-safe all his Sterling notes. He kept only a few to carry with him.

And being told that every apartment worth renting has a built-in wall-safe is also reason to expect a mugging—especially if one looks wealthy or gullibly remiss.

It was also clear what an expensive country he had come to.

"What should a fellow expect to pay for a bed-sitter with wall-safe?"

His friends both smiled, and Pascal answered. "Francoise has one. She pays four-fifty a month."

He dived for the note in his wallet, and his face went ashen.

"Three pounds fifteen? Before a man even has a bite to eat?"

He did some scribbling in his notepad and saw his entire bankroll eroding in only rent. He'd have not a penny left for food or anything else.

And here, one even has to buy drinking water!

He was really in a no-win situation.

Six

As weeks passed, he found many satisfactions as well as challenges and came to the decision that he would accept all. And, in fact, submit to no more disappointments.

"Disappointments are but states of mind," he told his friends one Saturday night when Francoise generally came for a barbecue dinner.

French style was to eat dinner late by English standards, starting around nine o'clock. And they took a long time over meals, eating slowly and talking a lot. The boys always walked her home, for it was not safe to be out alone at night, especially for a woman. She voiced her 'disappointment' at having to consider such a precaution.

"Disappointments are entirely personal outlooks," he declared. "Surely, as such, we all have the option of how we treat them."

He paused while attacking a drumstick with fingers and teeth, and French-style also, they patiently continued with their own meals until he was ready to continue.

"You people, for example," he said, which brought raised eyebrows all around. "You found in me one whose lifestyle had conditioned him to be selfish. And maybe I should add 'useless'. I was unaware of the share-and-share-alike ethic because domestic chores were always done by others. It was their role. So I was disappointed when, even so politely, you brought this to my attention. It taught me that if I were to continue happy within myself, helping out was a reasonable expectation. You chaps have always been so jolly decent in the way you've brought things to my attention that I've realised disappointment as a weakness in myself..."

He turned the drumstick and fed the other side to his teeth.

"...So I have determined that in future, I shall have no disappointments. Instead, I shall have only thanks for the help you people give so generously—apart from good company."

They all gave a little applause and raised their glasses in a toast.

Francoise elected to reply.

"That surely illustrates that it is not us who are the teachers, *mon ami*. Yes, if everyone saw the positive side of what contributes to disappointment, the entire world would be happier."

~ * ~

July was when Tahitian schools had their other holiday.

The fourteenth was Bastille Day, a celebration in all French territories. In French Polynesia, the week either side was given over to celebrating Polynesian culture. The *Heiva* Festival was two weeks of music and dancing. With Polynesians comprising seventy percent of the population, it was a major festival. Tribes in their several traditional costumes competed over the two weeks in musical recitals, dance performances and elocution. And for a newcomer to see so many demonstrations, Beresford felt privileged.

The Bastille Day parade was in itself a gala event. Re-enactments in costumes were a major part of it and even the Polynesians joined in.

He wrote home.

...I was particularly impressed by Polynesian dancing. The most popular is the 'hula', danced in rows of five or six. The women still with lithe bodies (for all seem to go to fat very quickly) wear grass skirts and use their hips and hands in

wonderful rhythm to music only from drums, although cleverly orchestrated. It was all a jolly good show. These competitions last two entire weeks. Bastille Day is a major celebration of course—re-enactments of the revolution. How much is factual and how much fictional cannot be known, yet it is surely a wonderful ceremony.

You were quite correct, Pater, in that I am not allowed to earn money here. The Frenchies have pointed out a public pin-board in the market, a sort of 'classified advertisement' board, quite large with a comprehensive array of needs and/or offers, and it lists opportunities. Yet if the gendarmes find me taking up even one of these offers for payment, I am in lots of trouble, even prison. So I have an essential need to find a way to Samoa. 'Work for passage' is a possibility. It is common in this part of the world that deckhand duty entitles one to free passage on private yachts, so I am every day checking the pin-board for such a notice. Twice I have applied for such, yet have lost out to fellows with experience. So maybe I am going to have to tell a lie or two.

Provided I do not run out of petty cash (oh, how can one call his only funds 'petty'?) I will continue enjoying my remaining confinement of nine hundred and forty-two days.

Your loving son...

~ * ~

Whilst Beresford had been at sea, Germany had marched into Czechoslovakia and occupied its two western provinces, Bohemia and Moravia. Hungary occupied remaining Ruthenia. It was clear that Hitler wanted more than only the return of German soil 'acquisitioned' by the Versailles Treaty. And as July moved into August and August into September, Hitler's haranguing of the German people became radio highlights. Every day they indicated that Germany was moving

closer to all-out war. World tensions were high, and in Europe all nations still free moved into 'alarm' mode.

With Germany, Russia, Italy, Austria, Hungary and Spain in the Axis bloc, and Czechoslovakia now taken, Hitler had incredible manufacturing resources behind him. World War 2 seemed imminent. And Japan also a member of the bloc, and seemingly taking all of China with ease, was a further fear.

"I still hold the hope, however," said a frightened Francoise, "that Hitler will be satisfied with so many conquests. What is the British attitude, Berry?"

He had seldom taken interest in politics, so had no measure.

"My father would have a feel for it, that I am now in no position to glean. He was a colonel in the Great War—served on the Marne. Too old for active service now, of course, but he keeps up with the politics. He was livid when our prime minister gave in so easily on the Sudetenland problem. 'It is like handing Hitler the key to a neighbour's larder', was his expression. So it seems Britain's attitude will be to complain again, but do nothing."

"France was also a signatory to the Sudetenland solution," said Gaston. "And I'm sure we are quite unready for war."

Pascal already had an arm around Francoise's shoulder. She was trembling, and tears were welling up.

"If there is a war," he added, "I'm not sure what our situation should be—whether or not to go home and enlist?"

The thought gave Beresford a start. *Then what shall I do?*

"If we do go to war," he said, "will it be safe going home? I read somewhere that Germany is building a fleet of U-boats. If there is a war, surely the first thing it will do is throw a cordon around English and French ports. And likely seal off the Mediterranean at Gibraltar. Spain would assist in that, I should expect."

He almost felt surprised at such spontaneous reasoning coming from his own lips. Back home he would have steered his mind away from such bothersome things. He hadn't liked feeling he should have to bother.

Yet such a bother could well be now laying itself at his very feet.

And on the first of September, when Germany invaded Poland, the tension over Papeete breakfast tables was extreme. Both France and Britain had a contract with Poland; if it be attacked, they would come to its aid.

And Russia, on that same day, invaded neutral Finland.

So it really seemed that a second World War was about to burst.

~ * ~

It did two days later when France, Great Britain, Australia and New Zealand declared war on Germany.

"U-boats could even be lurking outside Papeete harbour right now," the local radio warned. All shipping was being advised. The few German ships in port, mostly small because all large had left several days ago, were immediately impounded. French military and naval personal seemed suddenly everywhere.

The radio all day issued warnings that until sweeps were completed by the navy's limited resources, minefields outside the harbour were also possible. Gaston suggested it likely that Papeete's harbour was already closed, that every vessel trying to depart would be being searched for escaping Germans.

An enlistment booth was set up in the City Hall, uniformed soldiers on the footpath directing passers-by into the building. Gaston and Pascal agreed to wait until things sorted themselves out—until some official recommendation was given.

In the German Consulate on Monday, Zetan Dieter was being rushed off his feet. Every German still on the island was clamouring to know his position. Some ran their own innocent businesses; others were employed in French businesses. All now, it seemed, faced internment. In the Consulate's garden, incinerators made voluminous clouds of smoke—documents and records being burned.

The only Germans on the island not at sixes and sevens were of the diplomatic corps. An expulsion order under Diplomatic Immunity was expected any moment.

Beresford fronted up to the British Consulate.

"Do you want to enlist?" he was asked.

"Not yet. I want to go to Apia and see if I can join some British war service."

"Don't know, yet, how anyone can get to Samoa. All shipping is frozen until we get instructions from London."

"What would you suggest I do, then?"

"Cripes, mate, how would I know? Don't you know there's a war on?"

He went to the market to check the pin-board, and on it was a note dated only that morning.

URGENT. Help wanted—family yacht to Pago Pago. Telephone Papeete AP.487

He ran to the post office, groping in his pocket for a sou. He felt almost in a sweat as the call sign buzzed.

"AP.487."

"You are looking for a deckhand to Pago Pago?"

"Yes. You American?" inquired a heavy American accent—a woman.

"British."

"Experience?"

"Plenty. Suva to Tonga, then to here."

"Can you leave straight away? Sort of tomorrow?"

"Sure."

"Name?"

"Beresford Branson."

"Passport current?"

"Yes. Do I need a visa for American Samoa?"

"British Passport?"

"Yes."

"That's okay. We know the customs people."

"Aren't they stopping all vessels from departure?"

"We have authority."

He breathed a sigh of relief.

"Your yacht's name? Which wharf? What time?"

"*Teri's Magic*—that's T-E-R-I, the marina by the cargo pier, Run 4, Number 8. You got that?"

He repeated it.

"Go there now. See my husband, name Jerry Edwards. Okay?"

"Got it. And your name?"

"I'm Teri."

"Thanks, Mrs. Edwards, I'll go there right now."

He took a bicycle rickshaw, but did not feel too confident.

If he asks me which end is the prow, I'm done for!

Jerry Edwards was a guy in his forties, big, plenty of tight black curls, a bushy beard and thick hands with the scars of a hundred small but hurtful accidents.

The yacht wasn't a big one. *Only one mast? I was hoping for a big one with lots of hands.*

He eyed Beresford up and down in a fleeting second. "What've you done?"

"Not a lot. And I needed a lot of help, but I'm strong and willing."

Jerry could see he had a newbie. *But I'm desperate, and the weather reports are promising.*

"How many trips?"

"Two. Fiji to Tonga, then here."

Jerry sucked in his chin in a grimace. "Can you stow a sail?"

"Sure."

He already had Beresford pretty well summed up. *And there could still could be others applying. But I'll leave this door open.*

"You're hired. My daughter can help you with the rough stuff. When can you leave?"

"Your wife said tomorrow, but I can…"

Jerry grinned. "She was testing you. Two days okay? But if you're free tomorrow, you can help me load. You have much luggage?"

"One valise and a couple of satchels."

"What's your name?"

"Beresford Branson. I answer to Berry."

"British passport?"

He's picked my accent too. "Yes, and your wife said I can get a visa on arrival."

"No troubles if your passport is in order."

The American went below and returned with a note.

"Tomorrow, take a rickshaw to this address—a high hedge with a green gate. About nine? And bring your passport so I can sight it."

"Done."

He held out a hand, and Jerry pumped it two or three times—a grip like it was going to break two or three fingers.

Beresford left at a trot.

I only hope I can arrive in American Samoa without those big hands breaking more than just a few of my fingers!

Seven

The Frenchies were thrilled at him scoring a passage.

"But we shall sorely miss you. We have learned a lot from you."

"And me from you, dear friends. I shall miss not only you, but your kindnesses."

They told him how they wouldn't have expected that sort of comment from the Berry they'd met on the *Konig*. Those words in themselves made him feel great.

"Tomorrow night we shall pick up Francoise and take you to dinner. Where would you like to dine?"

"The Polynesian restaurant you first took me to."

So that was agreed. It was also agreed there would be no exchange of gifts. With all the problems the war was likely going to visit on all, everybody was avoiding expenses.

He gave them a note to the post office, asking it to forward mail for him to the post office at Apia, stamped *Hold for Collection*.

"Please deliver that for me," he pleaded. "And when I return your key to you tomorrow, please remind me to collect my assets from your wall-safe."

He was on time next morning, dressed for manual work, fingers crossed that an experienced deckhand had not since applied.

And he was surprised at the sign on the gate:

Consulate of the United States of America.

He wondered if what he was required to help load might be records the USA wanted in American Samoa rather than here.

But that's not my business. I don't really care.

"I need to quickly get home," Jerry Edwards explained. "I'm with the American Trade Office in Samoa. It is not a diplomatic assignment, but a government one nevertheless, and with this war breaking out, whilst the US isn't involved, it will play havoc with shipping reliabilities. I need to be there rather than here."

Beresford met both Teri and daughter Randi. Their visit to Tahiti had been the family's twentieth birthday present to Randi, and they had been on Bora Bora Island when the war erupted. They were from Santa Cruz in California but had been in Pago Pago (pronounced in the Polynesian language *"pango pango"* with a hard 'g') so long that Randi had few memories of the American mainland other than occasional visits 'home'.

And she looks a bit of all right—enough that I think she would have been on my list of those I asked wait for me in Durham. But then also, whilst the body might be trim, there are no fluttering eyelashes—only twittering muscles as she grabs a box, the weight of it suggesting paperwork, or bundle of what could be anything, to fling over the sideboards of the pick-up.

So he was prepared to deny himself the pleasure of watching her whilst endeavouring, almost unsuccessfully, to illustrate her same agility in loading.

Jerry asked him to drive it to the docks while he attended other business.

"You'll see a nigger guy lounging around waiting for someone to hire his muscles. His name is Henry. Offer him a franc or two to help you load this stuff—all thirty-three items, note,"—and he paused until

Beresford counted and nodded—"into the forward cabin. Floor space is already cleared. Lock the hatch when you leave and bring the key and pick-up back here. Okay?"

Beresford nodded, and Jerry gave him both the key to the pick-up and the key to the cabin hatch. He then clasped him by the shoulder.

"I will not be here when you return the pick-up, but you be at the Customs Office at 9 a.m. sharp. I'll have your passport with me, and we can all get our clearances together. We need to catch the morning's ebb tide, so don't be late."

Only then did he release the grip on the Englishman's shoulder, to laugh when Beresford walked to the wrong side of the vehicle.

Bloody hell. He wants me to drive on the wrong side of the road? Only experience I have of that is riding pillion on a scooter! Or like being an experienced deckhand on a yacht? Oh dear God, please have mercy on the English who declared the Pope awry and went our own errant way.

So he didn't feel too confidant on his drive, not only having to feel his way through the tangle of bicycles and rickshaws and mopeds by the score, snatching left for the gear lever every time he needed to change down and instinctively looking left for his rear vision mirror. Especially when he kept being dazzled by traffic overtaking on his left.

But he was breathing normally again by the time he got there, driving right up to Wharf 4 to park by *Teri's Magic*. He didn't have to find Henry, for Henry had followed from the gate at a leisurely pace. A pick-up driving up to a yacht usually meant lifting something. And all went smoothly.

Although I'd much rather Randi had come to help unload. Yet would I have been able to keep up with her?

Henry, however, was happy to work at Polynesian pace.

~ * ~

With sad farewells over, Berry, with his gear, was at the Customs Office in good time.

Cute of Jerry to keep my passport. That's all the insurance he needed, of course, in case I ran off with the pick-up and all the likely

clandestine records. Or could the US Consul have some means of having my passport checked out to see if I'm on the level? Maybe have a record or something?

He tossed the thought aside. He could do nothing about it one way or the other.

There were no problems getting his clearance. Jerry presented all four passports together and showed the clerk documents from his wallet—*no doubt authorities from the US Consul?*

Once aboard, Randi quickly illustrated that she was in command whenever out of her father's sight, and her idea of command was, fortunately, not giving orders, but rolling up her sleeves and doing!

I'm sure happy to go along with all that—so long as it looks like I'm willing to help. I just hope she just doesn't order me to climb the mast!

The weather remained fine, and he even began to feel that all three Edwards could easily spot not only his lack of expertise, but endeavours to at least try. And went along with it—not difficult when Randi was so expert, of course.

She is more than deckhand, I keep telling her—she is the subaltern captain, and she obviously enjoys being told it.

In the galley that night, with appropriate 'upstairs' lights lit and the wheel secured on its course, Jerry, Teri, Randi and Beresford sat over cold curried lobster with rice, yam and mashed coconut, bought that morning wrapped in banana leaves, and drinking warm Riesling.

"Where is home, Berry?" Teri asked.

"Durham," he replied, thankful no animosity on his sailing expertise had yet arisen.

"Durham? Is that a town?" asked Jerry.

"Both a county and town," he replied, endeavouring to make it sound like a sister city to London. "A small county, yet distinctive. In England's north-east."

He was desperately trying to make it sound significant.

But it didn't work because Teri came back with, "Is it near London, then?"

"Oh, not at all," he scoffed. "It is three hundred miles north."

He wasn't in the least realising that three hundred miles in American parlance made it almost 'next door'.

So a short silence reigned.

"Your family, Berry? What does your father do?"

He was taken aback. *Oh dear! What does a baronet do, that people in a republic would understand?*

He coughed. "He is... He is a baronet."

And he simply stopped, waiting for their reaction.

Jerry asked, "And what does a Baronet do?"

Beresford thought long and hard, coming down in favour of taking the superior position as all Englanders were taught.

"A baronet is part of the aristocracy—a heredity title. It entitles the first-born son to inherit the knight's title of 'Sir'. It is a dying practice, however. Time will decimate it. However, my family still enjoys its tradition."

Suddenly his audience became hesitant—Jerry raised a finger, and so did Randi. He called on Randi first.

"Does that mean you are royal?"

He laughed openly. "Good heavens no, Randi. Royals are princes or dukes or earls. My father is merely the son of an antecedent who had been honoured by the royals of his day—having a knighthood conferred on him. The title dies out once a first son has no male offspring. "

Jerry now asked, "So what does this make you, a 'Sir' somebody? Or will you become Sir Beresford when your father passes on?"

Berry laughed again. He was now enjoying himself. "Not at all. I have an elder brother. Thomas will inherit the title."

"And if Thomas dies before you?" This came from Teri.

"The title lapses. Only the first son can inherit."

There was a silence.

"Oh," said Teri, "all that is so romantic. Those old European customs have so much tradition tied to them. You must feel very proud?"

And that really threw him. So it took him some time to answer.

"Proud? What have I to be proud of? Pride is surely something one earns. I've always believed that this 'baronet' thing is only part

of the old world. No inherent earns it—it is simply doled out. In fact the reason I am in the South Seas right now is what my father calls 'blooding' me. I think I'm in training for somehow earning a respect in life."

So now there was almost a full minute's silence.

"Well," said Randi. "And here was I starting to think we had a prince or something on board, and you tell us we don't even have a nobleman?"

There was lots of laughter, and Berry had to think hard on how to respond.

"You have only a nobleman's son who has been common enough to tell lies to you all, because I have no money and need to get to Apia so I can find work."

All three collapsed in a paroxysm of laughter.

Eight

In clear weather for the entire fifteen hundred miles and with Randi's propensity for wanting to illustrate her superiority working in his favour, Berry had an enjoyable excursion. And made new friends. Nor had he been seasick.

It was not only enjoyable but educational in that it was his first voyage in a sail vessel. And on arrival, although not part of the agreement, he was given a bonus of twenty American dollars for having fitted into the 'family' so well.

And I expected nowt! And here I am within a shout of Apia, where I can work for a wage!

So he was feeling high.

"How are you getting to Apia?" Teri asked.

"Same way I got here, I guess. Let my sailing skills work for me?"

She put her arms about his shoulders and hugged him. "I could go for you, if twenty years younger," she told him. "But come stay with us tonight."

"I don't want to be a problem," he answered, "unless you have a guest room."

This time, she laughed aloud. "We don't have a guest room. We have a guest bungalow if that suits Your Highness?"

His turn to laugh.

"And tonight," she added, "with the staff not expecting us, we shall dine out and I will ask Jerry if he can get you to Apia."

Beresford Branson was beginning to realise what made people in the world tick.

~ * ~

And he was to quickly discover that Western Samoa was a different world from Tahiti, despite both being Polynesian.

Jerry Edwards had indeed found a berth for him to transfer from American Samoa on a trading vessel that plied backwards and forwards between the two ports. Teri had armed him with names of cheap restaurants, Randi had planted a teasingly delightful kiss full on the mouth, and Jerry gave him a letter addressed to a friend in Sydney.

"Please post this for me," he said. "This Sydney friend is a philatelist who wants Samoan stamps. Maybe you could please ask the clerk to neatly stamp them?"

Beresford was so chuffed at Randi's kiss, and the family had indeed been so helpful, that he was happy to do anything for them.

And whilst it was only some seventy nautical miles, the two small nations were split by the International Date Line. He left American Samoa on Friday morning, arriving a few hours later in Western Samoa, to find it was Saturday afternoon.

Whatever happened to the rest of Friday?

He found it incredible that time could simply be snatched out of a person's life.

He could see the mechanics of it. There had to be a beginning and end of everything. The date line had to be somewhere, and it made sense that American Samoa should be the same date as the USA rather than a day ahead. And likewise Western Samoa be the same day and date as New Zealand, which administered it.

So the dateline officially took a bypass to accommodate the tiny nations.

But Western Samoa wasn't a happy place. A gloomy atmosphere dwelt in the air, so much so that he had difficulty relating to the Polynesian people here with those in Tahiti. The women were still big-hearted and buxom, and they wore the same brightly coloured smocks and big old woven straw hats, yet were nowhere near as effervescent and bubbly. They didn't go about giggling as if enjoying life.

As the twentieth century began, the old Samoa divided. The smallest of the three 'big' islands became a USA dependency, the larger western islands going to Germany. Early in WW1, New Zealand troops landed unopposed on the German islands, and after the war, Western Samoa was placed under New Zealand administration. But with the majority of the European population of German descent and culture, the transition had never really worked. Allegiances of many remained with the Fatherland—the British influence was resented.

During the twenty intervening years there were many riots and many deaths. The Polynesian majority, while tending to carry on with their traditional lives much as their brethren in Tahiti did, lacked support through both the German discontent and New Zealand's failure to earn respect as an administrator.

So Beresford, on arrival, hoping to here find employment and a satisfying life, found his philosophy on disappointment, so enthusiastically grasped when in Tahiti, was in Samoa difficult to justify.

Should I try closing my mind to that? I've got to get used to trying to look outside the box, seeing that the new day dawning is also the old night dying. Or that the sun setting is more a matter of the earth's rim rising? But being British has me, here, from the start, offside with the majority. I will not easily find friendships. And the likelihood of work will be more limited. I simply had not given thought to the fact that German influence would be rife in this British protectorate. Yet where should I go? Geographically, Fiji and Tonga are close, and to the north are the Gilbert and Ellice Islands—all British protectorates.

On the veranda of the Customs Office had been a pin-board offering accommodation at various hotels and guesthouses. Several offered shared accommodation, such rates being the cheapest. He noted the four addresses, then studied the town map alongside.

He noted also, the address of the civic library. He intended reading up on neighbouring countries—a precaution he hadn't taken in choosing Samoa.

I chose here because it was closest. I expected it to suit me even better than Tahiti.

He then smiled inside at the thought of how pleased 'Pater' would be with him, now planning on tomorrows.

Albeit too late of course. I should have done Forward Vision homework in Papeete!

His heart sank even at the sight of the nearest of the four guesthouses on his list.

It is filthy. I dare not lay my head on a pillow in such a place.

And without another thought, he moved further up the same street to the second, which was little more encouraging. As was the third.

"They seem to improve the further you walk," Ego tried adding a silver lining to his master's despondency.

The last house, however, didn't excite him, yet seemed from the outside, at least bearable.

But it is the most expensive of the three. Yet it must do for a few days to look further. Maybe there are families that take in boarders? Yet that would mean a private room, which immediately is more expensive than sharing.

He was shown a room in which he would share with two others. Neither were there at the time. The office could confine sealed envelopes with valuables in its safe. The room's only doorway was off a veranda, so he would have his own key to come and go.

The place is at least clean, even to the blanket. And pillow. And it offered an optional light breakfast for sixpence.

He checked in, paying the minimum seven nights in advance, fourteen shillings.

He walked back to the Customs House, where he had left his luggage for a fee of tuppence, and installed it in his digs. He consigned his cash into an envelope that cost a ha'penny, and asked the German woman in attendance to recommend him to a café or wherever he might find a meal at that hour. It was late afternoon, and he had eaten nowt since breakfast in Pago Pago.

A tasty yam and pork stew at an eatery stall in the Polynesian market cost one and threepence, and a small bottle of drinking water, a penny.

He decided to leave the library until checking the pin-board here in the market, for jobs.

Maybe with Germans here being interred for the duration, there will be vacancies?

It was the first positive hope he'd found.

~ * ~

On return to the guesthouse, his roommates were home. They were young Polynesian brothers from the other western island, come here where paying jobs were better than 'at home'. They had very little English, yet with the few words of Polynesian Berry had gleaned in Tahiti, they managed to understand each other a little. He spoke slowly, to make it easier for them, and waited patiently while the more literate of the two, Elo, thought about responses to Beresford's many questions. He found out that the German woman who had installed him was wife of the owner. Only two days ago, he had been interned. She was believed safe enough, it seemed, to leave free to run her guesthouse. Only Germans not locally born were confined, so her two sons could at least work to help support her. All three, however, had been deeply interrogated by the British Diplomatic Office before being allowed their 'freedom'.

Yes, since the internment of many Germans, jobs were available.

Oh what a stroke of luck this timing is!

He was told where he should apply, come Monday, and given directions. They were not difficult, for the town was small—but a

fraction of Papeete's size. In fact he must go to the Town Hall, which was right next door to the library.

He listened to the radio that night in Frau Auberling's sitting room. Her teenage sons, Otto and Erik, were home, although the Polynesians were not there. Unable to understand the fast-speaking English announcer, his roommates' nightly wont was to eat at a Polynesian café that Beresford was anxious to get an introduction to. And the news was not pleasant for even 'abstract' Germans to hear. Canada had declared war on Germany, and neutral USA had promised to sell on credit airplane fighters to Britain. They would be flown there by Canadian Air Force pilots.

Beresford was given permission to use Frau Auberling's World Atlas, and deduced that delivery flights would refuel at Iceland.

Surely then, Iceland will already be fortified with British or Canadian troops, to keep it safe from the Germans.

And when the news finished and the Auberling boys retired to their room while their mother cleaned up in the kitchen, he asked if he might use the desk to write a letter home. Permission was given, provided he switched off the light when finished.

Dear Mater and Pater,

What an unhappy time this is. Have you yet received my letter telling of Bastille Day and the exciting Polynesian Festival? I guess mail everywhere will be slow from now on, for I'm told even all mail here is being opened by censors. 'Here' is no longer Papeete for me—it is Apia. I arrived only today with the assistance of a jolly nice family that brought me on their yacht from Tahiti. With war breaking out, that American family was as anxious to get to American soil as was I to get to British. Not that either had anything against the French, in fact the reverse. My objective was to quickly get where I can work and have happily arrived here where jobs are available, I'm told, because so many of German extraction have been interned.

Maybe I shouldn't be making too many comments about war things, in case your censors take exception and chop more copy from this than I should wish. My French friends in Papeete will forward mail from you that arrives there. Until further notice, please use 'c/- Post Office Apia, Western Samoa' as my address. Until I know about employment here, I don't know how long I shall stay.

You will no doubt be pleased to hear, Pater, that I intend visiting the civic library and reading up on work situations in each of Fiji, Gilbert and Ellice Islands, Solomon Islands and even The Friendly Islands, which the people here call Tonga. I am led to believe that whilst Tonga is a delightful place and again ninety-percent Polynesian population, with whom I would feel much at ease, it is very small and little developed. Work opportunities are limited. And the Solomon Islands too, it also having one time been a German dependency, may have limitations. But Fiji is British to the core—well at least for those not lost to cannibalism, I am warned!

Naturally I am devastated at the danger all in Britain face. I am hoping that in this age of such high technology, the war might be quickly over. Dare I go so far as to risk censorship by saying that Hitler may be satisfied with attacking only Continental Europe—draw his line through the English Channel? I do so ever hope so!

I love you both, and brother Thomas of course, who is included in all my news and good wishes. I would imagine Britain has introduced conscription of some form? I haven't here seen or heard anything on that. I shall be enquiring at the Diplomatic Office here if I should be thinking of coming home and enlisting. I cannot telephone you yet because I was told at the Customs Office only this morning that calls to Britain are, until further notice, restricted to only approved officials—it seems there are but few lines available. No one in authority in this part of the world seems ready to answer direct questions

on this sort of thing. I guess they are still waiting to be told what to do.

Time-wise, failing a patriotic need to try getting home earlier, I have but eight hundred and ninety days before seeing you again. I hope during that interim you all keep well, safe and as happy as the times allow.

Your loving son...

Nine

At 9:30 Monday morning he was told at the Employment counter in the British Residents Enquiries office, the sign carrying in small type, 'including citizens of British Empire nations', that he was too late. They had had four only vacancies on their book, and all had been given the names and address of the applicants.

"So if you like, you can wait in case any applicant informs us none were suitable. Otherwise, I recommend you be waiting tomorrow morning at 9 o'clock, and I shall see you first. Do you want to register your name and address and a preference for the type of work?"

All that peeled off the fellow's tongue as if recorded on a gramophone record.

"Yes, please. My name is Beresford Brans..."

"We have a form here, for filling in. You may sit at that desk," he said, pointing to a high bench with several stools. You will find pen and ink there."

And the fellow, with a practised hand, plucked a printed sheet from beneath the counter desk and pushed it towards Beresford.

"Obviously reared in the British public service," Beresford whispered to Ego as he took the form to the bench, climbing up on a high stool.

But shall I wait or come back tomorrow? It would seem this fellow expects more to come. And my time today could be well spent at the library. If I were to find my waiting several hours fruitful, and find a position, then it could be a long time before getting to the library. And Saturday afternoons could be busy there, it being the only time it is open for those with regular work.

So having exercised such deep Forward Vision, he filled out the form, waiting for the public servant to check that it was completed to his satisfaction.

"I appreciate you offering to see me first tomorrow, sir," he fawned. "I shall be waiting when the doors open at 9 o'clock."

Outdoors the sun was still climbing, yet the brilliant sky, with hardly a cloud to be seen, was in itself dazzling. The square on which the civic buildings stood was shaded with rows of various palms. Most were coconuts, for several such lay scattered even in the roadway. There was plenty of room to skirt them, for the thoroughfare was wide, the traffic thin.

Yet it's highly likely the driver of any vehicle, other than hand-drawn rickshaws, is keeping a careful watch in any case. It's just that sort of town.

The traffic was less dense than in Papeete, though at least here they drove on the left. In fact it was not dense at all. Even sparse, he ended up with.

It certainly is a lazy atmosphere. But I suppose being two hundred miles closer to the equator than Papeete, one should expect both heat and additional humidity to make life slower. And both Ellice Islands and Solomon Islands are further north again, so that is something a man should consider. Heat in itself is enough to make an Englander suffer, let alone the agony of high humidity.

The library indeed had some major newspapers of South Pacific nations, albeit a few days old, and even dated issues from London, New York, Paris, Berlin, Sydney and Auckland. No European editions of course, had anything as recent as the outbreak of war in Europe.

"But Sydney and Auckland should be dependable if you was lookin' fer anythink dependable, Guv," said the perky little male attendant in 'e broadest Cockney even Beresford had ever heard.

And the 'Guv' expression tells me he's recognised my accent as the Queen's English! It would seem the library should be looking for someone with better language than this pearly little tart.

"I should like to read the *Fiji Times*, please. And I see nothing here from The Ellice Islands. Do they have a newspaper?"

"No, Guv. They depend on Fiji for gettin' their name out into the world. Can't help yer there. How about American Samoa? New Zealand? We get all their stuff."

Yes, definitely a job here if I can locate the manager. Or even the mayor?

He took the *Fiji Times* to a reading table and spent an hour making notes.

Fiji had no Polynesians. Its natives were Melanesian, photographs showing them with black faces, bones stuck through cheekbones, black hair in tight curls, gleaming white teeth in black lips. The only 'nice' thing he found out about Fiji's black people was that he could find no stains on their teeth that might hint of human blood.

Cannibalism died out in most areas once Christianity took a hold in the late 1800s through the early 1900s... it read.

Bloody hell! What do they mean by 'most areas'? Do they have them signposted? And 'today' is still the early 1900s. Does that mean that some, albeit Christian, still practise cannibalism? That's taking the body and blood of Christ a bit too far for my liking.

He was beginning to take an intense dislike to Fiji, yet pictures showed women in the marketplace giggling pretty much like Tahitian women. And Suva streets had lots of motorcars. And buildings were three and four stories high. None of the images of those in the several photographs hinted of black savagery. And the English language in the articles was literate.

Near forty percent of the population Indian? Brought there by the British in the 1800s as slave labourers in the cane fields and sugar factories? And their descendants now proving the main traders in Suva, outnumbering locals in manufacturing and retailing?

He read further down the column that indigenous natives "*would rather sing, dance and enjoy life, than work for a living.*"

Bloody hell! From cannibalism to embracing the Charleston?

He finished his note taking on Fiji with absolute confusion in mind.

But it certainly would be worth a look if things here don't work out.

~ * ~

Elo and Rano asked him to join them for dinner.

"Beware a Polynesian suggesting you eat or drink with him," he had been warned by Gaston and Pascal. "That invariably ends up with you having to pay his or their shares. It is an unfortunate habit they have—stemming from Europeans having better jobs than them or at least having a few more coins in their pockets than can natives."

So he was on guard. He realised these lads would not have much money to their name, or they wouldn't have come to Apia. Yet he needed to make his situation clear.

"Yes, but I hope it is not expensive. I can barely cover the cost of my rent here and am desperate to get a job. I hope to be lucky tomorrow."

"Tevake is a café owned by our countrymen. It serves only Polynesian food. Do you know it?"

"Of course. I ate much of it in Tahiti. I find it delightful."

So he joined them—only a block away in the Polynesian quarter. And he was pleased to find that the similar food was considerably cheaper than Papeete.

This all bodes well, provided I have work.

And he enjoyed his roommates' company and conversation, broken and thought provoking though it was. Yet he had much to learn, and they seemed to appreciate his situation.

"You paint pictures?" they asked, which amused him. He had read that Gauguin had lived in this town for part of his life and that it had become a Mecca for artists as well as the hopeful triers.

"Not at all. If I can find work as a clerk, I shall be delighted. Even sales work, although I've no experience. What do you fellows do?"

"Me gardener," said Elo. "Work for council. Me know many fruit, many flower."

"Me make boats," said Rano.

"Canoes from trees?" Beresford asked in all seriousness.

Both lads laughed.

"Not here," replied Rano. "In village, make canoe from tree. In Apia make big boat for man catch fish. Or sailboat."

"I had my first journey on a sailboat last week, Rano. I was lucky enough to get passage with an American family to Pago Pago. Then came here by steamer."

And so dinner went. All three drank nowt but coconut juice, and Beresford was pleased at so conveniently finding reference to such a place.

And establishing such a rapport with my roommates. And being with them likely saved me paying more than if, as a European, I had come alone.

Provided the proprietors remembered him, the low-price standard had been struck.

He came home in a considerably happier mood than during recent days, and happy too, that communicating with the lads was becoming easier.

They were home in time for him to catch the radio news, so whilst the lads went to their room and beds, Beresford joined the family listening to the broadband. It was telling of dreadful hardships in Poland. The Germans were advancing, having decimated areas ahead with artillery and Stuka bombers. The Luftwaffe was bombing Warsaw. The Polish people were strung out along roads leading east wheeling every type of conveyance imaginable—from baby prams and wheelbarrows to horse and carts—loaded with whatever furniture and belongings would fit. Gasoline was available only for Poland's retreating army vehicles. Its small air force had already been decimated.

Ah, what terrible times.

~ * ~

Yet on the morrow, he got a job.

His first appointment was with an insurance company.

"Thank heavens for an Englishman," the manager, Arthur Priest, told him. "If you can type, that would be an added blessing."

The company had one only English housewife proficient in typing. She was old enough that her children were grown, so she was able to come out to work. "My contribution to helping the war effort," she later told him.

"She is the only one we have who can convert 'German-English' into the English we prefer," Mr. Priest continued. "We have lost five German employees with good English to internment. So you are welcome. We have the daughter of one, who can show you what we need. It is not onerous. And feel free to come to me if you need help. We were paying her father £3.3.6 per week. Is that satisfactory?"

What? An employer asking if it is enough? What has the war already done to these people who are an entire half the world from it? Of course it is not enough!

"Oh dear. I was earning £3.12.0 in Papeete. And Mr. Jerry Edwards, a trader in Pago Pago, offered me £3.17.6 had I been American. Do you know him? He told me he trades here often."

The manager looked amiss.

"No. I don't have that honour. But we couldn't pay anything like that. If you will accept £3.10.0, you can start right away. And we do not work Saturday afternoons like in Papeete."

Beresford put on a show of disappointment, yet acceptance.

"But please, Mr. Branson, do not tell anyone else what we pay you," Mr. Priest whispered as they shook hands on the deal.

Beresford was shown a desk in an office with five others and introduced to Greta Sneider.

"Greta will introduce you around," Mr. Priest told him.

So things were going well. He had been in the country only three days and was already employed. He would be paid every Friday and could already see that, having paid his rent and breakfast, he would have £2.12.6 left to live on. He could even save something out of that towards his fare home.

Ten

Three days later

Berry came out of a coma to find himself on a hard concrete floor in a corrugated iron shed, his hands tied behind his back, alone and the heat unbearable. The temperature seemed over a century, and sweat dripped from his brow, nose and chin. He was hungry, his throat parched, and he had shit his pants.

If only I could somehow get these sweat drops into my mouth! They'd be salty, yet I guess that salt might only replace what is oozing out of me. Yet how come I am here? And at whose hands?

The knowledge of having defecated in his shorts horrified him.

How could such have happened? And when? How long can I have been here? And why?

He could smell his own stink, and every little movement he made only exacerbated the mess of it.

He had left work late after his second day, feeling chuffed that he was beginning to get the hang of things, overly conscious of it being the first time in his life that he was experiencing 'working for a living'—petrified of making a mistake and being fired. He had worked late, knowing his boss liked to see his clerks with empty IN baskets and full

OUT baskets, so had gone straight to Tevake's. He would eat there, whether Elo and Rano were there or not.

Maybe they'll come later, yet I know they don't come every night, he recalled thinking.

He remembered walking down the street for the house. It was dark by then.

But that is all I remember...

His legs itched, and the stink of his own mess was worse than it might have seemed, purely for not being able to do anything about it. And his hip hurt, his entire weight seeming to be forcing it harder into the concrete. It was not dark now. Daylight gleamed through chinks in the rusted iron in several places. In all four walls. There was no furniture other than old wooden workbenches along two of the walls. The two only windows, glassless yet iron barred, were hung with Hessian flour sacks as curtains, half closed. The timber-framed corrugated iron door was closed.

And likely bolted on the outside—even padlocked.

Why, oh why? kept snagging at his mind.

He lay coiled in a ball, tense like a snake ready to tighten at the first hint of danger. He'd been left undisturbed, since becoming conscious, for an indeterminable time. He could remember walking home. He'd passed a wooden house built right on to the roadway and the open gate of a yard, to suddenly feel himself grasped from behind—a hand coming over his shoulder. And the smell—there was no mistaking it: ether.

Again came the questions that kept bombarding his mind. *Why? Who? Not as if anyone could think I had a wallet full of banknotes in my pocket.*

And he couldn't even bring a hand to check in his hip pocket to see if his wallet were still there. He was laying on the wrong side for that.

And the stench of his excretion still infuriated him.

And now I want to piss!

He tried wiggling his pelvis, trying to gauge if the crotch of his walk-shorts and under-shorts were wet. But he was unsuccessful there too.

If they wanted to drug me and lock me in a cell, why did they bind my hands also? And so tightly? Enough that I think they are becoming numb. It's just too difficult to tell if it's numbness or just my tension.

~ * ~

But then, for the first time, he heard something from outside other than a dog that had been yapping for quite a time, a long way off.

Footsteps. And more than one pair. But they're not talking.

The footsteps were heavy enough on what sounded like sparse bracken to be not likely more than two men.

But ears play tricks on people concentrating too hard on a sound, I remember reading somewhere.

So he tried easing his impatience.

I'm going to find out soon enough.

Then a recognisable sound reached him: a padlock clicking open and a chain being pulled through a hasp—*or should that be staple? I've never known which is which.*

Yet the chain was finally through, and the door opened. He could twist his head far enough to see two men, and behind them what looked like open country, or farmland?

A spark of electricity seemed to surge through him—he recognised the lead man, even though the light was behind him.

It was Jerry Edwards!

Ah, hallelujah! Help at last!

"Oh, Jerry. Thank God it's you," he said to the face that stood looking down at him.

He saw Jerry put a hand to his nose.

"What's he doing in this state?"

Jerry sounded terse and demanding of the other man, a Polynesian, big, burly and ugly.

"Clean him and bring him into the house," Jerry said briskly and turned on his heels to disappear out the door.

Wh..wha...what is all this? Jerry not helping me? Seeming to know I would be here, somehow confined even if not tethered?

If Beresford had been confused before, he was now doubly confused. And frightened. The surge of relief that had flashed through his mind had been dashed so quickly, to be replaced by a dreadful fear. He simply could not believe that Jerry was suddenly a man connected to the plight he was in.

Jerry's the most considerate of friends...a husband—a father. He gave me a twenty-dollar bonus because of my situation. "It's for having fitted so well into my family" were his very words. And now? What the dickens is going on?

But the brute was already attacking binding around his wrists, whatever it was, with a knife. And he was none too gentle.

Beresford felt a nick, yet was thankful it hadn't been his throat.

The fellow pulled him to his feet, then began pushing him to the door. Yet Beresford's feet wouldn't hold him—his circulation had somehow gone awry and muscles had stiffened.

He fell.

The beast kicked him in the ribs.

"Get up," he shouted—reaching down and grabbing Beresford's shirtfront. He felt and heard something rip, but his feet now came into play and helped him stand. He was led on still trembling limbs into a farmhouse yard and to a bench outside what looked like a laundry. The ape then reached for a milk urn filled with water.

Should I run? This big oaf is so cumbersome he'd never catch me.

He began the movement, but his legs again went from under him. The pain in his ribs from the kick added to his body faltering. He'd have fallen again, except that the bench was right there for him to throw his weight against. And with hands pressing down on it, he was again upright. The great oaf smirked as if congratulating himself for having so weakened his catch, and dragged the urn to where Berry stood.

"You strip," he said, pointing to Berry's shorts.

So he pulled both of his shorts down around his feet, and even before he could kick them away, the giant lifted the urn as easily as if it were a watering can and upended it over Beresford's head and shoulders.

He pulled up another urn full of water...

Obviously in the throes of being cleaned after the morning's milking?

...and set it beside Berry. He then stood back and pointed.

"You clean."

Berry had to use his under-shorts as a sponge and almost sensed a flash of pleasure as he cleaned himself down to the knees and beyond, to then rinse out everything in the milk-urn. Only then did he notice Jerry leaning on a doorpost to the cottage, arms folded, watching.

Is that a smile on the bastard's face? Or a smirk? Oh, have I ever been a gullible fool? I'm still not sure what this is all about, yet it's clear he was expecting to find me here—and in this sort of circumstance, so he isn't the friend I took him for.

And again came the same questions. *What? Why? At least I now know who!*

His mind was turning double somersaults trying to come up why Jerry had proved such a friend in so many ways only days ago...

...when now he seems party to my being kidnapped and maltreated. And Teri and Randi? Where do they fit into all this?

Jerry went back into the house and returned with a cotton sarong.

The oaf went to it and brought it to Beresford. He held it in a hand thrust forward, in jerks, urging Beresford to take it. Berry ignored him, simply continuing rinsing socks, under-shorts and dress-shorts until satisfied he'd left all the shit possible in the urn. Then he turned and walked to a clothesline. He let down the prop, tossed each garment in turn over the wire, then raised the prop as if the procedure were one he went through daily.

Let the bastards wait, he mused. *I'm as anxious as hell to find out what all this is about, but I'm damned if I'm going to let them see how bloody scared I am. And I still need that piss.*

He walked over to a shed wall where lettuces were growing and pissed on them.

Only then did he turn and walk to where Jerry stood, by now openly smiling.

~ * ~

The evening prior

Frau Auberling wondered at her English boarder not coming home from work.

The last two nights he had come directly home, then gone to dinner with Elo and Rano.

This night they waited a while for him, but then went to dinner on their own. Already they had told Erik Auberling that tonight they wanted to take Beresford to a different restaurant. But when nine o'clock arrived, they went without him.

"Home, he is still not," she told them when they arrived, ready to retire.

And her sons were concerned but not worried.

"He could have gone anywhere, *Mutte*. With friends from work he could have gone to dinner," Otto reasoned. "If he is not here come morning, I will go to his work and ask where he might be."

So she was satisfied, yet still concerned. She liked the lad, *Englander* or not. He was one of those in the town who did not seem to hold the world against her. Since the war started and her Otto was interned, even the British women who had always been friendly now looked the other way on the street and in the market. But her young boarder didn't treat her so. He was one of the nicer *Englanders*, and she hoped he wasn't in trouble. Her sister in *Munchen* had said in a letter a while back that in Germany now, many people disappeared. They were seen to leave their homes to go to work, or such, yet simply never came home.

Humph! Maybe here, too, now?

~ * ~

Life in Polynesian societies was laid back. It was easy and gentle, and nothing much happened to change it. Anything in the least bit dramatic happened elsewhere. There was the occasional murder, but even then, most knew the circumstances, and that in itself relieved life of any real trauma.

So in that the young Englishman had not come overnight, breakfast in the Auberling guesthouse was one of all smiles and winks and hoping Beresford's evening had proved a happy one for him.

"I will call at his office nevertheless," said Otto. "It is likely I will find him there with either a smile on his face, or a black eye." And everybody laughed.

Life in the South Pacific was like that.

But when he arrived, the door was not yet open. Several people were waiting for the manager to arrive. None, however, knew other than that, when they left, Beresford was still catching up on his day's work. And once the manager arrived and found everything in order as Beresford had promised to leave it, no new light was forthcoming. Beresford, by intent, had been left alone to finish his work, to then slam the front door with its click-lock.

"Well, Otto," declared Mr. Priest, "it is no use us thinking he might be ill or delayed at home. We can only conclude that he might have met with some accident. If nobody else knows where he might be...?" He perused all faces, to glean no response. "Then I shall telephone the police and report a missing person."

Otto went away much more worried than when arriving. So with brother Erik already gone to work, and the Polynesian boys also, he decided not to go home and inform his mother.

Better Mutte spends her day thinking he may just have had a fun evening, than fret alone, as I must, worrying about what can have happened to him.

So he went off to work.

Eleven

Beresford and Jerry Edwards sat across a table staring at each other—each trying to read more in the other's mind than in what came from their mouths.

In Beresford's mind was that he must doubt every word Jerry muttered.

And Jerry had to wonder the truth of every Beresford answer.

"Did you post the letter?"

"What, the one to Sydney?"

"There was no other."

"Yes, I posted it. Is it your change that you now want?"

Jerry couldn't help but smile. But he couldn't let up on the pressure. "How much did it cost?"

"Nine-pence ha'penny. So do you want your tuppence-ha'penny change?"

"No. Who was it addressed to?"

"I don't know—you didn't put a name, only a post-box number."

"What was the number?"

Damn, what is it with Jerry? He wrote the bloody number!

"I don't know. I didn't read it. I was just surprised at it not having somebody's name."

"Why should it?"

"All letters are addressed to somebody. You said your friend was a philatelist wanting the stamps."

"All that is true. I wouldn't tell you a lie."

"Well, why am I here?"

"That's beside the point. I need to know that post box number, and you are the only other who ever saw it. Now what was it?"

Sheesh! He's paranoid about this number!

"I've already told you I don't know."

"Did you insure it?"

"Yes. The postage was six-pence-ha'penny and the insurance threepence."

"You thought to remember all that. Why don't you remember the post box number?"

"What is this, Jerry? Is it you who had me kidnapped, tied up for so long I shit my trousers? And am as hungry as hell because I've had nothing to eat and the only water I've been given is now full of shit!"

He was furious.

Jerry smiled again. He turned and shouted, "Keno!"

Within a minute, the most repugnant and significant adversary Beresford had ever held a grudge against lumbered into the doorway.

"Bring drinking water and food. Quickly!"

The oaf came through the doorway and lumbered into an adjoining room.

"And shut the door while you get it," Jerry yelled.

The door between them slammed.

"Have you got the insurance receipt?"

"They didn't give me one."

"You didn't ask?"

"I thought that in this hick town, they mightn't do that."

Jerry gave a look that Beresford wasn't sure was a smile or a sneer.

"What's today?" Beresford asked.

"Friday. Why?"

"Because I don't know how long I've been in fairyland."

"So what's the day got to do with it?"

"Well, I posted it only on Monday. It was the only free day I had, because I started work Tuesday. So it's too soon for your friend in Sydney to be complaining, even by telegram or telephone, that he hasn't received it. Especially when it must have taken you yesterday to get here. And it was last night your goon chloroformed me."

Jerry gave the sneer-smile again.

Into Beresford's mind flashed the memory of a report on Papeete news of a flying-boat passenger and mail service beginning operation between Southampton in England and Sydney in Australia, with an on-flight to New Zealand's Auckland. And then when the postal clerk in Apia had excitedly told him that Apia had a daily float-plane mail service to Auckland via Nukualofa in Tonga, he had added up the days it would take Jerry's letter to reach Sydney.

Yet Jerry's agro isn't about how bloody long it took to get there. Only this number thing.

"Why do you smile? Because I was a chump you found it so easy to suck in to some plot? A gullible greenie who trusted you? Took you at your word? And if not all those things, why have me kidnapped? That's a federal offence all over the world."

Jerry now looked dead serious. His eyes showed not even the glimmer of a smile.

He spelled out his next words very slowly... "I simply need to know that post box number. If you know it, I advise you to tell me."

Bloody hell. What's a man to do? I've already told the liar I didn't read it, let alone remember it. If he really needs to know, it means he'll not going to kill me, for only I saw that envelope since he handed it to me. What his purpose is, I still don't know—any more than knowing what was in it.

"If I knew it, I would tell you. I don't tell lies like some I now know better. I thought I was your friend and doing you a favour. Do you want your twenty dollars back?"

For an instant Jerry really looked like he was ready to lean over and punch his victim into the next world. His eyes were glowing livid.

"Did you write the number down?"

"No, why should I? I was only asked to post the bloody thing. What is so important about remembering that number?"

Now Jerry spoke even more slowly. "Whether you remember it or not, might just have a bearing on whether you live or not. That is what is important in this little *tête-à-tête*. So tell me!"

Jerry's eyes now looked like icicles, and Beresford was getting a real lesson in learning to read people's expressions.

And certainly learning never again to sum people up on first meeting!

Fortunately, just then, for Jerry had reached a pitch where Beresford thought he might really get physical, the food arrived. And a bottle of drinking water.

Beresford didn't waste a second—he opened the bottle by holding the crown-seal on the edge of the table and thumping it with his other fist. The cap flew so far it hit a window—and Beresford began draining the small bottleful as fast as his throat could swallow. The food was banana and mango slices, and he grabbed these by the handful and stuffed them in his mouth.

Jerry took the moment to calm down. He knew that for the next minute he was getting no answers out of Beresford.

He even waited long enough for the Englishman to reopen the conversation.

"What did you, Teri and Randi have for dinner last night Jerry? Did it refresh you? Did you give me even a thought?"

Beresford was also learning not only how to read other people, but how to cower them—how to stand up for himself.

"I came to Apia today to find out from you the number on that envelope. And I do not leave until I have it."

"Go to the post office. Ask them if you can see the insurance receipt."

Jerry's eyes seemed to spin.

He gave no answer but turned again, and again yelled, "Keno!"

When the man arrived, Jerry put an arm across the table and, with a quick gesture, swept everything onto the floor.

"Clean that up, then get out," he told the ape.

In that moment, Beresford lost every skerrick of respect for Jerry Edwards.

From here on, he is enemy!

Twelve

On Saturday the sixteenth of September, the radio news bulletin, after all the disheartening news of Germany's *Blitzkrieg* through Poland, and Britain and France still muddling through the mechanics of their promise to come to Poland's aid, reached its local news.

The Auberling household was at breakfast: bread, cheese, cold sausage and coffee.

All listened wide-eyed when the announcer reported the finding of a young white male found in the early hours of Saturday morning on the outskirts of town, near naked and badly beaten. He had been robbed and dumped beside the road for early travellers to find. He had been admitted to the hospital for observation.

Almost as one, Elo, Rano, Otto and Erik stuffed the rest of their breakfasts into their valises, left the balance of their coffee mugs and bounded out the door. They ran all the way to the hospital. There Mr. Priest was waiting to see 'the surgeon who attended the patient found by the roadside this morning'.

"Surgeon?" Mr Priest was asking the receptionist. "Has surgery been necessary?'

She didn't know.

"We call doctors 'surgeon' sometimes," she said with the hint of a German accent.

The five introduced themselves, if not by individual names then as 'Beresford's room-mates' or 'sons of the Auberling Guest House'.

They had not long to wait. The receptionist returned behind a doctor wiping his hands on his apron, the telltale stethoscope dangling from his neck.

"Yes, you may come to see him," he told them. "He has a split cheek, many bruises and what I think may be a broken or at least split ribs. We have bound up his ribs and fed him morphine."

He beckoned them to follow and led off down the hallway.

"If he is asleep, we must not wake him. Morphine sedates a patient for several hours."

In a ward of several other patients, the visitors were ushered behind a closed screen. It was indeed Beresford Branson, and he was asleep. The doctor beckoned them back into the hallway.

"I ask if you will please give his name and whatever information you have of him to the receptionist. He had no identification when brought in by a farmer on his way to the market. Then you can please come back later in the day or this evening. Not all together. Maybe one or two at a time."

So his friends now knew where he was and that he was safe. Yet each was frustratingly curious to know what had happened to him Thursday night through Saturday morning.

~ * ~

Beresford remained nonplussed as to the importance to Jerry Edwards of the post office box number.

He came all the way from Pago Pago to ask me that question. He obviously had me, by telephone or coded telegram, kidnapped by that oaf and held until he arrived. It is still too early for the letter to have arrived in Sydney for him to make those arrangements on Thursday. I mailed it early Monday. Float plane services would not fly overnight, so even if it was picked up early enough Monday for the pilot to reach Nukualofa by nightfall, it couldn't get to Auckland

before late Tuesday. And even if the weekly flying boat left there Wednesday for Sydney, it surely would take at least four hours to cross the Tasman Sea. Mail would then get to the GPO Thursday morning. The crux is that, could all those 'ifs' fall into place on the one incident? I'm no mathematician, but I think that coincidence impossible. It is far more likely that the earliest mail delivery in Sydney could be Friday and more likely Monday—yet Jerry made all these arrangements on Thursday.

He rapped his knuckles on the side of his skull to make sure he was awake and not dreaming. He was awake, because the rapping caused a spasm of pain to his plastered cheek, and his ribs hurt every time he tried to shift his body into a more comfortable lie. Whilst he couldn't see the rest of his body, clad in a hospital robe with tie-tapes down the sides, he could also feel bruises where the great oaf had obviously kicked him again, many times.

And doctor said I had no clothes on my lower body when found. Nor any wallet or wristwatch or gold ring the family gave me when graduating. So even the little money I had, and my photographs, and my ID card, are gone. Thank God my passport and cash are in the guesthouse safe. But my clothes? Are they still there on the drying line? And I've no idea where that farm was. There must be hundreds like it on this island. At least I pissed on that oaf's lettuces—that's maybe why the second bashing.

Yet his mind kept flitting back to Jerry's questioning.

If not because of delivery in Sydney, why would he, only a few days after entrusting the letter to me, go to all this trouble to see if I remembered the number? And what sort of clandestine business can he be in, that he has 'operators' like the fat oaf, on his payroll— and on his payroll he must be, or why else would he take the insults and demanding attitudes Jerry kept tossing at him, the "Clean up his shit!" for instance. And sweeping all that stuff off the table in a fit of pique and just demanding the oaf clean it up? That's not the Jerry who brought me from Papeete and paid me that bonus and let me lodge at his house.

He wondered if Jerry had gone to the post office to ask for the insurance receipt.

Nor could he get out of his mind that Teri, even if not Randi also, must know the second man inside Jerry's skin.

So are they, too, clever enough to hide all that from me? Am I so gullible as to get taken in by all three?

He was still mulling these things when the nurse ushered in two policemen.

Ah! I hadn't expected this. Although, on reflection, I guess I should have.

He had to think quickly.

Until I've come to some sort of consensus on the why and how of things, I really don't want to commit to anything. I only know the 'who' if it, and how do I know what can of worms I'm going to open if I blurt out Jerry Edward's name? If I can, I'll lead them to the site best I can, and they can take things from there. But I have to have at least a clearer sight of the target before I start chucking darts.

"These gentlemen wish to ask you some questions, sir. The receptionist has given them your name and address, yet they still want to talk to you. Do you want me to give you another pillow? Or raise your backrest?"

"Thank you, nurse. Another pillow would be jolly good."

That gives me a few more seconds…

And when she'd finished, the sergeant asked, "Can we have your name please?"

"The receptionist told you. The nurse just said so."

The sergeant sighed. "We have to ask. It is the law."

"Beresford Branson."

"Is that all?"

"Beresford Wansworth Branson."

"W-A-N-S-W-O-R-T-H?"

"Yes."

"You are a visitor here, Mr. Branson?"

"Yes."

"English, I gather?"

"Yes."

"What happened to you?"

"I guess you'd call it 'mugged'."

"You were robbed?"

"Yes."

The constable was taking notes.

Well, my answers are brief, so I guess that makes his job easier.

He could see that the book he was writing in had a sheet of carbon paper...

So there are likely little boxes to tick for some answers.

"What did he or they take?"

"My wallet, and fountain pen, and wrist-watch and a gold ring."

"A leather wallet?"

"Yes."

"Can you describe it?"

"The initials BB were engraved on the front. Inside..."

"What colour was the engraving?

"No colour. It was blind embossed. A Christmas gift from family."

"And inside?"

"It had a coin pouch and a pocket for folded notes one side, and a pocket for photographs the other."

"Folded banknotes?"

"Yes."

"Can you tell us just what banknotes?"

"A one-pound note and a ten-shilling note."

"Photographs? Other personal notes? Business cards?"

"Family photographs. No notes or business cards."

"A wrist-watch, you say?"

"Yes."

"Can you describe it?"

"A Timepiece with a round face, black hands on a white dial, Roman numerals. And a well-worn black leather band."

"A gold watch?"

"White gold."

"And fountain pen, you say?"

"Yes. A black one with a gold metal band around the cap edge, and gold pocket clip."

"Real gold?"

"I doubt it."

"And a ring, you say?"

"A gold ring with the initials BB etched into it, in italics."

He was beginning to weary of all this and was trying to hurry the fellow up.

"When and where were you accosted?"

"Thursday evening about eight o'clock. I had just dined at Tevake Restaurant and was walking towards the Auberling Guest House, where I live."

The constable was now writing furiously.

"And how did the assault occur?"

"I felt an arm come over my shoulder, and a pad of ether was clasped to my face. The fellow was very strong."

"And what happened then?"

"I don't know."

The sergeant coughed slightly and moved on.

"You were unconscious, then?"

"I guess so. It was daylight when I came to. Then I shit my trousers because my hands were tied behind my back, and I was lying on a concrete floor in a corrugated iron shed with only a tool bench for furniture, and the door was closed. Many rusted holes were in the walls, and daylight was beaming through them. Nobody came—"

The sergeant held up his hands, and the constable now sat on the foot of the bed, still writing.

Beresford waited.

But it was the constable who spoke. "You were on a concrete floor and... what happened then?"

"I shit my trousers because my hands were tied—"

The sergeant again held up a hand.

~ * ~

They must have been there an hour or more.

I wonder how long it takes them to attend a murder scene? Or a major traffic accident? No wonder criminal cases take so long getting to the courts.

They eventually got around to asking where he was between 'about 8 p.m. Thursday and the 6:20 a.m. Saturday when brought to the hospital'.

He told them he had no idea of the time of day he came to on Friday but had then been taken outside and told to strip off his walk-shorts and under-shorts and was then doused with a milk-urn full of washing water, after which he'd draped his clothes over a washing line behind the farmhouse. They then asked what kind of farm it was and to describe the house and outbuildings or anything distinctive about the site he could remember, as well as the people he'd seen.

He told them what he could of buildings he had seen, chickens he'd heard as if in great numbers, that banana trees in abundance and corn were growing in a field to the left of the shed and sugar-cane to the right—and that he'd seen no one but the great ox of a smelly Polynesian man who had beaten him dreadfully until he'd passed out again.

"For all I know, he could have dosed me with more chloroform or ether or whatever it was. But I remember nothing more than coming to, here in this bed."

As the policemen disappeared around the screen that surrounded his bed, other visitors were waiting.

Mr. Priest and Greta Sneider peeped around the screen, and he smiled happily at seeing them. Greta carried a small basket of fruit. The questioning looks on both faces lasted only a minute, then changed to smiles.

"We have been worried," said his manager. "And your head bandaged? At least the doctor says you are recovering well, so that prognosis is good news."

"We brought you these," Greta said, holding up the basket.

"Oh, thank you both. But can you please push this screen out of the way? I asked Nurse, but it seems she forgot."

"Nurses can be like that," Priest said, as if it were the sort of thing Beresford might want to hear. He had Greta slide it all the way around so the patient could see, for the first time, all other patients in the ward—several of whom gave him a welcoming wave.

Priest asked all the appropriate questions of how, and who, and why, and Beresford answered each as appropriately as he could, without mentioning the Jerry connection.

"There are simply so many things to do with it, that I am also in a quandary. Why he should chloroform me and lock me up overnight, and not release me until the next night, or at least by dawn the following morning, just to rob me, I have no idea. Unless he thought I might be worth holding to ransom."

He tried passing off the entire thing as if all were an absolute conundrum.

Which of course, it is. If the Jerry thing gets back to the police, there could be more repercussions against me. It was only when I got the feel that Jerry finally believed me in not knowing that number that he gave up. And by then it was dusk and I was locked back in the shed. It was only later the obnoxious 'hulk' must have come in and begun knocking me around again.

"...only when you're fully recovered," Mr. Priest was saying.

Beresford's mind suddenly clicked back in. He hadn't been listening.

"Look, you're understandably not too alert yet," his boss added. "You just get yourself well soon, then we shall see you back at work."

Greta gave him a little smile, and they left, turning at the door, both just showing a palm by way of farewell.

~ * ~

The following day they let him up, not to try walking, but into a wheelchair that he could self-propel on to a veranda, all wire screened yet too rusted to be insect-proof.

Yet a chap can still see all that is out there, and it's a big ocean. And even here is the distinct smell of salt. And seaweed.

His head didn't ache so much now, and the morphine doses had been discontinued, so he was in hopes of soon being released. The mugging and cross-examination had indeed left him shaken, yet he didn't hold anything against Apia for it. He couldn't get out of his mind that the entire thing was to do with Jerry Edwards having used him to post off something that was obviously clandestine. Or was it just the address that was significant?

If it was so easy for Jerry to come on to Apia now, why couldn't he have come to Apia himself to post it? Or sent Randi? Why was it so essential to hire someone in Papeete who would have been absolutely useless as a deckhand if the weather had turned bad? Could it have been so important time-wise that he couldn't post it from Pago Pago? Yet, then, there is the fact that he told me the friend in Sydney had asked for Samoan stamps.

"It all simply doesn't make sense!" he said aloud to a sparrow that alighted on the veranda railing to peck at something lodged in the rusted wire.

It made no answer but simply flew off. He envied it.

Its only problem is finding grass seeds and puddles of water enough to satisfy it one day at a time. And somewhere under the building's eaves to make a nest. And feed its babies if it has any. And...

He then realised that even the insignificant sparrow would have things to ponder on, things essential to its well-being.

I wonder how the war is going? Will Britain's 'tommies' be trekking through France on their way to attack Germany—the Rhinelands they only so recently, without a murmur of protest, allowed Germany to reclaim? Oh the world is in such a mess. And, I guess, the stresses I have in not having answers must pale into insignificance compared to the stresses the Poles are suffering.

The thought of writing a letter home crossed his mind, seeing he had nowt else to fill his time, yet he realised it was only a few days since last writing. And he certainly didn't want to tell them about his last few days.

And, of course, with now the air-clipper service operating, the Sydney-Southampton leg taking but nine days, my letters should

reach home within a fortnight instead of six weeks by steamer. And surely Pater, whose mind seems to encompass absolutely everything that happens at home, will, once receiving my last letter, send his despatches to me air-mail.

Then he suddenly realised that he had not specified sending his letter airmail. Not only had he not thought about the air service, he would likely not have wanted to pay the up-charge anyway. He didn't, then, have his job with the insurance company.

So it will be another six weeks before they have that letter.

And then another thought struck. *Will the air-clipper service be still running? This is as much an aerial war as a land-based war, the wireless has been saying quite frequently. Now that we are at war too, will the Luftwaffe be bombing England? And if Canadian pilots can ferry fighter aircraft via Iceland, then surely Germany's fighter aircraft will be a threat to the cumbersome and unarmed Flying Boats.*

So his surety of fast mail in future seemed already dashed. And he had still not heard from home about his suggestion of returning in order to enlist.

So again his mind returned to the fact that the sparrow surely had the better life.

Thirteen

Yesterday in Europe, German forces had reached the Polish-Russian border in the north, and in the south, Russia invaded Poland.

So the Poles fleeing east with their loaded prams, wheelbarrows and wagons, were sandwiched. And the Polish army trying to stop the German advance in the south were now being attacked from behind. And further south, their only remaining avenue of retreat, was the German-occupied Czechoslovakia.

There is simply nowhere left for the Poles to flee. They must now sit in the mud beside their pram-cars and wait to see what God has in store for them next!

His mind was imagining every Polish ship and aircraft not already destroyed, heading north to neutral Sweden seeking refugee status.

What a dilemma for Sweden! With Hitler already illustrating that he holds no agreements sacred, it places them in a no-win situation. It cannot afford to earn Germany's displeasure. So what will happen, I wonder, to all the Poles who have already taken ship and fled there? And surely such refugees risk falling prey to the cordon of U-boats Germany will have strung across Poland's Baltic Sea ports?

It was proving a very one-sided war.

And every day that Britain and France do not invade Germany, only lets the Huns occupy more territory to later have to be reclaimed. This could very well become a more prolonged war than it first seemed.

Again he wondered if he should risk taking a cargo ship home.

Risking the U-boats that is, not risking Pater's wrath. In the circumstance, I'm sure he would be happy to see me home—proud that I'd taken such a risk in order to enlist. Or I could go to New Zealand or Australia. Surely those countries have some provision for British passport holders. There is still the risk of having to sail from there to wherever they would send me, of course—but it is most likely England.

The thought that Australia would then be paying his passage home held considerable appeal.

It was Monday, and he was discharged from hospital and would go to work on the morrow. He was not concerned that they would have filled his post, for Mr. Priest had assured him that his job waited. He was concerned, however, that he might be docked payment for every day he didn't attend; it had already been three workdays.

He was happily welcomed at the guesthouse by Frau Auberling. Each day since his arrival, she had become more disappointed with her reception by British people in the town. Whilst she had illustrated genuine joy at seeing him home, he could tell that she had been recently weeping. The hair-bun on her head was somewhat awry, and her eyes were red. But he said nothing. He would ask her sons when they came home.

And that evening, Otto whispered to him that a woman shopping in the market had leaned close behind his mother's back and hissed *"Kraut-frau!* Killing children!"

"She is very upset," he said. "My *Mutte* is a sensitive woman. She is proud of being German, yet does not approve of the Nazis or what they have turned her country into. She is very distressed about this war. Erik and I are even considering that we should not listen to the news any more. But then, we cannot stop her listening to it during the day, hoping for some good sign that it will all end quickly."

"How long has she been here, Otto?"

"Twenty-five or maybe twenty-six years. She and my father married in 1912. He was a mechanic for motorcars, and Samoa advertised for such men to migrate. So they came. I was born just after they arrived. When the Great War began, he returned to Germany because they needed mechanics, and just after he left, *Mutte* brought brother Erik into the world. After the war, Father returned and worked still, in motor repairs. There was not so much work here of course, so they opened the guesthouse. It is because he was in War Service that he is now interned. *Mutte* is free so long as she keeps the guesthouse open. The authorities watch us, we are sure, but we accept that. It is that friends of years are now turning against her that hurts so much."

"I think so too, Otto. She is a very kind and good sort. She has a friend in this English person, to be sure."

Erik too made a fuss of him, even apologising on Samoa's behalf, for the terror he had been put through. The Polynesian lads illustrated regret bordering on embarrassment that he had been attacked and held by a Polynesian.

"He bad rogue man," they insisted. "Rogue. Is that the word for bad man?"

He told them yes.

They insisted that they would spread Beresford's description of the fellow, in the hope the police would be led to him.

Beresford was having second thoughts on whether he wanted the fellow found.

Not that I don't want him to suffer lots and lots of unpleasantness, even physical retribution. My Christian ethics don't extend that far. An eye for an eye and a tooth for a tooth and a split cheek and split rib for a split cheek and split rib is my philosophy. Yet I don't want the relationship of me and the treacherous Jerry thing opened up, at least until I have some sort of answer to the 'why' question. Such would only introduce difficulties I can do without.

He wondered what the common sparrow might do in such a situation, and the answer was easy. *It would simply carry on with*

life, realising that even once knowing, what could he do about it? He has no more hope of changing the world any more than I can.

So he decided that even to all his friends, he would, until Ego urged him otherwise, keep it to himself.

~ * ~

Tuesday morning he was back at work and made a fuss of. Everyone was apologising for him being taken advantage of by a local rascal. And he was happy that that was the way everybody saw it. In Tahiti, the Polynesians had been under French domination since white man first intervened into the Pacific. Here, however, each native had had to face change in acclimatising to a new culture.

The Tahitians were never asked to suddenly switch their French influence to a different culture. The one they had simply persisted, so became easier to bear with in time. In Samoa it was first the Germans who began imposing a new culture and religion on them, only to be faced with a British takeover. And the British have never yet won the respect of even the New Zealand Maoris who they have administered for as long as the French have been in Tahiti. So I can understand why there are some native people unprepared to wipe all the German traits they learned off the blackboard.

He had learned to have great respect for Polynesians... *Except for one disgustingly odious ogre!*

So he was now ready to try fitting into the culture, confused as it was.

The *fale* in Polynesian culture was the village meetinghouse. It had no walls, only a floor of grass mats for all to sit on, chiefs, other dignitaries and commoners, and a thatched roof sound enough to keep out the heaviest rain. *Fale* was the place for free expression, the raising of problems of all kinds, that debate would settle them. Sometimes. None believed there was a perfect way to solve problems, political, civil or personal. Yet there all sides could be heard and resolutions mooted. Sometimes things got fixed to the satisfactions of the majority—sometimes not.

Traditional customs still ruled there. The old tribal chiefs were still accorded due deference in matters, all somehow intertwined with British law, that people could get along. Beresford was beginning to sense an understanding of that situation.

He had enjoyed the similar gala occasions as the *Heiva* Festival in Papeete, the hypnotic grace of the dancing, the mystical rhythm of the drums and bright floral tribal costumes. They were all here too. He realised that Polynesians didn't seem to mind a westerner sitting on a mango-tree stump looking on, so long as he didn't begin interfering in their way of life, yet there was a line—a line never mentioned, yet as clearly defined as the territorial spoor-marks of wild animals. So he accepted that he must still observe caution in reacting to the friendship Elo and Rano offered, especially when realising that whilst they were themselves visitors, they were accorded seats in Apia's *fale*.

Yet the war wouldn't go away. Poland surrendered, and the Nazis began building a wall around parts of Warsaw, delivering into the ghetto every Jew they could identify. And the black-shirted SS were brutal in their searching. In early November, Germany announced formal annexation of Western Poland into the Third Reich—it was now officially a part of Germany. The Russians annexed Eastern Poland. So the entire country of Poland had been swept off the face of the earth. Poles now had no homeland.

In mid-November Beresford received a letter from home dated 4 September. It had been readdressed from Papeete. It was old news of course, England just having declared war on Germany and everyone expecting to again have air raids, not from Zeppelins dropping bombs at random this time but from *Stukas* and *Heinkels* that were then devastating Polish cities. The family sent love, with the telling message that they were just thankful that he was safe in the Pacific and didn't have to be called up.

...The Huns cannot keep up the pressure they are throwing at Poland, son. And I repeat what I said to you in my other letter—that Germany will try swallowing more than it can

chew and that, with today's technology, it will be a quick war. So stay where you are, boy, until further notice.

The family professed itself all well and wished their son plenty of love and best wishes.

He was able to kiss the smudges where tears had made the ink run.

Fourteen

The New Year 1940 wasn't a jolly affair in Apia. Folk were hesitant about turning on the radio, expecting to hear only deeper depths of despair at what was happening in Europe. On land, news was leaking out of the inhumane treatment of the Poles—especially the Jewish people. And the Soviets had introduced yet another front—it invaded Finland for the second time—having, since the first, agreed to a cease-fire on Finland conceding considerable territory to Russia.

Another example of the Axis bloc breaking treaties!

On the seas, however, the war was proving more even, despite heavy loss of life. At least one German U-boat had managed to somehow sneak through the boom-nets shielding Scotland's Scapa Flow anchorage in the Orkneys, to sink *HMS Royal Oak* with the loss of eight hundred seamen. In December was the great drama of Germany's cruiser *Admiral Graf Spee*. Crippled in battle, she had fled into Uruguay's Montevideo harbour. International law demanded that in a neutral port she was allowed remain only seventy-two hours for minor repairs or be interned, with all her crew, for the duration of the war. She bravely sent all her wounded and the majority of her crew into internment and sailed out to face expected slaughter from

the three British cruisers that had crippled her in the first place. Her captain scuttled her once in international waters.

"Well, that was indeed a gentlemanly way of handling a difficult situation," Beresford told Frau Auberling over a cup of tea. "It should make you feel very proud."

She responded by patting the back of his hand and wiping away a tear.

Yet it was the Jerry Episode, as he called that particular confrontation that still bugged him. It was the threat on his life that irked more than any other facet.

Whether you remember it or not, might just have a bearing on whether you live or not. That is what is important in this little tête-à-tête. So tell me!

I shall never forget the look in his eyes as he said that. They showed everything but friendship—it was hate and determination. Yet determination about what? Finding the number?

He tried switching his mind onto a different set of rails—manoeuvring it through intersection points in a new direction...

My life depended on whether I remembered or not? Hey! That can be looked at two ways. Maybe his threat was taking my life based on me remembering it. Was I to be killed if I could remember it? Am I still alive only because he finally realised I didn't?

That would make sense of the entire thing! If there were really things covert in the package, it is natural he wouldn't want me to remember it. Yet what could those contents have been? Photographs? Newspaper clippings? Any-bloody-thing I guess—well, anything that could get through censors.

So where does that take me now? Only into the realisation that I now have a different burning curiosity!

He sat back, as exhausted as if he'd just moved a ten-ton lorry.

The bastard, the utter bastard. I don't have to die because I cannot trace that package! Or the addressee. But it still doesn't answer why

he couldn't have come here and posted it himself. Unless he has a criminal record here and wouldn't get through customs? Nor his family?

He was again clapping hands to his forehead. If he'd solved yesterday's problem, he had only introduced another entire bundle of unknowns.

Yet I am obliged to follow none. I'm here, I'm hale and I'm a hero to all the locals.

Why shouldn't I adopt the Polynesian philosophy of life and simply sit back and make myself happy with what 'is'?

~ * ~

In Sydney's Double Bay, a harbour-side suburb of exclusive mansions and expensive apartments, Yoshida Kaito received mail from Apia.

It had been opened, undoubtedly by censors, and re-closed with staples. Yet nothing had been deleted by cut-outs, and no marks had been made. So he smiled.

The living room of his small flat was entirely misplaced in Australia. It was a genuine *washitsu*, a traditionally styled Japanese room. There was no clutter, leaving every item accentuated. It doubled as his bedroom, for he had *tatami* mats for both sitting and sleeping. *Shoji* screens hid his kitchen, wind chimes of baby gongs tinkled softly and both *ninja* and *samurai* swords graced his walls. Mock *shoji* lamps and *chouchin* lanterns provided the lighting, and on a wall was a *hokora*, a miniature Shinto shrine, the building that housed sacred Shinto relics. His *hokora*, however, was but a plaster façade that opened to reveal a wall-safe where he stored his 'sacred relics', documents and films that he need keep secret.

Indoors he wore a kimono and slippers and prepared his own food—he considered Australians the worst cooks he'd ever experienced.

Even 'Japanese' restaurants here flavour food so it tastes like things Australians already like—additives people in Japan have never heard of.

The 'sacred relics' he received from Peter Rabbit, once having been decoded, he placed in the *hokora*; he then worked on his decoded copies.

He'd often wondered who Peter Rabbit really was, yet had to remain satisfied with the fact all spies had such anonymous names.

His submissions always seem thorough, however.

All had been carefully schooled to simply accept what the 'Almighty' had declared. He alone controlled what he called Enlightened Protocol, and protocol in this sense, was to simply do as told.

Japanese were good at that; it was part of their culture.

He went to the refrigerator and poured a beer.

How lucky am I to have scored Australia as my base. I don't like its food, but its beer is even better than the choicest sake.

At which thought he looked over both shoulders to ensure no countryman could have heard such blasphemy.

Kaito had been in Australia five years. The Yoshida Enterprises Pty Ltd he'd founded imported Japanese toys and exported stuffed koala, kangaroo and wombat 'cuddlies' home. His wife ran the Nagoya end of the business while maids tended their three children. He travelled home every other year. Most of what he received from 'out in the field' he despatched home inside his cuddly toys—paperwork photographically reduced to miniature size in small cuddlies and 8mm films in larger cuddlies. Yet simply receiving information wasn't his only task.

Business took a decreasing proportion of his working time as his spying work took more and more. He had a variety of western tourist outfits. His facial image being so conspicuous, he needed attire that wouldn't attract attention—so he looked quite the normal tourist as he rode Sydney Harbour ferries. His 8mm camera worked overtime, especially around the Naval Base. He felt safe there because it was right by the scenic Botanic Gardens in one direction and the famous Harbour Bridge in the other—one of the most photographed areas of the entire harbour. And he spent considerable time filming the areas he believed likely as sites, should Sydney build a protective boom across the harbour—a boom ensuring every ship or submarine entering must

declare itself before given access to downtown. He narrowed down the possibilities to two.

If the 'Almighty' has both options to work with, along with the aerial photos already despatched, that is insurance.

He had already sent aerial photos of both Sydney's Mascot and Bankstown airports, and many of the Rose Bay base in the harbour from where the Flying Boat service operated. From other personnel he had done the same for Brisbane's Eagle Farm and Melbourne's Essendon. His next project was Sydney's railway grid.

But I'll hire a different company this time. I don't want to risk getting the same pilot.

The documents he received from Peter Rabbit were copies of all available maritime maps of Tahiti's several islands. The accompanying note simply said:

> *Dear James and Shirley,*
> *I'm sending all the maps, just in case the weather influences you to approach by one direction or another. Have a good trip, and I look forward to seeing you.*
> *Peter*

Fifteen

Beresford continued working for Mr. Priest and twice took Greta on dates to Apia's open-air movie cinema, though he wasn't interested in fostering an attachment. He simply didn't know how long he might be there; fostering affairs of the heart could only further complicate life. He was beginning to consider the option of going to Australia—heavily influenced by the fear that Jerry Edwards might yet take it into his head to have the 'ape' actually murder him.

Should such a situation arise, there is less chance he could find me, if in Australia.

So the easy Polynesian lifestyle continued to hold him, even if temporarily. He took his measure by the fact that the war seemed to make little difference to everybody's life, other than the simmering Anglo-Germanic tension.

In February, the British despatched a destroyer into a neutral Norway fjord to board the German prison ship *Altmark* and rescue two hundred and ninety-nine British seamen. Yet during the following months, hope by some that Germany might indeed have been satisfied with its new boundaries was shattered. It invaded neighbouring

Denmark and also Norway, both countries not only having declared themselves neutral, but with significant ports to the North Sea...

Right on my Britain's doorstep!

And within another month it invaded neighbours Holland, Belgium, Luxembourg and France! Devastating news to all the hopeful pacifists. All hope of a short war was now shattered. Hitler had declared his hand in no uncertain terms. He wanted all of Europe.

"Can Sweden, Switzerland and Portugal really, now, hope to remain neutral? Even Spain, whilst declaring itself pro-Nazi is entirely helpless after its long civil war," was the conversation piece in the Auberling sitting room, night after night as the wireless gave increasingly bad news.

"Hungary and Italy having now signed allegiances to the Nazi cause just proves them cowards," Otto declared. Beresford had realised that none of the Auberlings referred to the enemy as Germany. It was ever 'the Nazis'. So he endeavoured, for their sake, to follow suit.

Day after day, the radio illustrated that no punches were being pulled—it was indeed a bloody war. Rotterdam was so mercilessly bombed that thirty thousand Dutch people died, their entire city flattened—a statement to bring, within days of its invasion, Holland's surrender. Like Poland, it had been utterly vanquished. Then Belgium surrendered.

Germany invaded France, not through its Maginot Line, the chain of forts along the German border; it simply went around them, invading through Belgium. France's 'multi-million dollar' impregnable defensive line never fired a shot.

In London, Prime Minister Chamberlain came under such scathing attacks condemning his handling of Britain's crisis and want of diplomatic competence that he resigned. A National Parliament was formed with the controversial Winston Churchill its prime minister.

At least the fellow is blue blooded!

Beresford was getting mail from home much the faster since introduction of the airmail service via Auckland and Sydney, despite that all mail both in and out of Britain was censored if even hinting at anything that might help the enemy. It was understood that spies in

undetectable disguise could be operating everywhere. Every tiny scrap of good news that found its way to the radio script writers was given wide circulation. Much was made of the fact that the RAF had bombed Germany's port cities of Bremen and Hamburg.

Yet how would these compare, I wonder, with Holland's port of Rotterdam? Is such news just to give us hope? No matter how fragile?

And before the end of the same month of swallowing up the entire northwest of Europe, Nazi forces reached the English Channel at the French city of Dunkirk, not forty-five miles off England's coast. Near a million British and French troops were stranded on its beaches.

And Norwegian airfields but four hundred miles from Scotland? The Luftwaffe is now going to find every day a 'field day' for bombing Britain. And Nazi troops just thirty miles away?

He was aghast at the thought, again weighing up the option of going home. His mind flew to wondering the cost of getting there by air. He enquired at the British Consulate.

"Haven't a clue, old chap," he was told. "But we could find out for you. Leave me your contact address, and I shall get back to you when I have an answer. Don't hold your breath, though. It's likely that these days, every seat is taken by naval and military bigwigs or diplomats. Maybe you might even have to get a permit to travel—you know, security and such?"

So he left his enquiry with the fellow, who gave every impression he was thankful to be stationed here and not there.

He felt utterly despondent about everything in general.

And the work I do is also utter—utterly boring and utterly thankless. I achieve nothing purposeful out of it but salary. And why do I need the salary? Just so I can pay board and have access to a wireless that in one sense I feel is defeatist simply listening to, yet remain agog to hear it again tomorrow. All I have to live for is wishful thinking! There are simply no more opportunities to hope for! Except, maybe, to wait for news on getting home by air. If I can find enough money! And I'm damned if I'm going to ask Pater, even if circumstances have themselves quashed that embargo.

He tossed up his chances of robbing the bank if a flight ticket became available, although Ego quickly quenched that.

~ * ~

Come Friday night when each had a week's salary in their pockets, Elo, Rano and Beresford met for dinner as usual at Tevake. Yet what was different about this Friday, for Beresford, from any other?

Did I trip over a black cat on my way here? Or fall over to 'break a leg'? And I certainly wasn't wearing a four-leaf clover.

Yet luck was to hover over him in the form of Joshua Noble, an Englishman eating alone at the next table, his back to Beresford's back. He knocked a spoon off his table. It bounced on hitting his chair-leg, to settle where Beresford had but to lean down and pick it up. He reached back behind him to hand it to the unseen fellow.

He felt it taken from his grasp.

"Well, thank you indeed, sir. Very gentlemanly of you," the stranger replied.

Beresford quickly twisted about.

"Geordie, eh? Tyneside or Sunderland?"

The man now jumped his chair somewhat sideways so he could twist, to see who asked.

Beresford proffered his hand. "Beresford Branson—Durham."

"Well, I'll be," said the stranger, getting to his feet. "A real Englander, eh? Joshua Noble at your service, sir. Whereabouts in Durham, then?"

"You probably wouldn't know it. Spennymoor. It's..."

"I know it indeed. Branson, you say? Sir Thomas Branson?"

Beresford was now more than taken aback, and his surprise showed. He was conscious of his Polynesian friends watching in wonder.

"I am his younger son, sir. And am indeed astounded that you know him—I mean—here in Samoa? An entire world away from your home and mine."

He then turned to his friends. "This gentleman's home, and mine, are but thirty miles apart. And he knows my father."

He turned back to Joshua Noble, a man likely nearing fifty and beginning to bald.

"Here, move your chair...bring your food...sit with us," exclaimed Beresford. "You and I have much to talk about."

Noble looked at the two Polynesians. "I don't want to intrude, but..."

"Come along, man. These chaps are learning English and don't often get the chance to hear such a conversation. Especially between Geordies."

Noble laughed. Beresford took his chair and placed it opposite his own, that they had one of the lads either side.

"Now they have to listen to us," explained Beresford, with a grin.

"This is a time to celebrate, Master Beresford. Do you like a glass of wine?"

"I do indeed, yet their selection is small. And expensive. It comes all the way from Australia."

"Then it's likely a good drop." He turned and called the waiter.

Yes, they had three only bottles of a Penfolds *Cabernet*.

"Three of the same means there's no choice. But I know of them— been in the business a hundred years. I'll guarantee it's good."

He went through the tasting procedure. "Not that we've a choice," he said with a half-giggle, "but it has a taste and bouquet to please you too, I am sure."

The Polynesian lads hesitated. They had never drunk wine.

"Then try a sip," Joshua said, pouring a thumbnail for each.

And while they smiled, it was noticeably false, but Joshua slipped a small extra for each, then generously poured for Beresford and himself.

"Joshua," Beresford began, but was interrupted.

"Call me Josh. I ask that of friends."

"Then please call me Berry. These two lads do, as do all Apians who know me."

Somewhere in the back of Beresford's mind he could feel Ego knocking. Jerry Edwards' 'ape' was in the picture. Yes, this meeting was in just such a jovial and 'no expense spared' sort of introduction as with the Edwards—an almost too good a 'hail fellow well met' situation.

It threw him right on the defensive.

Yet this fellow, with no prompt from me, knows Pater. Or at least knows of him. So he's worth a hearing. Yet I'm going to keep my guard up, just in case.

Ego relaxed.

"Josh, I was about to ask how you know my father. Spennymoor is hardly a metropolis. It's highly likely that nobody outside Durham County, but you, it seems, has ever heard of it."

"I have, in fact, Berry, visited your home—ah... *Folly...ah...*"

"Folly Drift."

"Yes, that's it. It must be ten years since. A partner and I were floating a company to manufacture *cassava* or *tapioca* as some call it—even *sago* as you probably know it in Fiji. It's grown in many tropical countries, Brazil, Kenya, the Dutch East Indies and such. I had dabbled in business there, and people in this part of the world eat things like yam and taro—all sort of sister plants..."

He stopped, looking at the lads, who both had illustrated interest at the *cassava* word.

"You lads know this plant?"

Elo spoke up. "We grow *cassava* in our village. Make good pudding. And bread. Not easy to find. We like. Yam and taro we grow easy."

"*Cassava* is difficult to extract from the root without machinery," replied Noble.

Then he turned back to his fellow Englishman.

"We looked at various sites on Viti Levu, Fiji's main island, which has high mountains—ideal climate at altitude for this product, for it needs soil that will drain itself quickly of water. We saw a site and firmed a price, with three months to find the capital. We had some, yet not enough. I guess you know your father has several investments in agriculture in Africa?"

Berry shrugged his shoulders and showed palms up.

"So we took our paperwork of government permissions, deposits paid etc, seeking some backing. We'd put pretty well all our own assets into it, and I think that's what persuaded your father to come in. He

asked for a week to make his enquiries, like to our bank and our legal people et cetera, and he came good with half what we needed. So when we raised the other half, we bought our land, planted our crops and built our processing plant. We run it with about half Fijian staff, half Indian. So there you have it. Your father is one of my shareholders—not 'our' anymore, because I bought out my partner two years ago when he ran off with my bloody wife. So your father's share of my now profits, help pay your bib and tucker, young Berry."

And young Berry was indeed astounded at such a coincidence befalling him.

"And what brings the son of an English knight to this nether part of the world? It's hardly Oxford or Cambridge."

Berry smiled. "I'm being blooded. I'm expected to return home having earned respect for my contributions to mankind or something like that. I think you know the sort of story."

Josh smiled. "And how does your father keep? He must be a fair age by now?"

"Seventy-one. But keeps good health. Yet his letters illustrate great heartache with what is happening in Europe. And with such stringent rationing now, he foregoes many pleasures, what with Spanish and French wines now impossible to obtain. In fact I'm tossing around the thought that I should go home to enlist—pull my weight at the front."

"You any good at running backwards? That's the way it is," said the practical businessman. "It's not men we're short of, Berry, it's equipment—military supplies and food to feed not only the people, but the forces. That's why I'm not called up—I'm part of 'essential services'. I'm exporting eighty percent of my entire output to Britain. It needs more people to do things like this. Are you working here?"

Berry told him what he was doing.

Josh sat back and threw up his hands.

"I'm here in Apia now because I'm so short-staffed. Melanesians don't like work. They would rather dance, sing their beautiful ballads and douse their worries with *kava*—it's not alcohol, rather narcotic, yet quickly induces languor and a sense of well-being. So I have to

have Indians who harbour a great sense of the work ethic—and the penny! Yet Melanesians and Indians don't get on—the blacks believe the Indians intruders. Yet it's the Indians who do all the work so the natives can play. And if I employ more Indians than natives, I lose my license to manufacture. It's a real merry-go-round. I'm here trying to organise alternative shipping routes to the UK. U-boats are sinking two in ten of my shipments, so I have to find alternative transport so I can make more shipments in smaller quantities. And nobody's looking after the plant. Not looking for a job, are you?"

Sixteen

10 June 1940

Dear Mater, Pater and Thomas,

    I hope this finds you all well.

    I shall not find the ease of posting from Apia any more, as I have moved—both location and job. And there is good news attached to it. However, be patient because I first want to say that the move may make it more difficult to get mail to Auckland for the clipper. I am now resident in Fiji. My new mail address is c/- Post Office Lautoka. Mail you have already despatched to Apia will be forwarded. So you see I am already looking at things with Forward Vision. Fiji is not Polynesian but Melanesian, the local people quite black—the men robust but strongly proportioned and the women taller and slimmer, yet all with a great mop of curly black hair.

    What I didn't envision when struggling in Samoa was a chance meeting with my new employer. His name is known to you, Pater. It is Joshua Noble. I don't have to tell you what he does, for you know even better, yet, than me. I have just arrived here and am waiting for Josh to return from his present business that I dare not put in writing. It is that role, plus 'general salesmanship', that I am to be instructed in. So I have plenty of travel ahead. However, please continue mail to Lautoka.

Josh is particularly pleased about me having French as a language, for the introduction of French territories to his business provides further outlet in both sales and despatch—if you get my meaning. He really is a jolly good sort of fellow, I find. I only hope that I don't have any unpleasant surprises in this. Have you any comments on him, Pater?

Mater, darling, how are your ladies' baking classes going? I do hope all proceeds end up in the right sort of places. It must be difficult for you with the rationing, but I hear most colonies have established "Food for Britain" parcels—despatching on vessels that hopefully avoid the U-boats.

And, dear Thomas, give me some news on what are your eager interests in the moment. Mine seem like making my remaining six hundred and fifteen days of penance before seeing you all considerably more purposeful.

All the best to you,
Your loving son and brother...

~ * ~

He had been told to book himself into Tanoa Guest House and spend his days looking over the town and beaches.

"By the time you get there, Berry," Josh had said, "I'll likely be only a few days behind you."

He had also said, "Don't wear a wrist-watch and don't keep wads of cash on you. The place is not dangerous except for lone foreigners wandering in lonely places and looking wealthy. Dress as you see other local white people dressing—simple and sensible for the weather and conditions."

He had also advised Berry to open his own bank account. "I will be paying you by monthly cheque. I don't believe in giving people cash to carry around in these times. In a community where there are many unemployed, there will be muggers. One simply has to be careful. It is, unfortunately, a sign of the times."

So once warned, Berry did as recommended. And he was not in the least concerned at the casual way even businessmen dressed— shorts, long-socks and sandals with an open-neck short-sleeved shirt. Some wore pith helmets, others plain panamas. Even police wore the traditional *sulu*, the sarong-type skirt worn by most natives, as a uniform. The uniform even called for bare legs and open leather sandals.

He had Josh's business card, yet the physical address given was but the name of a village that didn't show on the town map. He would simply have to curtail his curiosity until Josh arrived. Meanwhile he purchased daily newspapers to familiarise himself with not only Lautoka but Fiji in general.

So he had lots of time for thinking, to talk with Ego...

'All journeys start with a small step', I remember Pater telling me that one time when I was, as usual, only half listening. But, gee-whiz, I've taken so many steps since leaving home, and everyone seems to begin with a great leap. Travel is not just an education in geography—I have found it a path to humanity. Jerry Edwards, the Frenchies, the Auberlings, the Mr. Priests...all revelations, bombshells if you like, of which there must be millions scattered across the world. And is Josh to prove another? I'd reckon so, because no two people I have met have been even alike, let alone the same.

And he listened to the radio news on the wireless in his room. The Nazis had bombed Paris, and there was exciting news of the evacuation of British and French troops stranded on Dunkirk beaches. Over an entire week, thousands of boats from weekend runabouts to commercial ferry-boats had crossed the channel backwards and forwards, twenty-four hours a day, bringing both hale and wounded soldiers to waiting arms and care centres on the Kentish coast. Nearly a million souls had been saved from imprisonment or worse.

Was its God's intervention that the Nazi's stayed their advance through the town, waiting for supplies to catch up?

He at least felt safer here than if still back in Apia, despite Josh's warning. He had indeed feared for his safety there when even the newspapers were daily reporting that the police were still searching for the man who had attacked Beresford Branson.

I was the only one who could proffer identification.

Yet his departure had been so quick he gave up hope of getting his wallet, wrist-watch and gold ring back.

At least, should they eventually be recovered, the Auberlings have my address here.

He did not buy replacements. He had already delved into his cash capital as far as he wanted to risk, before getting his first pay packet from Josh Noble. Not that he mistrusted the man, but that after the Jerry Episode, he wanted to be cautious—let things come in their turn rather than ruing loss should they go awry.

Josh having a heart attack before getting back, for instance!

Yet nearly a week later, Josh arrived hale and hearty.

"I docked about midday," he told Berry over the phone about five o'clock one evening, "in the packet that commutes with passengers, mail and cargo to Apia, Tokelau, Ellice, Honiara and Port Vila. One can take side trips from any of those, but that's the regular round trip. Do you have anything planned for dinner?"

"No, Josh. I've been eating here at Tanoa's café."

"Okay. Ask directions to the Isa Lei. It's only two streets from you. I'll be there at seven-thirty. That all right with you?"

"Jolly good. I shall be there."

~ * ~

Jerry Edwards gently lowered the handpiece into its cradle, Leo Ferguson's final words ringing loudly in his ears.

Ferguson was the FBI's area boss for Pacific Oceania, operating out of Washington DC. He masterminded counter-intelligence from China and Japan to Australia and all points east to the Americas.

He had agents operating out of fourteen centres in the area, and Jerry Edwards was his agent for Melanesia and Polynesia—the most extensive, yet least populated. It had no independent nation; all were dependencies of either Great Britain, Australia, New Zealand or France. The exception was Easter Island. Despite its Polynesian culture, it was part of Chile and came under the FBI's South American office.

Jerry's counter-intelligence responsibilities fell mainly in the area of espionage—observation, spying and reporting. Threat to the USA had not been as high since World War 1, and despite its neutrality in WW2, threat from the Axis Pact bloc was paramount. The US was every part a component of the Allies except active on the field of battle. It was knowingly providing Britain with not only machines of war—military equipment from rifles to tanks and fighter aircraft and bombers—but intelligence. Japan, a major partner of the Axis bloc was seen through FBI eyes, therefore, a major threat—and the US Mariana dependencies lay less than a thousand miles off Japan's coast.

Despite Japan having fought with the Allies in the Great War, there ever remained a deep-hearted resentment against the nation that had, in 1853, despatched a fleet of four warships into Yokohama Bay. Japan had elected to live in seclusion for two hundred years and was still enjoying its solitude from the rest of the world's problems. Under the threat of America's might, Japan had been forced to open its doors to international trade.

"Gunboat Diplomacy" Japan had called it. Diplomatic tensions between the two had simmered ever since.

Leo Ferguson had summed up his call to Jerry Edwards with… "…and in this God-awful war in Europe, Jerry, and Japan a fully-fledged member of the Axis bloc, Hitler has shown that it will be fought more in the air than on the ground or at sea. Nothing, if we are forced into this war, as seems Goddam certain, is going to stop Japan attacking by air, in turn, every island in the Pacific, including Hawaii."

The resonance of his voice pealed loudly.

Yet Jerry could smile while Leo Ferguson could but tremor.

What Leo couldn't know, nor even Jerry's own Teri and Randi, was that Jerry was a rogue spy, a double agent. He was highly paid by the Empire of Japan for information. With an island trading business as well being a trusted agent for the FBI, he was ideally placed both geographically and politically in Pago Pago—central in Japan's quest to rule the Pacific all the way to Tahiti.

Seventeen

Beresford found Isa Lei without trouble. It was a mid-class eatery chosen by both locals and westerners.

"Where locals eat, Berry, the food is both good and authentic. Isa Lei is the tearful Fijian song of farewell, the most haunting melody and lyrics I have heard anywhere. It bemoans the fact you are leaving, and begs you to return—just like this restaurant, you will find."

They quickly dispensed with Beresford's arrival and settling in, to talk on Josh's business in outline. And by the time food came, it had, to Beresford, all seemed so rushed.

"In this part of the world, Berry, 'rushed' has a vastly different meaning from home. Here, as you will find, nothing is done at a fast pace. Such is simply a way of life here. What I call rushed is only that one must ensure you don't miss connections. Missing a boat is different from missing a tramcar or bus. It means many days or even weeks of waiting. And waiting also falls into the 'vastly' range. It is vastly frustrating when there is so much work to be done. Lack of having dependable staff contributes to that—this is why I have great hopes that the son of Sir Thomas Branson can take some pressure off me."

"I have very little experience of working, Josh. Back home, the nearest I came to it was helping out at fetes or the incessant galas one's mother indulges in. Or running messages. Or helping out if the gardener was indisposed. That boring job as a clerk in Apia is the only time I have worked for a wage."

"But I see you have a way with people. And with language. You had not only won the respect of Polynesians, you had picked up snippets of their language. There are thousands of English, German and French who have come here and been here for years without even attempting to earn respect or even liaise on a social basis with locals. It is in this area that you have work skills that those businessmen lack. It is this experience that gives you what the work I have for you calls for."

They then casually talked business over delightful food and a bottle of wine, and Berry found himself feeling involved with something of merit.

It might be but a modest product from a modest plant, yet it offers challenge—a challenge far from modest—one with goals, one with satisfactions if I play it right.

It was agreed they start with servicing their marketplace in two areas—easterly and westerly circuits.

"You take the easterly, Berry—the Polynesian area. It is the bigger although the less populated, and the most time-consuming because there is more travelling. I designed it around the timetable of the good little ship *Mbula*. Its home base is Lautoka."

Then he smiled. "Whilst *Isa Lei* is the song of farewell, *Mbula* is the word of greeting. A coincidence for sure yet maybe, for us, prophetic. I know her owner and captain well. She loads and offloads mail and cargo, plying here to Suva, then to Tonga's two ports, Vava'u and Nukualofa, then Rarotonga in the Lower Cook Islands and on to Papeete. Then to Tongareva in the Upper Cook Islands, then Tokelau, another NZ dependency, then Pago Pago and Apia. Then it's Suva again and home."

Berry's eyes widened.

"That is a huge part of the world, Josh. My mind is spinning."

"It's about the area of the USA or Australia—certainly bigger than all of Europe. But most of it is ocean. You'll certainly see a lot more of that, than terra-firma."

Josh would, while Berry found his feet, continue the western circuit.

"Six months around those eastern islands, lad, will blood you. Then we can look at basing you in Honiara where you've easy access not only to all the New Guinea islands in its north, but to the French communities—New Caledonia and New Hebrides. They will be new markets to cultivate."

~ * ~

June 1940 was a significant time in the war. Only days after the Germans invaded France, which had had a ten-year warning of Nazis building strength, the French were caught so unprepared that they capitulated. On the very day Italy declared war on Britain and France, it despatched its navy to seal off France's southern coast, and also, the Nazis entered Paris—it was already all over.

The very next day, however, Britain sent an answer to Mussolini. It despatched bombers, devastating the Fiat factory in Turin. But the morale-building raid was too late to help the French.

Marshal Pétain became the French prime minister and did a deal with Germany. France was divided. The northern half and the Atlantic coast fell under German administration. The south, administered by Pétain, would work hand in glove with the Germans. Its capital would be the city of Vichy.

General Charles de Gaulle, next most senior French officer, escaped to Britain. He was there recognised as the French leader. He felt highly humiliated when cinema film of Hitler sightseeing in Paris was deliberately leaked to the Allies. Of interest to Joshua Noble, however, was that de Gaulle declared both New Caledonia and New Hebrides to be Free French possessions, and Australia was invited to use them at their discretion...

"What I think he means by that, lad," Josh declared, "is that he wants Aussie troops there, even if, I reckon, it is only, ostensibly, to train for jungle warfare."

"Yes, Josh. But Australia already has New Guinea for that."

"But New Guinea is British, lad. De Gaulle wants them on French soil. The Australian Army might be small, but it's the only one we've got in the entire Pacific."

Beresford couldn't see why, yet considered it not worth risking argument. He simply let it slide.

Another Pétain move, however, surely at the insistence of Japan, was to declare French Indo-China, the three dependencies of Vietnam, Cambodia and Laos, available to Japanese interests. This was obviously to aid Japan in its war with China. It already occupied China's eastern coastline and had recently made concerted advances in China's south yet was hampered by the fact that Britain had been helping China by landing military hardware and supplies for them in Vietnamese ports. Vietnam shared its northern border with China's inland south, so there was an overland corridor. Pétain's move now allowed Japan to close that door.

Josh also realised that if Japan did decide to move its war south, giving it access to the rice-growing areas Japan lacked, the entire Dutch East Indies was now without protection. With Holland vanquished, its oil-rich East Indies was defenceless. And Japan was now desperate for oil to keep its forces both supplied and offensive.

Only Britain's Hong Kong, Singapore, Australia and New Zealand remained as military bases in the entire South Pacific—and with Australia's forces now numbering a half-million and New Zealand's less than a quarter, what hope had they against Japan's seven or eight million?

~ * ~

Josh came dockside, not only to farewell Beresford on his first career venture, but to introduce him to *SS Mbula*'s owner-captain, a Welshman with some fifty years of sailing the southern ocean behind him. Master Evans hated being ashore anywhere yet, despite all those years mixing with personnel from just about every country in the world but Wales, had never lost his accent. Occasional idiom wheezed through whiskers that sprouted from his entire face aplenty.

"Ach, be-heavens, laddie," Berry heard through the spittle sticking to the whiskers, "I be sailin' these sea along such I know every wave. Each up and now flings hisself aboard ter slaps me in me face acos I forget ter say *Shwmae*."

"*Shwmae* is 'hello'," Josh whispered.

He had a private cabin, seventy-two by forty-two.

Inches, that is. I measured it. It is bed length. And width-wise, the bunk is twenty-four and the spare area in which I have to turn about and stow my gear but eighteen. The under-bed area belongs to downstairs. What it might be headroom for, I've no idea.

But he had a porthole with brass surrounds, polished such that it was painful if there were sunshine wanting in. All was as clean as was the shower cubicle filthy. A single shower, but a fraction the size of his cabin, was used by Mr. Evans, his three officers, the doctor-come-cook, and the passengers.

And I am but the one passenger so far it seems. Yet we've many a port during the journey. At least I don't expect to be asked to share.

The shower cubicle doubled as a toilet. What one did to relieve oneself if the shower were being used, he was yet to discover.

The stern rail it would seem, along with the rest of the crew.

He certainly felt a long way from *Folly Drift*.

He looked on it, however, as all part of a worthwhile experience.

...All part of what I was sent away to discover. I simply hope I never despair at the number of times I must remind myself.

He had spent his last two weeks being shown through Noble Mill Pty. Ltd., seeing how Noble Cassava was made from dirty, scrawny, earth-covered roots to pristine powder in brown paper bags printed with green and yellow coconut palms (*as if they had anything to do with cassava*) and packed for transport to everywhere in the South Pacific and to Britain. The pockets on the several starched short-sleeved shirts in his 'south-seas' uniform packed in the spare eighteen inches of his cabin were emblazoned with the same Noble crest.

He now knew how cassava was refined and packed. He now knew what was here known as tapioca and there known as sago. The roots grew in, fortunately, any sort of soil so long as it had clear drainage of water—an ideal requirement of the many mountainsides of Viti Levu Island, almost rivalling its sugar plantations. It was 'bread' to islanders. Or, in East Asian terms, 'rice'. It was part of every meal, baked as bread type products or used in stews and desserts. There was a use for it in every Polynesian and Melanesian dish. Village food was designed around it though its extraction from the root was dreadfully tedious to accomplish in villages. It was still done, yet part of Berry's job was to endeavour to influence remote village people how easy it would be if they could raise the few pence needed to buy it ready powdered...

"There are ample opportunities for visiting such villages, Berry. The *Mbula* will be in port four days, three days longer than you need to see each island's buyers. You can travel and find these markets anew."

"But where do they find the pennies when they know nowt of money? Doesn't that only invite petty crime?"

"That is not our concern, Berry-me-boy. That is a police problem. We need only to find more customers."

And he was shown how it could be cooked. It could become like the 'chips' of an Englishman's 'fish and chips'. It could be boiled up with sugar into the most taste-marvellous pudding. It could be boiled into stews of whatever animal was being cooked—it was the 'potato' of western people.

So he was ready.

It was a short sail to Suva, the country's capital, in which he found even three-storied buildings. It was quite a metropolis—indeed the largest city in the South Pacific, its only rival being Papeete. He had even reached the stage of feeling glad that he was in quiet Lautoka, Fiji's second city.

Yet that thump, thump, thump, of the ship's engine! Oh, dear God, how I wished it would stop! Yet knowing it cannot, I have to satisfy my mind that I need to find some pleasure in it...

"You'll spend much more time afloat than ashore," Josh had said, and that continued ringing in his ears.

So he conditioned himself for finding a rhythm in it, putting the rhythm into song or verse, even composing words. And he found he could make the same sounds—depending on how he wanted them—melodic or sinister, loud or soft, measured or wild, demonstrative or soothing. He found he could make anything out of them that he wanted.

I suddenly realised I could make them! I could influence my mind to actually enjoy the previous boredom of them.

And people? What an incredibly eclectic mix! At every port they were different—the customs people who were the first to greet him, the buyers in the distributing companies, each of whom Josh had listed and made comments on, the present village buyers, suggesting further recipes they could use the product for—learning more of the language from each in turn. On one occasion while waiting for *Mbula* to sail, he sat with his atlas listing villages not already on his 'buyer' list. If there were time he would visit one or two. If not, he made a note to do so next time.

He was getting excited at discovering all such different types of people—seeing how they lived. He found culture differed in minor ways at each port and put it down to travel being more primitive in past times, so development took different tangents in different places.

And is still doing so, he also realised, *though maybe not so quickly.*

He was thoroughly enjoying himself. This was living!

All the people I meet are actually real! Oh what a narrow world I have been living in. Had been living in? My parents have always lived in?

Yet, he wondered, *doesn't this make that world, in its way, as unworldly as this one?*

Oh what a fortunate opportunity has fallen my way.

He again got to thinking on the Frenchies, the Jerry Edwards family, the Auberlings, Josh Noble, etc...

And I am adding to that list, now, every day.

He wasn't hearing the thump of the motors any more. He was making plans on what he could do with all he was learning.

Oh to have a goal. Josh has his, and it is the saviour of his soul. Frau Auberling has none—she accepted defeat—yet maybe because of that her sons have goals for having recognised her dilemma. Jerry has his goals, whatever they are, yet they drive him to the desperation he illustrated to me. So what is my goal? Right now I know it—it starts with the challenge Josh set me. Yet it is but a stage. And I am learning that I should not, yet, be carried away with that, because there are next stages to be achieved. So I need to help Josh achieve his, then mine are in the picture. I cannot decide the programme— other forces are doing that. I simply have to recognise and read the signs as each comes along.

Eighteen

Oh, so much had happened in his life since arriving in Lautoka.

Now being so far from it, he realised how he had come to see even it through different eyes. It became so much more than being just a busy port, commercial development having destroyed much of its beauty. He learned to look for natural beauty—wild blackberries growing by roadsides, ferns of all kinds gracing hillsides that development hadn't spoiled, hibiscus and poinsettia trees that seemed to defy development, simply growing wherever they could find space, bougainvillea that grew wild even in council parks and gardens in an explosive array of colours. Lautoka had become, to his eyes, quite a beautiful place.

And every port since, he had looked not for the development that had taken place, but for the natural beauties illustrating what a paradise it all would have looked before—the place that developed the culture that shaped the modern people.

His eastern journey took sixty-five days, a journey into dreamland.

He had seen more islands than he could count, many of which it was doubtful had ever known the footstep of man, experienced sunsets that he simply couldn't have believed had never been seen by millions—sunsets that screamed out at him how privileged he was in that moment, every one lasting a glorious hour for him. Coconut palms and white sandy beaches by the million graced his eyes—each its own magnetic lure. Sometimes they sailed so close he could hear the beat of drums and strumming of guitars that no doubt played for dancing maidens. It was all indeed a paradise—all indeed a million miles from the screams of Europe's tortured.

Before leaving, Josh had wanted him to look up a Jerry Edwards in Pago Pago.

"I am told he has trading boats shuffling around the islands, and there could be some help for us here. You will touch Pago Pago on your trip, Berry. Go see him. See what he has to offer that might help streamline our distribution. There's also the fact that he may have contacts for despatch to Britain. These days we need look at every alternative."

Berry had, at the time, agonised. Yet his young mind snapped at a tangent...

"Why not wait until I get some experience under my belt, Josh? I don't want to be fronting up to the CEO of a trading company and stuffing up. Can I put that on the back-burner, or, if it's urgent, you do this one until I'm at least a little blooded?"

Josh went along—it added up to common sense.

Beresford had now to catch up on what had been happening in Europe. Aboard *Mbula*, Master Evans would permit no wireless other than weather reports.

"That war is not part of our world," he declared. He had many years ago divorced himself from it.

"'Tis a madman's world, that one is, to be sure," he declared over dinner early in the cruise when Berry asked about radio news.

"It be like herrings in salt," he admonished—his way of saying it was a war restricted to a small part of the world 'like sardines in a can'. Here was a different world... "And I will have nowt of any other. Let them rave all they like and spill blood all they like. Give me instead, *kava* and native love songs."

He had had a son killed in the Great War, Berry was told by the first mate. "'He was the candle of my eye,' the skipper will keep telling us when in his cups," the mate had said. "But he got snuffed out in the trenches of Flanders when but a lad of eighteen."

So now home, there was much catch-up for Berry to discover.

London was being bombed nightly by waves of German airplanes, thousands of civilians being killed. The Russians had taken all three Baltic states, and the Italians had stripped Britain of its Somalia and as well invaded Egypt. German air raids had devastated much of Southampton, Bristol, Cardiff, Liverpool and Manchester.

Oh, and Manchester is so near home. A hundred miles? I doubt it.

But he was agog to hear from Josh if he had been to see Jerry Edwards.

Yet I dare not let him suspect my eagerness.

He decided to simply wait and see if Josh mentioned it. The last thing he wanted was Jerry Edwards learning his whereabouts, and he mulled on the negative sides of such a thing happening.

I thought that Fiji would make me safe from the fellow. And I still cannot fathom what was his so desperate interest in all that. Oh, the dangers involved in needing to have trust in people! I never realized that so many avenues of doubt could cloud a person's mind. I'm beginning to wonder what honesty is all about. Look at the dreadful example Hitler is setting—so how can I believe that now even Winston Churchill is telling us the truths of this war?

~ * ~

The thick clouds hovering over the world of international politics kept much of it in darkness. Few, in the time, saw what was going on behind the scenes.

The neutral United States view was that the best defence against foreign attack or infiltration was intelligence. Intelligence against hostile services. They called it counter-espionage—measures taken to detect enemy espionage and, where possible, to turn the attempt back against its perpetrator. Counter-espionage went beyond being reactive. It actively tried subverting hostile intelligence services by recruiting agents in the foreign service, by discrediting personnel actually loyal to their own service—thus taking away resources useful to the hostile service.

All such actions applied to non-national threats as well as to national organizations. Wheels worked within wheels more intricately woven than the most magnificent timepiece. People were cogs meshing with other cogs to allay threats or even kill threats. The intelligence priority oft-times conflicted with a nation's own law enforcement policies, especially when foreign threats involved foreign personnel with citizens of one's own country. It in itself was wheels working within wheels. Co-operation with other operations? Covert or friendly? Who was to know?

Cooperation could include telling all one knew about the other service, yet preferably in doing so, actively assisting in deceptive actions against it. Offensive counter-espionage was one of the most powerful tools for finding agents and neutralizing them. But not the only tool. Understanding what led individuals to turn on their own side became a skill recognised only by those who possessed it. And the Japanese agent who influenced Jerry Edwards had proved a jewel. He had won Jerry Edwards over—or had it been simply that the price was right?

Japan had long-term plans, it needed information and Jerry was getting it for them—paid on results. He boarded one of his own small fleet, an eight-hundred-ton cargo steamer, to alight at Honiara, capital of the Solomon Islands. Guadalcanal was a picturesque island with the highest mountains in the entire South Pacific, including several volcanos, active and dormant. It was rumoured that high up where white men had yet to penetrate, cannibal tribes still practised their grisly rituals. Yet Jerry's interest didn't include foraging.

The nation was a 'loop' of near a thousand islands, its most northerly but a couple of miles from Papua New Guinea's island of Bougainville, and it stretched southeast a thousand miles towards France's New Hebrides (later Vanuatu). The sea channel within the 'loop' was known as The Slot, a nautical 'highway' to every other island.

Guadalcanal was central and had the nation's only airport serviceable to anything larger than local 'flip-flops'. Its jungles were a veritable garden of tropical flowers including some two hundred varieties of orchid.

Neither was Jerry Edwards interested in the floral delights, however. He was a rich American fisherman seeking nautical maps of The Slot.

~ * ~

During his four days in Papeete on his Norton tour, which fortunately included a weekend, Beresford had been quick to seek out Gaston and Pascal. And of course, Francoise. Yet only Pascal was there, delighted to see Beresford, yet severely suffering the traumas visited on all French people.

"We are all three absolute loyalists," he stressed, "utterly aghast at Pétain selling out to the Germans. Not that we could want to see Paris go the way of Warsaw and Rotterdam, but oh, saving it at such a cost of deserting to the enemy? Francoise shocked us both when she almost spat the words when talking about Pétain... *Crotte de chien!* she called him."

Beresford could tell how much she must have been moved.

Gaston and Francoise had quickly, then, left for London, eager to join de Gaulle's Free French movement.

"Both are hoping they can be trained for underground service in France. They fully realise that it means firing squad if discovered. Gaston and I talked about it deeply and agreed that he would go, to see if such a route is possible. If he writes me saying simply 'Yes', then I too will go. As soon as we told Francoise our decision, she insisted she go with Gaston. I am sure she already sees herself as this war's Nurse Edith Cavell."

Beresford conducted his business there with Josh's two customers on the Friday, then moved into Gaston's now empty bed, that he and Pascal had the fullest time available for swapping news. Beresford told him about the outcome of his departing Papeete as deckhand for Jerry Edwards. Pascal was amazed of course.

"But he was doing work for the American Consul, wasn't he?"

"Indeed. But I am simply lost in trying to see how all the loose ends fit together."

Yet he now felt better about it, having at last found someone who he could tell the whole truths of his frightening abduction in Apia.

And despite it was too cold at that time of year for swimming, they still lunched, come Sunday, at the Beachcomber Hotel.

It had been agreed between Beresford's two French friends that if Pascal were to depart for London, he would mail a picture postcard to Beresford, saying simply, "I am off for holidays. Wish me luck."

Beresford gave him the *Folly Drift* telephone number, so he would have local friends 'on-side' during his training.

Nineteen

In Pago Pago he had gone ashore with an entirely opposite purpose: only to meet Josh's customer and to wave the company flag. For the rest, he sought incognito status.

To and from the ship he wore his pith helmet pulled uncomfortably low. Last thing he wanted was to be recognised by any of the Edwards trio. He otherwise hid aboard.

In Apia, he had not only visited Frau Auberling, who clasped him in her arms as if returning like a prodigal son, but dined with them one night and with Elo and Rano at Tevake on another. All were interested in how his job was faring. He also visited the police. He had tossed up the *for* and *against* options, yet would dearly love to recover his watch and signet ring—and to identify the oaf against whom he still held a grudge. Yet he still remained careful not to divulge, even to the police, his present address or even career. They had no good news for him.

Waiting for him on return to Lautoka, however, were two letters from home telling him that Thomas had joined the navy.

...I should put no more than that snippet in writing, son, for reasons you will understand. But he is gone with all the love and best wishes we could give him. We feel very proud.

Until New Year he learned much more about the business, and Josh included him in all deliberations on shipping to Britain in such risky times—none guaranteed of course.

"Poor old England is having a hard time of it," he told Beresford on his complaints about Captain Evans' embargo on news. "London is getting thoroughly pasted. All major industrial centres are copping it. And U-boats seem to patrol outside most British ports."

And the next week's news declared Germany had invaded Romania, to now have that nation's massive oil reserves. And Italy had invaded Greece. And within another week Germany had flattened Coventry, killing more than a thousand civilians.

Everything was gloom for the Allies.

"Will 1941 prove kinder?" was the question on all lips as the bells tolled in a doubtful New Year.

~ * ~

"The war is simply forcing me into it, Berry. Getting supplies into England is a no-win situation. Whether we ship through the Panama or around South Africa, we still have that USA-to-England traffic lane to enter, where U-boats are having a turkey shoot. I can mount extra shifts, but the losses are hurting. Our options are either forget shipping to dear old England, or finding more sales locally, to make a second shift pay. How would you like to move to Honiara?"

Beresford realized Josh was in a spot.

"I would hate to see us stop our shipments home, yet realize Fiji isn't as helpful on insurance as larger nations in times of war. So I see that you're losing a lot, Josh." Then, for the heck of it, he tossed in a joke. "Why don't you ask our workers all to take a pay cut?"

Josh thumped him on the shoulder.

"The Indians who count every ha'penny? And the Melanesians who are as likely to instead move back to their village and live on roots and wild boar again?"

They shared a sick giggle over it.

"Berry, my boy, Honiara is the only sophisticated town in all the Solomon Islands. And there, you are right next door to the New Hebrides and New Caledonia. The French may not be *cassava* enthusiasts, but there's a million natives in their islands who are. They currently go through the tedious routine of refining it by hand—extremely laborious. We can give it to them ready for the cook-pot. Few will have money, of course. You know, by now, that in these islands, the majority of natives don't need money. Their work is subsistence living off what their jungle or seashore gives them. However, maybe if some French farmer wants to set up a packing plant, we could ship to him in bulk and his family could weigh it into paper bags. He can then make it into his bartering product that the native world lives on—goods or service exchange instead of money. It means you have to sell the idea to the French authorities first. And you now know enough to be able to do that. What you reckon?"

He's mentioned Honiara before, with always the thought that I'd "grow into it". Yes, and now I'm ready. And if he has to add a shift, he will need to be here full time. And I see no real reason why I shouldn't, nor can't, help out. I've got used to the Melanesian people—they're like their Polynesian cousins in every way except looks. They'd rather sing and dance than work—that is their ethic. I envy them. It was me before coming here. It's just my instinct that's different from theirs.

"Is there a Tanoa Guest House in Honiara? Or a near look-alike?"

"I'll come with you, to settle you in, and we'll find one."

~ * ~

Beresford thought it time to tell Josh about Jerry Edwards.

"I've deliberately kept it to myself, Josh, because it had nothing to do with you or my work here. It was before I met you—not long before, but when I was still sensitive about it. And you coming up with his name just before I left for the east, worried me. I just didn't want to see the guy again."

"You're talking in riddles, lad. Tell me all."

So Beresford told him all—including the line he would never forget...

"Whether you remember it or not, might just have a bearing on whether you live or not. That is what is important in this little tête-à-tête. So tell me!"

"And I'm still alive, Josh—and he had me hidden away so well that the police still haven't found that farm. So it must have been that my life was forfeit if I 'had' remembered. I still don't know what to make of it all. The address from which I had to drive his pick-up full of documents was the US Consulate in Papeete. So he is well connected, yet I don't know in what capacity. I just thought that, as I'm now about to leave you, you should know this before contacting him."

Joshua Noble was scratching his head. "I see your confusion in all that, lad. And I know you well enough to know you don't go off in fanciful flights of mind. So this is worrying. But yes, lad, thanks for the telling. I don't need his help such that I need to take risks. It might be a big part of the world, around here, but at the same time, it's very small. I shall keep what you've told me confidential, despite I too, would love to know the answers."

~ * ~

15th March 1941

Dear Mater and Pater,

I hope this finds you well and that you are managing to avoid the terrible bombings we hear about. They likely don't tell us the 'very' bad news, yet even what they do, is oft-times dreadful. We are divorced from it, of course. If we were not listening to radio, we would not realise there is a war on, which makes us lucky.

I was particularly pleased to hear from you, Pater, your glowing impression of Josh Noble. I have worked closely with him for near a year and have learned to respect him as a gentleman and as well as both his acumen and advice. I was indeed fortunate to meet him.

I recently toured, for him, several colonies east of here and found some of my French friends had gone to England to 'help' in their country's crisis. If I were to tell you what they think of Pétain, I'm sure you would find just a hole in the paper. They may contact you.

My new address is c/- PO Honiara, Solomon Islands. I have just arrived here, and it is a backward place although the people seem little different from Fiji, if not a little more withdrawn from strangers. I think I shall really have to earn my way here. My reason for being here is its proximity to the French territories, that I can try developing a market for cassava. Just looking around here, I feel I have a challenge ahead. It is near as far west as one can get in what is called the South Pacific Islands. If I go further I am in either Papua New Guinea or Australia, but so far here, the sunsets are as brilliant as further east. I think if I were asked to nominate this entire quarter of the world in a phrase, I would have to say "A place of memorably spectacular sunsets".

Just before departing Fiji I deposited at the post office a free despatch, seeing it is Food for Britain. It contains cans of processed meats, coconut juice, desiccated coconut and, of course, cassava. I do hope God will give it clear passage to you.

If I cannot wish you a Happy New Year, I certainly wish you a safe one—for the entire year and beyond. If I hold true to a prompt return from my penance, I shall be pulling on Foggy Drift's doorbell in three hundred and thirty-seven days.

Your loving son...

Twenty

March 1941

By now the Japanese had free access to the entire French Indo-China peninsula, so China had lost its path to the Vietnamese ports. The only access remaining open to China was the lonely road north through Burma's Mandalay to Kunming.

Sasaki Takashi, advisor to the Japanese War Office for Asia South, recommended that a vital part of Japan's attack south, "in the event of war", must be Burma. Closing off that supply route would leave China devoid of all imported assistance. China would quickly become paralysed.

Japan was indeed, itself getting somewhat over-extended. Its naval strengths were inadequate to defend new conquests. To cut China off from Allied aid would indeed be a bonus in this respect. The report was noted by General Tojo's advisors—a giant nail in Burma's coffin. In the south, Japan eyed Malaya's rubber and overland access to Singapore, the 'state of the art' shipping facility in that entire quarter of the world—its marine workshops and control of trade-routes. Singapore was adequately fortified from attacks by sea and felt safe from overland attack in that Malaya's jungles were too dense even to build any sort of road—or so thought the Allies.

What lay in the path of attacks on both Burma and Malaya was Thailand—recently renamed from Siam. On Thailand's western border was Burma, and on its southern, Malaya.

Thailand, a militarily weak nation, was already in Japan's debt. It was ruled by an authoritarian government, its prime minister an affirmed fascist with a grudge against France for stripping territory from it to add to the Laos/Cambodia segment of French Indo-China. When Thai Prime Minister Plaek turned to Japan for support as sporadic fighting between Thai and French forces broke out again along Thailand's eastern frontier, Japan used its influence with the Vichy regime in France to obtain concessions for Thailand. As a result, France agreed to give a small portion of the territory back.

Sasaki Takashi made a note that here was a plan for Japan, come a convenient time to invade both Burma and Malaya, to provide access via Thailand. He submitted it, too, to his report for General Tojo.

Surely, he mused, *one good turn deserves another, unless Thailand wants to be invaded in lieu.*

~ * ~

In early 1941, Australian forces were attempting to drive the Italians out of North Africa. On 21 January, they captured the Italian garrison-port of Tobruk, one of the few well-equipped harbours along the Mediterranean coast—a prize site for provisioning any army in the North African deserts. The Australians lost forty-nine dead yet captured twenty-seven thousand Italian POWs, two hundred and eight guns, twenty-eight tanks and the general. Add to that a fleet of trucks and supplies, the Italians having being all prepared to 'charge east and take Cairo'. A month later, the entire Italian Tenth Army surrendered.

So Hitler despatched Rommel's Afrika Korps into the fray. He wanted Egypt's access to the Suez Canal. Winston Churchill, however, believed that with Tobruk in British hands, the experienced brigades could now serve a better purpose in defending Greece. So he sent the larger portion of Australia's army there.

It was a topsy-turvy war all right. German Field Marshal Irwin Rommel was suddenly rubbing his hands in glee. Experienced Australian forces in Egypt being sent to Greece?

~ * ~

By now, Beresford had met Andy Everton, Josh's buyer in Honiara.

Like many Australians, thirty-year-old Andy had been in the Solomons a handful of years, not in his case farming coconuts but trading in everything from packaged *cassava* to grain harvesters. The two fellows clicked—Beresford enjoying the brash, open style of the 'dinkum Aussie' who had few set ideas but would 'have a crack at any bloody thing'. Andy for his part was amused at Beresford's obvious "good breeding" yet enjoying the primitive, laid-back lifestyle of the South Pacific. It was indeed a case of 'opposites attract'.

Beresford hinted at the entrepreneur Andy about starting a small packing operation in a corner of his storehouse, weighing a pound of *cassava* powder bought in bulk from Noble Mill into brown paper bags in lieu of ready packed.

"I like the idea, mate, but the niggers here simply don't wanna work. As soon as they get their week's pay, they go walkabout—well at least as far as their home village, where they throw a party for its entire populace until their belly-bag's empty, maybe a week later. Only then do they come back to work."

Beresford then learned that a 'belly-bag' was exactly that—a purse tied around their waists. For many, that was about all they wore other than a g-string-type village-made jock-strap.

Andy was from Dubbo, "Central West of New South Wales," he had said.

"Is that the 'outback', then?"

"Well, let's say it's sort of half-bloody-way, mate. I still wouldn't recommend you try wanderin' too far off the bitumen, but, unless you wanna die from bloody thirst."

Beresford still wasn't sure if Andy were joking. It was somewhat difficult to tell with Aussies, he was beginning to learn. But they had become great mates so quickly that they were already in digs together.

And Andy's first order for cassava in bulk was already telegraphed to Lautoka. Beresford even loaned his business shirt to the paper-bag printer, so that he could trace off the design.

~ * ~

During March, Bulgaria signed the Axis bloc. Britain shipped fifty thousand seasoned troops from North Africa to Greece, leaving Tobruk vulnerable, and the Luftwaffe dropped magnetic mines into the Suez Canal, which stuffed things up properly. And in April, Rommel captured Benghazi and started advancing, again, on Tobruk. Germany invaded Yugoslavia and Greece. The British hit the Italians in Libya and took a hundred and thirty thousand POWs—there were now more Italian prisoners in Africa, than troops. Yugoslavia surrendered two weeks later, and Greece in three. Of the fifty thousand British and Australian seasoned troops sent from Africa to Greece, twenty-two thousand were now prisoners of war. The war was not going well.

In May, Rommel began a major assault on Tobruk. The Aussies that were left, now vastly out-numbered, had dug themselves in.

The new German super-battleship *Bismarck* sank Britain's biggest, *HMS Hood.*

In heavy German bombing of London, its Houses of Parliament were destroyed.

The British navy crippled the *Bismarck* off the French Atlantic coast and pounded her to death; two thousand Germans sank with her. In June, Hitler again turned on friends. He took Russia by surprise, sending hundreds of thousands of German troops across the border the two had struck through central Poland. In a blitzkrieg charge through Russia's western states, he had, within a week, vanquished the three Baltic states and was two hundred miles into Russia proper. The Luftwaffe was bombing Moscow.

Major news in the Pacific, however, was that the USA not only froze all Japanese assets in its country, but stopped exports of oil to Japan. The writing was on the wall that war between them was imminent. Japan must take drastic measures if it were not to be starved of oil—a commodity by now precious to all warring nations. Russia and Britain joined forces and invaded Persia to prevent the Nazis reaching that southern Russian border and taking Persia's oil.

By September the Germans had interned more than a million Russian POWs.

In October, General Hideki Tojo, head of Imperial Japan's military forces and an aggressive fascist, was appointed prime minister; war seemed assured.

On December 7, Japan invaded Malaya at Kota Baru and two hours later attacked the US naval base in Hawaii. The following morning, having taken horrendous life and delivered almost a deathblow to America's navy, it declared war on both the USA and Britain. On 8 December while the US was licking its wounds in Hawaii, Japan began moving troops through Thailand to the Burmese border in its west and its Malay border in its south. Thailand ceded all facilities of railways, roads, airfields, naval bases, warehouses and communications systems to the Japanese.

On 9 December, Japanese bombers sank the pride of Britain's naval strength in the Pacific, there to defend Singapore, both the *HMS Repulse* and the *HMS Prince of Wales*.

Two days later Hitler and Mussolini declared war on the United States.

Two days before Christmas, America's Wake Island fell to the Japanese.

On Christmas Day, Japan occupied the British dependency of Hong Kong.

The war had certainly arrived in the Pacific.

Before the year finished, Australia suspended its flying boat service to London.

Twenty-one

With America in the war, the entire Pacific Ocean entered a new page of history.

Never could the old life return. Not only every native's life would change, but so would his culture, his very ethos. Also the lives of millions of men from many nations who would fight over every inch. In the transition, more blood would drench island sands and seas than all the war in Europe and Africa put together. Many new nations would evolve, 'western protectors' ceding nationhood to what had been protectorates.

Beresford, rather than finding himself come New Year 1942 with but forty-six days of penance to serve, became physically involved in proceedings. It was a part in neither army, navy nor air force of any nation, yet which put his life on the line as a volunteer fighter in a truly active sense.

It began with Thailand, under duress from the Japanese declaring war on Britain and the United States. Whilst it had no troops and armaments involved, it gave Japan open slather in using whatever facility Thailand had—a far easier choice than being invaded. It was the same sort of ready co-operation as had existed between England and the USA. Japanese troops were landing in Thailand same as, within thirty days of 'Pearl Harbor', American troops were landing in Britain as a gateway to Europe.

In February, the Japanese army took Singapore from the north— from the Malayan jungles the Allies had ever believed were so thick that no road was possible. The Japanese cleared one wide enough for troops on bicycles. One hundred thousand British and Australian prisoners were taken, all wounded being murdered where they lay.

Distant Australia wasn't to escape the war this early either. A Qantas flying boat, one of those grounded from the London run, now serving as a troop transport in the Pacific, was shot down by Japanese bombers off Timor. Another 'disappeared' on a flight between the Dutch East Indies and Broome, the bayside town on Australia's northwest coast, a pearl-fishing town being 'secretly' used as the flying-boat base.

A week later, Japanese troops were landed in force on Java. Without a Dutch force to defend it, landings on the nation's twelve thousand islands proved a turkey shoot. Many of the islands pumped up oil in abundance to now feed Japanese forces.

Two days later, Broome was bombed and two more Qantas flying boats were sunk.

During the first week of March, Honiara radio reported that eleven ships flying British, USA or Australian flags had been sunk in the South Pacific and Indian Oceans. The next week Japan invaded Papua New Guinea, the large Australian dependency immediately to its north. They landed almost unopposed in both Lae and Salamaua. Burma's Rangoon then fell to the Japanese army attacking via Thailand, China losing its last lifeline.

South, the Dutch East Indies capitulated, giving Japan the island nation's entire oil resources.

All Japan's six aircraft carriers attacked Ceylon to sink "near anything afloat".

During the next four days they sent a further twenty-eight Allied ships to the bottom of the Indian Ocean, then took possession of Australia's Christmas Island. Japan now 'owned' the Indian Ocean.

On 1 April they landed troops on Buka and Bougainville, the most northerly of Solomon Islands.

~ * ~

"I'm off," declared most of Solomon Island's white community, the vast majority Australians. They preferred to simply walk off their plantations than stay.

"I'll leave mine for the bloody Japs," each declared. "How am I going to defend my home and family? We've got no fuckin' army, no fuckin' air force, no fuckin' navy and there's a million fuckin' Japs shootin' holes in my house, and I've got kids."

The situation was as helpless as that.

Australia rushed aeroplanes to Honiara to evacuate, they thought, the entire white population. Yet along with Beresford Branson, both Andy Everton and Doug Kennedy said, "No."

Unbeknown to Beresford, Andy and his Aussie mate Dougie, both single, had been appointed "coast-watchers" in the event of a Japanese invasion. Their role was to be available for duty wherever the authority wanted them, living in caves or wherever they found even basically habitable accommodation, armed with walkie-talkie radios, reporting on Japanese shipping and aircraft movements. Not only Guadalcanal Island or even throughout The Slot, but as far afield as the New Hebrides and New Caledonia, coast-watchers were assigned duties. Beresford was invited to join, and he did so.

He felt like a kid at Christmas.

Here have I been trying to decide whether it is better to go home and enlist, or even go to Australia and enlist there, and now here is essential work right here. How else are the powers that be who control bombing raids or such to know where, unless someone is feeding them information?

It had taken but minutes to lodge a telegram to Josh Noble, telling him of his decision, knowing that he would have Josh's support. There would be no more normal business for Noble Mill for the duration of the war, in any case. Whatever Josh could produce now, would go to feeding local military forces.

Fiji is two thousand miles away. Maybe the Japs will never get that far.

Little did he know that Japan was intent on occupying the entire Pacific as far east as Hawaii and French Tahiti.

Japan, now in total control of the Dutch East Indies, already had its foothold in Papua New Guinea, the only island between its land forces and Australia.

Australia possessed some of the world's most desirable minerals—coal, iron ore, oil, copper, zinc, tin, bauxite and uranium, apart from gold and opals—all waiting to be served up on a platter to the Japanese. Australia might be a large country in geographical terms, but at the outbreak of WW2 its population was just seven million, of whom half were non-combative women and a quarter, those two young or too old. Of the remainder, near half were in essential services, leaving less than a million to spread across army, navy and air force. Discounting those fighting Rommel in Africa, the thirty thousand taken prisoner in Greece, Burma and Singapore and those building barriers against the imminent Japanese invasion of its homeland, there were few left to spread around the vast Pacific.

In the Solomon Islands, the entire Allied military force comprised the Australian Army's Captain Goode, his twenty-four commandos and the RAAF's Flight Officer Peagram with twenty-five pilots and ground crew with four PBYs. All were now under orders to evacuate to the New Hebrides, to save the Catalinas.

~ * ~

Beresford mulled over his 'survivor's kit'. It was a simply common-sense issue. *Yet had I been asked what should be included, I wonder how few of these I would have chosen.*

He had binoculars, food and water for when holed up in hiding for days on end. Even a cyanide pill rather than be taken prisoner by Japs, who were crucifying Aussie prisoners in Borneo, nails through hands and feet and all. His walkie-talkie, of course, with various channels, malaria pills, chocolate blocks, a revolver and shells, an oilcloth poncho, rain-hat, spare bootlaces, antiseptic cream, bandages and safety pins. And maps of course, and a box of matches to burn the maps before taking the cyanide pill.

Tulagi and Honiara had the only two landing strips in the entire Solomons; surely the Japanese would be intent on taking them first—and if they had taken possession of the island, it must be a prime target for coast-watchers...a large loading of bombers, for instance.

He realised how the Japanese must have had a long period of collecting information about places they would need to capture. And all research had to be done, of course, before the war started.

The Jerry Episode, for instance. Could they have been maps of South Pacific Islands?

But then he scratched his head again. *But if Jerry were in the CIA or FBI or whatever they call those clandestine organizations, why would he get so frantic about sending maps of Tahiti to Sydney? That sounds as sensible as sending secrets of rubber to Malaya.*

He felt no further to the truth of all that than ever.

And war news seems mostly bad things—like US troops conceding Bataan in the Philippines, Nazi and Italian bombers blitzing poor little Malta, and moral-busting things like the Nazis selecting Britain's cathedral cities for intensive night bombing, and all Jews throughout Europe must wear Star-of-David insignias. As if we don't have enough troubles here, now! If there had to be a war, why have Axis powers on both sides of the globe—east and west? It simply spreads the difficulties. And we had warnings of it all!

He persisted in thinking how Britain and France and all European Allies could readily see in advance what Hitler was doing. *Yet they trusted him when he told lies by the dozen. And never learned from any such incident, to be caught totally unprepared. And in the Pacific, the US was as blind as Britain had been in Europe. They had every opportunity to assess what Japan was doing behind the scenes. That Japan needed resources to survive was emblazoned in glittering gold in every action Japan did during the 1930s, yet the USA was still caught unprepared. They simply weren't ready to combat the obvious threat, or Pearl Harbor couldn't have happened! They were just like France with its Maginot line—whatever defences they built, didn't work.*

Nor could he forgive his own country's leaders back in 1938 and '39 for not being suspicious of what was going on behind others' closed doors.

Where were the spies then?

~ * ~

April in Honiara was pretty much more of the same. The Japs conducted "desultory" bombing raids on Tulagi that caused little if any damage, yet was prelude to later intentions. The coast-watchers on Guadalcanal were usually able to radio advance warning of approaching aircraft to the Australian commandos on Tulagi, but the troops had no weaponry to take action.

"Three Vickers machine guns and one Bren rifle aren't going to scare off Japanese bombers," they told him.

"But at least you can put on your helmets!" he replied.

Then suddenly the bombings increased. Eight bombers every day plastered everything that wasn't already flat.

But they were only buildings!

On 1 May, however, they attacked the 'secret' Catalina base at Gavutu, crippling one, yet the others managed to escape.

Coast-watchers in the north reported that the Japs were establishing a flying-boat base on Buka Island in the far north—within attacking distance of both New Guinea and Guadalcanal.

On May 2, Jack Rei, coast-watcher on Bougainville, reported a large contingent of Jap ships entering The Slot and moving south. A few hours later, Doug Kennedy, further south in The Slot, reported a 'massive' force heading for Tulagi or Honiara.

That was enough for Beresford... *Unlike Britain in '39 and the US in '41, I can take a bloody hint.*

He sounded the alarm. The Aussie commandos, as ordered on such a signal, began their evacuation. They flicked the switch to destroy their equipment. All PBYs other than the one left to take off the stragglers were already aboard two small ships to sail to the New Hebrides—there wasn't enough fuel for them to fly there by themselves.

Twenty-two

3 May 1942, 5 p.m.

Carriers *USS Lexington* and *Yorktown* and their accompanying task force were positioning themselves ready to attack the approaching Japanese fleet.

They were under orders not to break radio silence, so had no communication with each other. *Lexington* could see that the Japanese force had split—one half veering south into the Coral Sea, the other continuing towards Tulagi.

When *Yorktown* arrived at Tulagi, however, the Japanese were already landing—and finding no opposition, troops were digging in.

Beresford, the coast-watcher with a view to Tulagi, reported the Jap fleet comprising an aircraft carrier, four cruisers, two destroyers, six mine-layer-transports and two torpedo boats.

He had, sort of, become a temporary Australian. Should the coast-watchers be captured by the Japanese, it had been decided that to hopefully prevent them being executed as spies, they not being in uniform, they be appointed Royal Australian Naval Volunteer Reserve officers reporting to the Townsville naval office. With it came a salary of five shillings per day.

~ * ~

4 May, 7 a.m.

Yorktown launched twelve TBD Devastator torpedo bombers and twenty-eight SBD Dauntless dive-bombers against the ships at anchor in Tulagi. The attack caught the Japanese by surprise, and *Kikuzuki*, a destroyer, suffered such severe damage that it deliberately ran aground to save itself from sinking.

Beresford then, come high tide, watched it slip back off the beach into deep water and roll over. He made a tick in his notebook. He made another when one of the Japanese floatplanes was destroyed trying to take off into the safety of the clouds.

~ * ~

12:10 p.m.

He watched *Yorktown*'s planes, after returning for refuelling and rearming, make a second attack. They had come from the south, so he could only assume *Yorktown* had based itself off Guadalcanal's southern beaches.

What he could see from his vantage point was that on this second attack, the Americans sent two minesweeper-transports and three seaplanes to the harbour bottom.

What he couldn't know was that *Yorktown* had then sailed off for the Coral Sea.

The action-packed day was over, and suddenly silence reigned.

It was as if the war was over.

The sky began dressing for another brilliant sunset.

~ * ~

After two quiet days, quiet in that there was no attack by either side, he and Andy met in town to talk tactics. Dougie had been relocated to New Georgia, the major island north of Guadalcanal, centrally located on The Slot.

They met in 'Dog on the Tuckerbox', a bar come café run by natives since the Aussie owner had evacuated with his family, friends drinking what they could before the Japanese arrived to garner everything. The bar was on a wide balcony that reminded him of Gaston and Pascal's apartment in Papeete. Potted bougainvillea plants in a rainbow of colours bedecked the bar, and below them a cultured garden of hibiscus in as grand an array of colours, and poinsettias, glorified the landscape. It not only had grand views south to the mountains in the island's centre, like that in Papeete, but to the north, uninterrupted views across Honiara Harbour, to The Slot and its ocean horizon.

"Jesus, mate," Andy opened with as Beresford arrived, "what a bloody to-do."

Beresford had been brought the four miles from his 'hide' in a motorbike rickshaw. A lad from a nearby village had 'won' it when it had been abandoned by evacuees.

"Indeed, old chap. From my eyrie, the 'taking of Tulagi' was better than a box at The Royal Albert." Beresford had once been to a recital at London's famous music hall and came away believing he would likely never see a more spectacular performance.

The sheer noise of dive-bombers and the ensuing explosions just the length of his binocular lenses away, along with the shelling from the cruisers and aerial dogfights over several hours, had by far and away proved the most levelling experience ever.

"It makes one feel so insignificant in this world, without a doubt, Andy." *The mere sight of human bodies simply being blown skywards, some limbless, and just watching them fall again, is something to stick in one's mind forever.*

"And the bloody strafing on those landing barges, Berry. Twenty blokes at a time maybe coppin' it with nowhere to bloody hide."

And it was just as well they had chosen that site for their meeting, for sure enough, just after they'd mixed rum and cokes for themselves and young Lobo, the Melanesian lad, two Japanese torpedo-gunboats entered the deserted Honiara Harbour. They watched one tie up at a wharf while the other dropped anchor twenty yards off. Each had a half-dozen armed soldiers afoot, on guard, while each also had a mounted machine gun trained shorewards. Yet there was neither a ship nor defending soul present. All ships had steamed out as soon as they heard the Japs were in The Slot, and all but the airport personnel setting the detonation charges and the two coast-watchers had been passengers to Port Vila.

When there was no reaction from ashore, other soldiers appeared, and all from the moored gunboat stepped onto the wharf and fanned out, surveying the quiet scene.

"Should we scamper into the jungle?" Beresford suggested.

"No," said Andy. "They are too few to be about takin' over the town. And from here we can see where—"

He was interrupted by the sound of aircraft—and within seconds, three floatplanes could be seen approaching. The three, with their drinks, hastened under cover.

"This is why them gunboat blokes wasn't in no hurry to take the town," said Andy. "And if Honiara is to be bombed, why didn't it happen before the bloody aircraft carrier left? For the moment, mate, we're safe here, mate."

Lobo was trembling in fear. He wasn't even drinking, despite it being free, a situation confirming that he was very, very scared.

"Sit down, Lobo."

It was the first occasion any of the three had seen Japanese so close.

Beresford tried to sound blasé. "Well, the Japanese are here at last," he said slowly. "Are you going to stay in town, Lobo? Or go back to your village?"

The only other people left in the town, by now, were Melanesians. The coast-watchers and airport personnel were the only remaining white people on the entire island.

Lobo was one who had moved to town to attach himself to a white household, being housecleaner, messenger boy, cook and general roustabout—easy work for the several shillings white men paid each week. He had been with Beresford and Andy for some months, although at a whim, as was usual for locals, he would one day simply not turn up for work—usually the day following pay day. Then he would arrive as usual three or four days later as if it were the normal thing. Which it quickly became. That was their lifestyle.

Lobo's answer was a shrug of shoulders, meaning he hadn't yet thought on it.

Could it also indicate that he is amenable to whatever we might have in store for him?

Not that they had a plan, other than to avoid capture. And part of any plan was, separated or not, they would take to the jungle once the town was in Japanese hands, Andy east of the town and Beresford west, hiding in lookouts they had already prepared—two each—a mile or two apart. Beresford's first was a cave some three miles west of the harbour entrance, his second further west in a woven-reed hut that Lobo's friends had built on the jungle edge with a view to the western beaches and as far west up The Slot as eyesight permitted. Andy's first was close in with an overview of the harbour, like the spot they now were in, yet closer to the coast. His other overlooked the airport.

They had plenty of batteries for their radios but would use them sparingly—that is, infrequently and for short contacts. They could never know if the Japs might have stumbled on their frequency.

What they were certain of, however, was that in the entire crescent of islands in the south, the only sealed airports were Honiara and Tulagi in the Solomons, Port Moresby in New Guinea, Noumea in New Caledonia and Espiritu Santo in the New Hebrides. And Honiara and Tulagi were now in Japanese hands. And Honiara's airport, being large enough for the biggest bombers, was extremely important to the Japs.

"Even if only to keep it from our boys!"

Both lads considered their walkie-talkies more important possessions than guns.

They realised also that, during the six months since Pearl Harbor, the Americans would have been frantically rebuilding its naval resources—so every Japanese ship that could now be sunk, particularly aircraft carriers, was a significant stroke in shortening the days before America could fight back. So reporting the whereabouts of enemy vessels was an ever-essential task.

Right now, they knew some important action was taking place south. They had seen *Lexington* and *Yorktown* head that way, followed by all the Japanese fleet once Tulagi was occupied. How many more ships of each side had also gone into the Coral Sea, they could only guess at.

They had been told that Port Moresby and the Coral Sea were the only remaining gateways between the Japanese and Australia. Already Japan had the Indian Ocean to itself—it now needed only this Coral Sea territory for Australia to be quite isolated from any hope America had of saving its resources for the Allies.

"But," asked Beresford, "why would the Japs now come here just to fly over? They bombed Tulagi over several days before landing troops. Why not Honiara? This is a bigger town!"

"Why would they destroy it, mate? It ain't as if they're gonna meet opposition. This'll be their easiest pickin' in the entire Pacific. They're just tryin' to make a bloody statement! Them planes is likely spotter planes lookin' to see how well the airport's bloody defended. And the gunboats is just a lure to see if an army might be here to bloody front'em."

Then suddenly, an explosion far greater than any bomb could make came from the near east. All three jumped in surprise. Then it became a series of explosions.

"The airport?"

"Surely, mate. What else?"

The airport was on the coast a mile or two east of the town. They couldn't see it from their vantage point but knew that destruction of the runway, the terminal building with its equipment, the maintenance workshops and the fuel depot, were to occur before the last plane took off. And even as the explosions were still stunning the boys' ears, they couldn't hear but saw a DC3 banking above the hillside to their east, turning south.

"There goes the last authority we had to appeal to, mate. You, me and Dougie up on New Georgia are on our own. Does that make you feel like a king or something?"

"A king without a bodyguard, let alone an army—and with a horde of rebels at our gate!"

And when the Jap seaplanes had made an aerial inspection of what was left of the airfield, they returned to Tulagi. The foot soldiers on the wharf made inspections of several buildings before reboarding and then also sped off.

The boys then spent the last hour of daylight exploring for what might have been abandoned in the exodus from the 'Dog on the Tuckerbox'. Beresford's major find was a little folding table, useful if squatting on the floor cross-legged that he could eat more comfortably in his cave, and a double-pack of bridge cards that on the table he could play patience in the many idle hours. And some books to read. He reckoned that was about all, on one trip, along with a bottle each of Scotch and Coke, that he could get back to his lair.

Lobo, not wanting to be left alone, dropped Andy off the rickshaw at the crossroad leading east, and with Beresford aboard, sped along the road west.

En-route, Beresford switched on his radio and punched in his number for reporting. He advised of the invasion and that he and Andy had withdrawn to 'agreed positions'.

Next day, Japanese transports delivered what the boys estimated a thousand troops to beaches both west and east of the town, apparently with the prospect of one occupying the town and the other, the airport.

~ * ~

During the next week, Japan had air patrols over all islands. Beresford was sending in reports of the additional troops and construction workers being landed at Tulagi.

Only after several days was he informed that a major naval battle was in progress in the Coral Sea. It was believed the Japanese purpose was twofold. First, it was essential to have clear access to attack Port Moresby, capital of Papua New Guinea, by sea. Japan needed both its port facilities and its airport. Already its bombers could reach Australia's Darwin from airports in the north of New Guinea and were bombing it mercilessly, yet they could reach no other city.

The second reason was an all-out attempt to destroy America's only two aircraft carriers in the South Pacific. When America's navy was decimated at Pearl Harbor, its three aircraft carriers were luckily out on a training exercise. America was now denied all airports in the South Pacific, and if its mobile airports could be sunk, that could win the war for Japan. It was as simple as that.

"But there are many casualties on both sides," Beresford was told of the naval battle.

And two days later he learned that not only was *Lexington* sunk, but *Yorktown* was crippled. The Allies now had neither air defence nor air attack facilities. It looked grim indeed. It also lost a destroyer and an oiler.

He reckoned *Yorktown* was probably headed for Sydney. He knew of no other port in the South Pacific that could effect major repairs.

Japanese losses were the flagship of the Tulagi invasion *Okinoshima* as well as the aircraft carrier *Shoho*. A second aircraft carrier, *Shokaku*, was severely damaged.

The final outcome was that both sides retreated, *Yorktown* limping either to Sydney or Pearl Harbour.

Beresford was crestfallen.

Is there any stopping these Japanese? It seems the battle was a sort of draw, both losing a carrier and having another severely damaged. But at least it leaves Japan no closer to its objective of taking Port Moresby.

Had he known that Japan still had seven and a half aircraft carriers against America's one and a half, he would have indeed felt destitute.

Twenty-three

June 1942

The good news was that British forces had landed in Vichy French Madagascar, winning for itself a presence in the Indian Ocean. In Europe it despatched the first of what it promised would be many 'Thousand Bomber' raids on Germany; the first 'thousand-aeroplane fleet' ever in the world practically decimated the industrial Rhineland city of Cologne.

Beresford's other happy news was that he caught up with Andy. Yet they could only console each other over the bad news that America had conceded its last foothold in the Philippines: Corregidor. Japan now had total control of all South Asia except India and Ceylon. And all the Southwest Pacific except the southern half of New Guinea, Australia and New Zealand.

Beresford had noted during the previous few weeks how time and experience had helped Lobo gain confidence. He had somehow combated earlier fears. So with Lobo and several of his village friends, he made sorties towards the town so he could report on what was going on. Andy was doing the same at the airport. Lobo and friends even went into the town proper so they could return with information on Japanese vessels in the harbour. They reported many unloading manpower, tools and materials. All details were relayed back to base.

Andy reported major extensions at Honiara's airport—giant earthmoving and grading equipment having been landed. An airport for large bombers, and even troop carriers, boded ill for the entire rest of New Guinea.

Soon after, Andy surprisingly arrived at Beresford's hide.

"Reason I'm here, mate, is that me and you have to find our way to Visale on the west coast. We are to be in position three miles west and two miles out to sea on Sunday night by 10 p.m. We are to have torches to guide in a PBY. We need Lobo to arrange a fishing boat. Can you fix that?"

"I'll have to. Where are we going?"

"Don't know. It's all a bloody secret. Dougie's comin' too. Will Lobo be in it, or do you have to convince him?"

"I'll vouch for Lobo. We should leave now. His village is on the way, only a mile from here. I'll just grab my gear. Visale can't be more than a fishing village, do you realise? And a long way."

"I've got a map. Yes it's a long way by road but maybe Lobo knows a way across country. Japs could be on the road, but there's no word yet of Japs in the hinterland."

Beresford knew his way to Kokumbona, Lobo's village. For a young man who had been despatched from home just over three years ago, his only skill satisfying personal desires with no expense spared, he had proved himself a quick learner of how to exist even in jungles. He had been taken there by Lobo one time, to help carry back so much fruit and cooked food to his hide that he would have enough for a month. And he could still remember the jungle trails.

"As I'm sure you realise, Andy, it's *who* you know. I quickly learned that a white man left alone in a place like this couldn't survive. I've had to learn how to keep on the right side of people—to have them feeling they owe me something. Isn't that the way you find it?"

Andy chuckled. "That's how I keep a grip on you, mate. A bloke wot ain't learned that yet, can only stay lonely. And hungry. You know what I mean?"

And at Kokumbona, Lobo showed how he too, was an exponent of the same philosophy.

"Fishing boat easy. How many men?"

"Only as few as can handle the boat. Fewer the better, mate," Andy told him. "And there's a ten-shilling note for every man who keeps his mouth shut. Including you."

Andy illustrated knowing the Melanesian language very clearly too—that money talks everywhere.

Lobo also had a friend who knew the cross-country tracks. Bilo would lead the coast-watchers while Lobo went by road on his cycle, that he could be there quicker to arrange the boat.

Bilo was happy to "do anything make Japan man mad," he explained as the three scurried along the narrow trails in single file.

"Already Jap man rape wife and girl my village. Already stick bayonet in many man try help."

"Well, that's keepin' the Nips away from us, mate," Andy whispered to Beresford.

~ * ~

They arrived in the dark, on a sandy cove on which it was difficult to walk without tripping over fallen coconuts. Bilo picked up two and shoved them into the sisal sack slung on his back.

"In case we must wait long time," he announced with a grin.

Andy's single quick flash from his torch was answered by another further up the beach. It was Lobo. He led them around a point where a darkened fishing boat, larger than either white man had expected, was waiting off the beach. The trawler's skipper was waiting by a rubber dinghy pulled up on the sand. There was moonlight enough to make out that beyond the trawler was only endless ocean.

"This three mile west Visale," Lobo told them.

He introduced the skipper, by name Awali.

"He no talk English. I tell him go two mile out. Okay?"

Beresford nodded, and there was a brief conversation between the natives.

Andy checked his watch.

"Tell him he might have to wait an hour."

After another short exchange, Lobo turned.

"Awali happy. He catch fish."

Andy gave Lobo and Bilo each a soiled ten-shilling note and a hug. Beresford also gave each a hug and sent them on their way.

With a smile on his face, likely at the sight of the paper money, Awali ushered the two white friends into the dingy. He and Andy took a paddle each and rowed through the fortunately tiny surf to the trawler.

The two miles out had not been designated in any direction, so they took the ninety-degree angle from the coast and dropped anchor at an estimated two miles.

"When we hear a plane, mate, don't flash. Let's first be sure it is a Catalina. Okay?"

Beresford showed him a thumbs up.

The fishermen were already casting lines.

And when they heard it they waited while it flew directly overhead, then waited for it to turn. Then they flashed first above, then at the level of the sea for whatever help that might be for the pilot.

"He will have been briefed on wind direction for the area, the tidal flow and currents, I'd reckon, mate. We're all lucky it's a calm night."

~ * ~

They were flown to Townsville in Australia's far northeast—quite a little city, they realised on circling. The PBY had one of the longest flying ranges of any aircraft, and it was broad daylight when they arrived. Only the navigator had the correct time of day for all the coast-watchers to adjust their watches.

When Beresford and Andy were picked up, having paid Awali his promised ten shillings per man, ten other coast-watchers were already aboard, including Dougie. They made two further pick-ups—at the D'Entrecasteaux Islands and the Louisiade Archipelago. Each had gone smoothly.

Beresford had only the highest admiration for the Aussie crew, flying 'blind' all the way with no other help on landings than flashlights.

And the PBY itself was a slow but admirably comfortable voyage. It was part of USA's aid to its Allied friends.

The RAAF's (Royal Australian Air Force) Lieutenant Commander Eric Feldt was the coast-watcher's CEO—Chief Executive Officer of everything to do with coast-watching wherever Japan had designs of expected occupation.

"There are over four hundred of you altogether," Eric Feldt told them, "as many behind enemy lines as those stationed in expected targets. We already have information," he spelled out so slowly that he had everyone's careful attention, "that three of our volunteers, like yourselves, have so far been beheaded by Japanese captors, and a fourth literally crucified, I am sorry to report—four-inch nails through palms and feet. I tell you this only because I want to illustrate not only the danger you all face, but the pride in which we hold you."

Beresford couldn't finish noting all that because of tears.

Yet this is a moment I'm sure I shall never forget.

The seminar proceeded for three days. It was designed not only as an information panel in methods of operation, as well as to illustrate how essential was their service, but to give the guys a break. He used part of his leisure hours to write home while he had access to a postal service; he also wrote to Josh asking him to advise the Lautoka post office to continue holding his mail.

No expense seemed begrudged in entertaining them, for after two further days of briefing, they were given a tour. In the hinterland they saw kangaroos and other wildlife in their natural environment. Off the coast they dived into the wonders of coral delights. They surfed off Magnetic Island, one with so much mineral deposit that it sent every ships' compass haywire.

Beresford came away both informed and refreshed. And even further dedicated.

Twenty-four

Guadalcanal, June 1942

News came through of another major battle in the far north—the US island of Midway—with massive losses by the Japanese: four aircraft carriers and a heavy cruiser sunk. And 'hundreds' of aircraft. He ran about shouting in glee.

However the Americans lost *USS Yorktown*, she that had been so effective both in The Slot and so much a part of his 'watching' reports. He was severely distressed over that.

Yet there is a war to be won!

He took every opportunity to keep up with the construction going on at Honiara's airport. And reporting. He could now visualise how all the reports he submitted influenced Allied planning—especially when, come 25 June, he was utterly amazed when an entire fleet of PBYs flew down The Slot from somewhere and bombed every installation the Japs had built on Tulagi.

And just after American Independence Day, a twelve-ship convoy delivered what he estimated to be three thousand Japanese construction workers in Honiara. Whether or not it was his report that influenced it, Allied Catalinas and B17s began blasting both Tulagi and

Honiara in bombing raids every few days, week after week.

Are they softening up Jap defences against a retaliatory landing?

His mind began to absolutely boggle. *Was every Guadalcanal coast-watcher taken to Townsville to deliberately prepare us for an invasion here by Allied forces?*

The coincidence of that, and now all this bombing of every defence the Japs had built, was just too much to ignore. They had even now moved Dougie Kennedy to Guadalcanal's south coast.

Beresford had written a letter home from Townsville, knowing that he could send none from here. Yet oh, how he wished he could write of his hopes for such an Allied move. All he could think of now was keeping away from either the town, the airport or anything the Japs had built since arriving, for all such were likely to be bombed.

On 28 June, his spirits skyrocketed.

From his observation cave on Guadalcanal's northwest coast he watched a fleet of PBYs bomb Tulagi over several hours.

Can anything be left of that little island?

What he wasn't to know was that, at the same time, B17s were raining bombs on Japanese-held Lae in New Guinea, also pasting the Japanese naval and air stations in New Britain's Rabaul.

Is the face of war changing?

Three days later, B17s began an entire seven days bombing of Tulagi and the entire north coast of Guadalcanal. Beresford was confined within his cave.

I just hope those fisherman friends in Visale are not getting pasted.

~ * ~

It was a week later, 5 August, and the weather was dreadful. Rain was so heavy he couldn't even see Tulagi through his binoculars, let alone what might be happening there.

If there is anything left of it, that is, he mused.

Nor was his radio working. He had tried keeping it dry, yet the weather proved all-powerful.

He also knew by now that such weather in the Solomons could persist for several days. What he couldn't see were six US cruisers and nine destroyers moving into his normal line of vision. Three thousand marines landed on Tulagi. Japanese troops were outnumbered and slaughtered almost to a man.

Before noon the next day, the island was secured for the Allies.

~ * ~

Meanwhile, eleven thousand US marines landed on Guadalcanal Island. In all, it was to be learned later, eighty-two ships were in the invasion force. The USA had decided it was so imperative to protect Australian resources from the Japanese, that an all-out offensive against Guadalcanal was essential. So, desperate, it sent what was later to be assessed as an invasion force 'utterly unprepared' to retake Guadalcanal.

It was the biggest invasion force of the war so far.

Yet rushed.

Landings were made in five areas, each surprisingly unopposed. Yet unloading supplies was continually delayed when, within hours, enemy torpedo planes began attacking, inflicting vast US losses of both men and equipment. Betty bombers and Zero fighters wreaked havoc. Coast-watcher warnings had advised of the attack, so unloading had ceased, yet three hours later, twenty-one US navy fighter planes were lost.

On the good side, the airfield was retaken without resistance—a major concession.

The weather had, by then, cleared somewhat. Beresford's radio was working again, but what confronted him was bedlam.

The Japanese had obviously recovered from their surprise, and ships seemed to come from everywhere. And aircraft—fighters and bombers.

No doubt that getting here so quickly, they can only have come from Rabaul and Bougainville. And at that, they must have been armed and ready for immediate action.

He watched dumbfounded as two American ships went down, men leaping overboard into what he knew were shark-infested waters. The rain remained so heavy that he had little chance of making out the names of most ships. Nor see their flags. He could not report even which side beleaguered ships belonged to.

He called up Andy to find out what was happening in the east.

"It's bloody carnage, mate," Andy yelled. "Marines are landing here, but more poor bastards are being strafed and bombed before reaching the beach than those making it. The ocean's turning red!"

"Bloody hell, mate! What about those getting ashore? Are they—"

"The bloody Nips have got so many planes in the air, they're strafing the beaches too. With nowhere to hide, the poor bloody Yanks are running around in circles. They can't even make the jungle. Yesterday they had no opposition but now... Wait up!"

"What?"

"The bloody transports that were landing men are moving off! Jesus! Shut the bloody door, they have, on the blokes already landed. They're picking up steam and putting out to sea."

"Oh Christ!" Beresford all but whispered into his mouthpiece.

~ * ~

Having tried desperately to keep awake, realising the present lull could be short-lived, he knew nothing more until just before midnight, he was awakened in his cave, in which he now had a hard, thin mattress stuffed with coconut fibre that Lobo had brought him.

It's nearly as hard as the bloody rock, yet he couldn't say so to Lobo.

Gunfire had broken out almost in his ear it seemed—the big 'BOOM' of a large ship's guns. He could see nothing but flashes from out in The Slot to his left—well off the Florida Island shore where Tulagi lay.

Soon there were answering flashes and booms on his right. And more from around the headland even further to his right.

He grabbed his radio and punched Andy's number. His fingers were trembling, so it wasn't easy in the dark. And he daren't light even a match, let alone use his torch—the first rule for coast-watchers was "No lights after dark."

"The Nips must've slipped through our fleet to come all around the south of the island. I reckon they've got our blokes sandwiched— pounding 'em both from your end of the island and mine, mate."

And it certainly seemed that way.

As darkness began to wane, the barrages having continued all night, a dreadful sight began unfolding. Between him and little Savo Island, he slowly realised as each long minute brought a little more light, what had looked like giant whales were capsized ships—two of them, slowly settling. A little to his right was another sinking by the stern, and its name was now visible—*HMAS Canberra*. He knew it from his Townsville visit. Australia's two only heavy cruisers, flagship *Australia* and *Canberra,* had been in the Coral Sea battle.

He could tell by the configuration still above water just how mammoth she was. He watched as it increasingly quickly slid beneath the waves.

His body shivered. He could almost feel the final gurgle she must have made.

And how many poor beggars went down with her? And the other ships?

He agonised over not knowing whether they were Japanese, American or Australian.

He was only to find out later that the other two, also now completely gone, were two of three US heavy cruisers sent to the bottom in that midnight battle—the *Astoria,* the *Vincennes* and the *Quincy.*

Andy was soon on the phone again. "The Nips have pulled out. Our transports are starting to again unload, protected only by *HMAS Australia* lookin' awfully bloody lonely and vulnerable. If the Nips come back, she's on her own. She'll really cop a pasting. At the moment here, all is quiet. It's marines as well as stores coming ashore—right here in the harbour. I'm on duty here now. How's things at your end?"

"Not a ship in sight."

He told Andy of the three large ships he had seen go down, including *Canberra.* "And there must have been several small ones during the dark hours because I could see flashes coming from every direction. Planes were flying over, dropping flares, so I guess they helped pick out the cruisers."

"Dropping flares over several hours?"

"Absolutely."

"Then there must be a carrier offshore somewhere. Is Lobo with you?"

"No, but I can get to his village in an hour. You want me to go?"

"Yes. Ask him to send a runner to the west coast and see if there is a carrier offshore. You still have your spare binoculars?"

"Yes."

"Give him those. Even though it might take a couple of days to get back with news, it could mean pinpointing a Nip carrier for our PBY boys in Townsville or Noumea. Did you report the *Canberra* sinking?"

"Of course."

~ * ~

Oh, this dreadful war! How many lads went down on all those ships? Some left floundering in the dark until too exhausted to stay afloat? Some even too crippled from shrapnel blasts to even try staying afloat? And only, what? Two weeks ago that we were whooping and hollering about our big success at Midway? And now this? It seems we lost more ships last night than Japan did at Midway. And neither Andy nor me saw any Jap ship get even a scratch?

What went wrong?

Oh, what went bloody wrong?

And what's left of the eighty-two ships our report said were sent to Guadalcanal? Fled south, that's what—out of range of land-based Jap bombers. And we now haven't an aircraft carrier in the entire South Pacific? And now no airport!

It was quickly realised that whilst the Americans now held what had been the Honiara airport, much of the equipment the fleet had brought to rebuild it hadn't been unloaded before the entire fleet disappeared again. Nor had most of the supplies needed to feed the troops already landed. Nor arms to defend those who had landed, from the now expected retaliatory air attacks—and likely landings supported by an enemy with aeroplanes both carrier-and land-based.

It will be a slaughter!

Twenty-five

"O that this too, too solid flesh would melt, thaw and resolve itself into a dew..."

He cast his mind back to poor Hamlet, trapped in a despair and grief from which he could find no succour.

At school we needed to be told what trauma a man's very soul can find itself in.

Then, of course, it was something impossible for fellows like me to even begin to understand. I could then only be told what were the bases of trauma. Only now is it becoming clear, this thing they call the terrors of war. It surely can only be realised when seen through one's own eyes in such graphic pictures with thunderous cannon in the background and blinding stage-lights highlighting drama and death; stage-lights flashing with such deadly discord, despatching man from life, family and love with such abandon. And hate.

Am I sick that I try to excuse what my eyes have seen by even trying to weigh up numbers? This against that side, to justify an excuse? An excuse to excuse me from feeling all this is bad, seeking any edge of success to mean it ends up all right? Yet all right in what macabre context?

If this is being blooded, then surely I'll be welcomed home; even if my spirit be as dead as those corpses I see drifting in the ocean and the thousands more who went down with their ships. Will this then make life come out all right? Is this what I was sent to find? Sent to feel? Sent to ponder on what every man needs to know to make his life purposeful?

I couldn't hear the screams of those men I saw die through this day and night. Should I be feeling the more satisfied than had I done so? Should this be part of the test?

Yet why should I feel all these problems be only mine? Didn't every one of those men have questions going through his mind as he died in such agonized panic?

Where are the answers? At what stage of terrible death have our wrongs in the past been absolved? Made amends for? Or have I simply been singled out to have seen all this happening as if on a stage for my education if not amusement?

I think not. That could only be too presumptuous. So why are some chosen to be actors and others the audience? Is that Pater's doing? Or God's?

~ * ~

With superhuman physical effort by US marines and local labour, Honiara airport was, in just one week, ready to land fighter aircraft and light bombers. Also about that time four of the naval destroyer-transports that had fled returned to Honiara with badly needed supplies.

Beresford, Andy and Doug, the island's three coast-watchers, remained the only 'old white inhabitants'. Each had emerged from his 'hide', while engineers rebuilt the town's radio mast, to organise natives in help to the marines in their several tasks on the island.

Tulagi, meanwhile, had continued to suffer daily bombing raids.

Why the Nips hadn't taken advantage of the unprotected troops restoring the Guadalcanal airport was only known by Lady Luck. Yet in only two more days after the essential supplies had been received, 'Henderson Field' as the Yanks named it was declared 'Operational'.

Another two days later, six Japanese destroyers landed on a remote beach in the island's south, landing a thousand troops. Dougie not only reported it but had native runners running up and down behind the Japanese lines, reporting on where they were setting up camps. Native runners were also used in the north, delivering upgraded transmitter/receivers. With the airport now operational, an advanced radio mast had been installed, and the new walkie-talkies had stronger signals.

On 12 August, marines attacked the Japanese troops. Jungle fighting, however, required its own peculiar 'nous', and the marines who had arrived had yet to be 'blooded'. They had received only a week's basic training in Fiji but had never faced 'guerrilla'-type assailants. They were wiped out to a man.

A week later, not only had another small fleet of supply vessels returned to Honiara, but thirty-one marine fighters and bombers arrived from the USA.

As Japanese air raids strengthened, not only was some protection available from the land-based aircraft, but casualty cases could be evacuated to hospital in Espiritu Santo in the New Hebrides. And on 20 August, three destroyers arrived with a hundred and twenty tons of badly needed rations; a fourth had been sunk en-route.

Two days later, a shipment of nineteen Wildcat fighters and twelve Dauntless dive-bombers arrived. Things were starting to look up.

In the jungle war, Guadalcanal witnessed its first major land battle by the Tenaru River. Outnumbering the Japanese ten to one was a major advantage, and whilst the marines suffered badly, the entire Japanese unit was wiped out.

"Yet it is not a time for rejoicing," they were told. "The Japanese will find our Henderson Field too much of a threat to their advance on Port Moresby and Australia. They also know our shortage of carriers means we depend on that airport for both air defence and air attack—and everywhere are targets. So it is their prime target here."

All also knew how tenuous was the Allied hold on Guadalcanal in total.

On 24 August, day one of what was to be another resounding naval battle, Marine Wildcat fighters hastened into the air when Beresford reported 'something like' thirty enemy planes heading east over The Slot. A tremendously tight air battle was fought over the eastern end of the island, resulting in disaster for the enemy. It lost twenty-one fighters for the loss of three Wildcats.

What the Wildcat pilots were able to confirm was coast-watch reports of a major Japanese fleet assembling off Guadalcanal's eastern point. Here was a sixty-mile-wide channel to the San Cristobal Island, most easterly of the Solomons. The channel separated The Slot from the Coral Sea.

Allied ships had for days been racing for Guadalcanal, expecting a fully-fledged Japanese invasion to retake it. Japanese strength was counted by PBY surveillance craft at fifty-five vessels—three aircraft carriers, three battleships, thirteen heavy cruisers, three light cruisers, a seaplane carrier and thirty-one destroyers. Its escort was an auxiliary cruiser with troops, a hundred land-based aircraft in support above, and an estimated ten submarines below.

It was a tremendous force.

The Allies had three carriers now repaired, *Enterprise, Saratoga* and *Wasp*; the battleship *North Carolina*; five heavy cruisers, *Minneapolis, New Orleans, Portland, San Francisco* and *Salt Lake City*; two new anti-aircraft light cruisers, *Atlanta* and *San Juan*, and eighteen destroyers. Henderson Field was providing twenty-three fighters and thirty-nine PBYs. Thirty B17s arrived from Espiritu Santo. Three picket lines of submarines completed the force.

A major flaw in the Allied plan was that their ships, already outnumbered two to one, were on a rostered refuelling system, whilst the Japanese fleet was supported by tankers refuelling them at sea. When the battle broke out, the carrier *Wasp*, three cruisers and seven destroyers were in Honiara either in the throes of refuelling or cued up for their turn. All missed the battle.

Action began with a massive air-battle disastrously costly to both sides in terms of planes lost. The Japanese light carrier *Ryujo* was sunk and *Enterprise* so critically damaged that she limped off into the Coral Sea. She left her fighters and bombers to operate from Henderson Field.

The ensuing battle became, essentially, a giant air fight to disable aircraft carriers and to bomb Henderson Field. The US lost twenty more aircraft and the Japanese seventy. *North Carolina* took damage, as did three Japanese vessels.

Japanese destroyers however, bombarded Guadalcanal Island throughout the night.

Next morning, B17s arrived back from Espiritu Santo to sink a destroyer.

The third great Pacific naval battle of the war was a tacit victory for the Allies. The Japanese, with their air-strength so devastated despite vastly outnumbering its opposition, retired without landing any of the invasion troops it had brought or rendering Henderson Field inoperable. Both sides, however, were left licking deep wounds.

~ * ~

Beresford sat one day in the 'Dog on the Tuckerbox', the very bar where he and Andy had watched the Japanese invasion, drinking with several marines and pilots—all off duty.

Beresford, Andy and Doug were no longer permitted leave at the same time. The three coast-watchers were on watch twenty-four hours a day in their particular 'hides'. Now only one watcher at a time could be absent from his post for a half day off each week. And they travelled to and fro on their 'free' time, and these days it wasn't all by foot as they now had 'motor-scooters'. No longer was there need to keep tracks to their 'hides' secret, for all knew that any day from now there would be a major battle for the island—one that could change the course of the war.

"If the bloody Japs win this island," a PBY pilot expounded, "they've got Australia. And without Australia, the US has lost the Pacific. And that includes Hawaii and every opportunity to ever get close enough to attack Japan. Alaska is already under attack. Canada would be their next target, and the entire USA is then within range of their bombers. So this very island simply has to be taken off the Japs while we've got this airport open. I reckon the next fleet we see coming will be either the Japs with a million troops or our lads with a million troops. It's going to be first here wins the war—that's how I see it. I reckon that's what the Japs thought they were doing here last week."

A first lieutenant marine buddy looked around to see who might be listening, for all in the group were junior officers. "I agree, Mike. My captain's under instruction to issue no leave passes, and he hints that more troops are on the way in big numbers."

Beresford couldn't lose the feeling that nobody expected today's situation would be the same tomorrow. Imminent change was in the air, and everybody seemed to sense it.

He made his farewells, finished his beer, picked up his satchel stuffed with bread, cheese and pickled onions.

A good old English ploughman's lunch is just the shot when a man can't get hot food.

~ * ~

Dear folks at home...

I hope the Germans are giving you enough respite to enjoy your summer.

I am still in the same place though living a frugal sort of existence, with plenty of action to compensate for the boring hours of inaction. It is not summer here, of course, but then by British standards, it always seems so. I continue to keep well, despite the odd touch of malaria, but I'm lucky enough to have access to tablets that keep me safe from it developing. And in a jungle environment there is always food of some description to be had from natives. I do hope you get enough to keep healthy.

For two or three months I had no access to radio, but just this week I can get local news, which is mostly conjecture. We are told only what the powers believe appropriate, so it is difficult to get a true measure of things. You still cannot write to me here. I would suggest all mail to Fiji. One of these days I might get there again and collect it. Here, however I can give outgoing mail to fellows flying here, there and everywhere, to post wherever possible.

If dear Thomas is at sea, I have been seeing something of the sort of life he could be finding. In service life these days, of course, a lot of luck comes into it. One can simply never be sure. Sometimes one can feel highly elated that his contribution is helpful, yet at others, quite dejected. But that is war, and one has to realise that others must make all the decisions. Luck too, of course, can take a hand in it. Or so I am learning.

I think of you often, hoping that you are not having to sleep in uncomfortable places like the poor souls in the big cities. Where I am located now, I can get no news whatever of what is happening in Europe. I can only hope things are not too stressful.

Keep thinking of me as I do of you,

Your loving son...

Twenty-six

The very next day Beresford reported a lone Japanese destroyer heading south down The Slot. Fifteen minutes later he heard the drone of a B17 rising from Henderson Field. Right before his eyes, as his binoculars were trained on the tussle, a brace of bombs seemed from his angle to go straight down the destroyer's funnel. A deep explosion certainly ensued, and the ship listed and sank in about fifteen minutes.

A coast-watcher's dream! his inner voice chimed.

His radio reported that night that the Japs had occupied the Australian dependency of Nauru Island in the north, as well as three islands off the sou-east coast of New Guinea.

They will be either the d'Entrecasteaux Group or the Louisiade Archipelago, his memory told him. They were either side of the Jomard Channel from the Solomon Sea to the Coral Sea—where they'd picked up two of the watchers for Townsville.

So the Japs now have that channel to Australia in their pocket!

After three unsuccessful attempts by Nip destroyers trying to land troops on Guadalcanal, possibly due to coast-watch alarms Beresford liked to think, two of the eight destroyers involved were sunk.

"

Hopefully, with all the troops aboard, drowning, flashed through Beresford's mind at the time.

However on 31 August, a thousand Japanese troops were indeed landed.

Only a thousand? What are these Japanese on about? Do they want to really take this island or not? They must know we have some fifteen thousand troops ashore by now. They've had enough flyovers in their Kawanishi flying boats that, like our PBYs able to drop bombs, are certainly only reconnaissance aircraft.

And from thereon, the Japanese began what became known as the *Tokyo Express*. Every night one or two destroyers, always at differing hours, sped down The Slot to deposit a thousand troops here there and anywhere around the island's coastline—all three hundred miles of it. The entire Guadalcanal Island was just less than a hundred miles in length and thirty across, so by the time one added all the bays and bluffs, it was likely close to three hundred miles of shoreline.

Give or take the tide of course, Ego offered.

So with help from natives, it was quickly realised that the Japanese troops ashore, with supplies, could already have negated the advantage of numbers the US marines had held.

And the *Tokyo Express* didn't stop.

Why should it? The clever buggers have worked out that we can't patrol all the coastline, especially at night. So every night, they increase their advantage. They don't need to invade in bloody force! They don't need to put bloody aircraft at risk. Or carriers.

With quite some surprise, and relief, the three coast-watchers were advised that four more Australians had been installed so most of the coastline was now pretty well covered. Invitations were made over the radio loop as the new guys were welcomed.

"And not before bloody time," had been Andy's contribution, to which he added, "But you blokes are as welcome as ice cream. But then, mates, would I rather have the ice-cream and let the Japs have the bloody island?"

When the carrier *Saratoga* was torpedoed and slunk off for repairs until God knew when, morale dropped to zero. All realised how outnumbered they were.

None of the land-based Japanese had yet broken out, which meant they were under orders to wait.

Wait for how long is the big question for us too. They know they now have advantage of numbers, and that's why we cannot attack them like back on the Tenaru River. So they're obviously waiting for some event—and what can that be but a wholesale bloody Japanese invasion? Where the fuck is ours?

He gave himself a slap on the wrist for having sworn, but it illustrated his frustration. If the Americans really wanted Guadalcanal, he could see only that they were letting the Japs steal a march on them—gain the advantage before anything really happened.

War certainly left a lot of questions in a soldier's mind, even if he didn't wear a uniform.

~ * ~

Was it coincidence that it was the beginning of a new month when the first positive thing for the morale-ravished denizens of Guadalcanal was a spark of hope?

Not one or two nor even three, but an entire six big guns arrived and were unloaded ashore. Heavy stuff to return the shelling from Jap cruisers.

"Five-inch bloody bore!" was the cry.

The cheers were nearly drowned out by the now installed loudspeaker for calling attention to arms—yet in this case to advise that two US destroyers, the *Gregory* and the *Little*, had just been sunk off Lunga Point.

"Lunga Point? Why didn't we get a report from our coast-watcher there?"

An inspection party radioed through that they'd found the coast-watch newcomer dead and all his gear gone. His throat had been slashed.

"So much for tracks to our hides no longer needing to be kept secret," Beresford bemoaned on his radio to All Points.

"Well, mate, that speaks for itself," the positive Andy replied. "Go find yourself a new bloody lair. Surely Lobo knows somewhere?"

So Beresford moved. All coast-watchers, however, were now absolutely conscious of how dangerous were their roles.

Beresford simply hoped that whoever had used the knife couldn't read the label and swallowed the poor guy's cyanide pill, thinking it candy.

~ * ~

What he didn't witness on this occasion but heard about when next in the 'Dog on the Tuckerbox' was an aerial battle between a PBY and a Kawanishi—both alone on surveillance duty. Both were armed yet slow and cumbersome to manoeuvre. The Kawanishi was the one to go down in flames, along with the photographs of the island's shorelines it had obviously been taking. The Catalina boys made quite a tale of it—even reporting it over the coast-watcher loop. It was the sort of tale that took longer to tell than the actual combat, yet congratulations were profuse.

Twenty-seven

Randi Edwards arrived home from a dinner to find half of Pago Pago's natives, it seemed, crowded around her house. Gossip travelled swiftly in such communities, especially when it was a white dignitary in trouble. And Jerry was really in trouble.

The crowd was mostly agog not so much that police vehicles were present in numbers but that they'd brought with them a paddy wagon—a prison wagon. That meant something really special—a white man taken away not in just a police patrol car, but a wagon with wire grills and padlocked door. And a respected celebrity at that!

Randi had to force her way through the mob, quiet and patient, but tense.

She was far from either quiet or patient, yet was tensely eager to find out the 'why' of it all. She pressed past the guard on the door, he proving more timid than her, to find her mother in tears.

"What is it? What's going on? Why all the police?"

Teri grabbed at her daughter as if seeing her as the way out of the dilemma she suffered. "Your father, Randi. They've got him holed up in the kitchen—handcuffed, can you believe? And they've got men searching every drawer and cupboard in the house. They even pulled down the wall linings of his study looking for something apparently in some secret place. They've charged him with spying. A goddam *spy*!" she shouted in obvious distress.

They were in the living room. Randi quietly walked over to where decanters stood on a bar and poured two double-scotches. She handed one to her mother and began sipping the other.

"Do they realise he is an FBI agent?"

"Yes. He's not only told them a dozen times, he has shown them papers verifying it. And the awards he's won in the service. But they're simply not impressed. I'm at my wits' end what to do." She again broke into breath-jerking sobs.

Randi, surprised even at her own calm, held her mother's drink to her lips.

"Here, Mom. You cannot think straight when so distraught. Just sit a while and sip this. Then we can talk more on it."

She waited then, for a few minutes.

"Have you eaten? I had dinner two hours ago. How long has this been going on?"

"No. Yes—oh, I don't know. No, I was just about to serve dinner when they came crashing through the door. It's all in the kitchen. That mob of officers and brigands have probably devoured it by now."

Randi didn't speak; she simply rose, showed a single forefinger to the mother as much as to say, "Sit," and strode to the kitchen.

Ah! She had never seen her father look so deflated. He had ever been her knight in shining amour, he who was always in total control, not only of himself but of every situation. Now he couldn't even smile at her. She was shocked to see that he almost cringed. And it hurt, right down to the gut!

He even looks guilty of whatever it is they accuse him of! Wherever has his fighting spirit gone? He looks utterly defeated!

She had gone in there not only to get food for her mother, but to see what she could do to help her father. Yet his attitude in a flash convinced her there was nothing she could do. And she could read in his eyes, which never left hers, that he also knew it.

She was utterly devastated.

A spy? His entire demeanour, his very eyes are telling me Yes! That, yes, he is indeed guilty as charged.

Yet still she couldn't bring herself to believe it.

A spy for what? For whom? In what sort of capacity? Doing what?

Nothing made sense. Yes, she knew he was an FBI agent. A good one. She knew his shipping and trading business around the islands was but a front, yet he had ever ensured it, too, was successful in its own right.

Yet now? What on earth is all this about?

From upstairs she could hear noisy banging of this, bumping of that. Then came the sound of breaking glass, not too loud, but without cries of shock.

She looked around the table and kitchen benches, and, yes, her mother had been right. Everything was a mess. She went to the fridge and extracted two chilled but roasted chicken legs. They were always there for people who just 'dropped in'. She tossed them on a plate, grabbed some bread rolls and took them to her mother.

Then, without a word, she marched upstairs.

Doors to cupboards hung open so she could see that all inside walls in each had been torn down except where they were painted concrete. Each bathroom cupboard was the same, all contents of shelves swept into the basin or on the floor. Every picture and wall hanging had been pulled down and timber-framed veneers stripped to see what might be hidden inside. She gave up after two rooms. She knew all would be the same and no single 'daughter of the accused' was going to influence them one way or another.

She felt sick, but there was nothing she could do.

She returned to her mother. That was one area where maybe she could do something.

She just sat by her, holding one hand and, with the other, offering a drumstick.

Teri heaved a great sigh, then took it. And bit into it.

"I'm glad you are home, my pet. I feel absolutely washed out. I still cannot believe all this is happening."

"It's happening, Ma, because they don't trust leaving you or me in the house when they take Pa off, in case we retrieve what they think is hidden somewhere."

"But what, my pet, can they find other than what is genuine FBI material? And everything in that line is surely above the level of even the highest authority in this little province."

It was beyond them both.

Spy? Randi thought. *Spying is helping enemies of the nation—surely Pa isn't involved with either Germany or Japan in such a sense. He is a true-blue Republican and fervent supporter of everything American. Isn't he an Exalted Ruler or something in the Elks? He has everything going for him—absolutely the last sort of man to start helping our enemy. This entire thing is crazy! Absolutely crazy!*

Yet nor could she delete from her mind the look in his face when she fronted him in the kitchen.

Everything there said, 'Yes, I am guilty as charged.'

~ * ~

Morale in Honiara was dead low. The Americans had just watched eleven of their fourteen P400 fighter aircraft shot out of the sky—absolutely outclassed by the Mitsubishi Zeros. No pilot wanted to take out the other three.

Everything suddenly, again, seemed working for the Japs. In New Guinea, after several months of severe jungle fighting against the Australians, they had broken through the Owen Stanley Gap, to begin the descent to Port Moresby.

Jap battleships bombarded Guadalcanal from every direction, and there wasn't an Allied ship in sight. The *USS Hornet* was now the only Allied carrier in service in the entire Pacific Ocean, and she was helpless against the might of the opposition. Terrified natives and military personnel were being killed by the hundreds. The southern beachhead was now five miles long and nearly three deep—hand-to-hand fighting was the order of the day, and the Japs were refusing to be pushed back. Reports from a coast-watcher still secreted in occupied Rabaul got word out that the Japanese had just unloaded from transports one hundred new fighters and eighty new bombers. All knew that these meant more bombardment for both the New Guinea front and the Guadalcanal front.

On the other hand, marines began moving into Beresford's hide area near Point Cruz. The significant Matanikau River ran south from The Slot near Lobo's village of Kokumbona, and the Japanese now occupied the entire area. After quite a scuffle the marines came out of it far better in terms of manpower, yet they could still not budge the Japs, who lost some hundred and fifty against the marines' forty. There were many wounded, however, with the worst cases flown to Espiritu Santo.

Then a whisper of hope came over the radio waves. In New Guinea, not only had the Australians halted the Japanese drive only twenty miles from Port Moresby, but the Aussies had them in retreat, back up the mountainside. And at month's end, the air war over Guadalcanal took a turn for the better. Sixty-two Zeros attacked Henderson Field; twenty-three were shot down for the loss of one Wildcat.

It was a 'cake-walk' victory to lift many a flagging spirit.

~ * ~

Yet on the ground, Beresford found himself in a sticky situation.

All he was armed with to defend himself was a British Sten Gun and a cyanide pill. Sten Guns Mark 2, with a Canadian imprint engraved into the metal stock, had arrived with a shipment a month ago. A thousand, with ammunition, were offloaded in Guadalcanal for combatants other than US military, and the word from seamen on the ship was that it was proceeding to Darwin with an entire cargo of military small arms. The coast-watchers on Guadalcanal were able to advise them that the last they'd heard was that Darwin was being evacuated. Japanese bombers had destroyed most of it, and its harbour was a junkyard of rusting, sunken vessels.

Why that ship hadn't been advised of it, Beresford wondered, *I can't imagine—observing radio silence is one thing, but if it leads them astray like that, it seems to defeat the purpose of bringing the armaments.*

Yet every man was becoming used to hearing such questionable decisions being taken, so realised it was useless hoping for answers to such a paradox.

It was by now realised 'upstairs' that the Japanese took no cognisance of international agreements on the rights of prisoners. Japan, in fact, was not even a signatory to the rights of the Red Cross during wartime. And coast-watchers wore no uniform, so were doubly vulnerable to instant death if captured. Being volunteers and therefore unarmed, each carried in a pocket a lethal pill to be taken rather than risk capture. Yet now it was decided they might as well have the means to protect themselves. They were offered the option of carrying a Sten Gun.

Beresford thought it strange that in their particular instance they should be offered a rifle rather than revolver, but again put the question aside in that same paradox basket. He accepted the Sten and was drilled in its use. He had it slung over his shoulder when realising that, moving from one hide to another, he had stumbled on a Japanese patrol wading the Matanikau River. They were heading right for him. And he was alone.

Oh, oh, decision time!

The mere fact there was no movement or shout to illustrate that any of the enemy had seen him, about a dozen in all, satisfied him that he had but two options—quietly retreat and hide, or quietly retreat and run.

The soldiers were talking amongst themselves—the 'wading' had them in various stages of it, all strung in a line. On the far bank, they were just entering the water; in the middle of the thirty or forty yards wide river, they were up to their waists or even a little deeper; closest to him, the front man was still more than knee deep. All held rifles above their heads, in both hands.

And to climb the shallow bank, they must, once clear of the river, negotiate ten yards or so of slippery mud.

It was the talking that had alerted him, so he'd been able to stop when still partly hidden by jungle.

Either option is to first retreat quietly. I'll make the second when I know whether or not they've seen me.

He wore jungle slacks and army ration boots, yet a short-sleeved pale grey shirt. And no beret or cap. He hated headwear at any time yet kept a rain-bonnet in his backpack because when rain fell in the Solomons it could drown a man if he turned a face to it. Binoculars hung down his chest on a strap around his neck and his hands were free. What wasn't in pockets he had in his small backpack.

So my face is bare, quickly flashed through his mind, *and my arms are bare, so even if my shirt doesn't catch the immediate attention when any look up, my white skin may.*

He quickly turned, crossing his arms against his chest, and as quietly as he could, crept back on his own footsteps. There was a track, of sorts, from the village to the beach, a half-mile distant. About halfway along, his unbeaten track led off to his eastern hide. Once the Nips had invaded, he had lost the use of the motor scooter he'd had for a time because the marines needed every one for ferrying wounded.

After twenty paces and having heard no shout, he knew stage one of his plan had worked. But he still didn't want to quicken his pace so much that he might make a noise.

If I stay on the track for a way, there is less bracken. Yet if I step in a puddle they could note the difference between the sole of my boot and the bare foot of a native.

So he swung off into the jungle, crossing fingers that he didn't step on something dry enough to make a sound. Yet he wanted to see which way they went—might even follow them at a safe distance once they'd passed him.

He slid his entire body under the branches of a huge fern that touched the ground all around, hoping he wasn't disturbing a snake. Snakes abounded in the jungle, yet he'd been told only three in this area were lethal.

Little comfort to a man terrified of even safe ones.

Yet he had no option. He could see to where the Nips must travel if taking the path he'd been on, yet just hoped the jungle was thick enough that he could watch them without them sighting him.

Or is it just my luck that one might choose this very spot to take a leak?

They did come past, none now talking, and he could see enough—was even able to count them. Fourteen, all in jungle greens and all helmeted, some even with mosquito nets over their helmets. And none wanted to take a leak just there.

His mind flashed again to snakes, leeches, mosquitoes and spiders. It remembered the time when he first walked into a spider-web strung across a jungle path at just his face height—he had nearly gone berserk.

I remember it so well because Lobo had been following, and he fell about in fits of laughter because he knew the spider that made that web was not poisonous. He had the gall to explain that the poor spider was likely more frightened than me!

Yet right now, that recall had to be quickly dashed from mind.

He hadn't counted how many men had crossed the river.

Could that number have been fifteen?

He hadn't wanted to spend that much time. Yet he now realised that even if one had dropped off to relieve himself, he would have caught up by now. So he crept back to the track, looking back down it just in case. Here the jungle was so dense that little sunlight could penetrate the canopy; there was a dearth of colour, making it easier to spot even a yellow face. There were none, so he changed his mind about following them.

What could it achieve? Our fellows know the Nips are in this part of the island. They've likely got their own surveillance guys out and about. And it was just as likely for me to chance running across one our own patrols as a Nip.

He continued on his own journey, wading the river and cutting north to his alternate hide, from which he could see more of what was coming down The Slot from the north than from the eastern side of Point Cruz.

Twenty-eight

Andy called Beresford.

"Where are you? East or west hide?"

"West. Why?"

"Stay there and bog down. I'm coming to your east hide."

"What? Why?"

"Radio wise-talk, mate. You just take cover. Things'll soon bubble. You got plenty batteries?"

"Of course. What you know that I don't?"

"Big regatta day near."

"Picnic?"

"Yeah, mate. Guy Fawkes' Day'll be a month early, give a few days, right by your window. I'm on my way to your other pad. All leave cancelled."

The rest of their conversation was drowned out by a stream of B17s taking off from Henderson Field. Beresford had to stuff wadding in his ears because there was wave after wave. He had never seen so many planes in a raid, and curiosity had him counting them. He ran into the open, yet they were clustered too tightly. He wrote 'maybe thirty' in his notebook.

Northwest? Rabaul is my guess. Wow, those boys will wreak some havoc in that town.

He reckoned the targets were its airfield and the best equipped docking facility this side of Australia. Fifteen minutes later, twenty-eight fighter-bombers followed the B17s.

There's certainly something going on up there. Could this be in response to the Nip invasion everyone's been expecting the last month? Seeing they didn't succeed with their last? And this time they're coming down The Slot again? And Guy Fawkes Day a month early?

Everyone soul in the British Empire knew Guy Fawkes Day was 5 November—the night every family let off fireworks. The Spanish rebel Guy Fawkes had set several kegs of gunpowder and fuses under London's Westminster Palace in 1605, to blow the king sky-high. But he was discovered before he could light the fuses.

So that makes it the fifth of October. And give a few days? Hey, today is the fifth! So, I guess he means a few days from now. And regatta? Another naval battle? Yes, surely it is the expected invasion. Which of course would be despatched from Rabaul!

He was quite agog. He checked his food stocks. He had coconuts galore, of course. And mangoes and bananas galore. He had plenty of kerosene for his lamp and cooking, eight eggs, a large can of cassava, half a pumpkin and eight yams—a king's banquet. Only drinking water might prove a problem, yet coconut juice was always insurance in that part of the world. He would get by.

~ * ~

Two days later Andy called again.

"Put your tin hat on, mate."

"Gotcha, mate. You at my weekender?"

"Yep, settled in nicely. Brought me own tucker, I did. If our guys are readin' their signals right, our family should be here when the first batsman takes strike. Got me?"

Beresford thumped the heel of his hand on his temple. "No. You got a better clue?"

There was silence. "Just before the twelfth man comes in to bat?"

"Gotcha, mate. So you'll see them first and I'll see the others first. How about we call each other soon as get a sighting?"

"Birds'll be on the wing before that. A do or die party, I'm told."

All afternoon of October 11 he'd been mesmerised by the bombing of Henderson Field.

With Japan aware that *USS Hornet* was the only serviceable Allied carrier, Henderson Field was vital to Allied defence of the island. However, with the end of daylight, all flights had returned, no doubt, to Rabaul or carriers further north in The Slot.

He ate cold food, having been warned to show no light whatever, and turned in early to bed in his *bure*, the native hut built of woven reed walls with, under a mock thatch, a corrugated iron roof for weatherproofing. It was comfortable enough, with ample window-flaps for observing The Slot shoreline west and all the way to little Savo Island some six miles north. That was, for the nonce, his 'slot' for observing and reporting.

Just after dark, his radio beeped. Andy's voice came on the line. Hearing wasn't easy because his ears were still thumping from the hours of bombing so close.

"They've made a right mess of the field, mate. Our lads are working frantically to get the runway repaired. It's okay for fighters, but not for the big blokes. They're filling with crushed rock. They won't be able to pave it, they say, before the Nip fleet arrives."

"Filling in the dark?"

"Under floodlights. That's why I'm calling. Soon as you hear a plane from the north, bip the airport so they can black out. There's a man waiting for your signal."

"Gotcha, mate. When's the action going to start?"

"The Nip fleet could reach Savo within two hours, judging by Frank's report. We're all ready. Transports are unloading troops and supplies even now. Word is that America's 164th Regiment is unloading ten thousand troops. Our big guns are already cruising your way. You're gonna have a front stalls view, mate. Just best of bloody good luck."

"Is BB here?" BB was their code for *Hornet*, Big Bee.

"Dunno, mate. I know only what I get on the blower. I can't see bloody shit from here. There's not a trace of moon."

And he switched off.

Beresford felt about, checking that his helmet was to hand, and binoculars, notebook and pencil. He fumbled in the dark to ready a second pencil in case the first broke.

I want everything ready so I can snatch some shut-eye before things start happening. He knew that once it began, there would be no let-up and could go on for hours.

He checked his watch. It was nine-thirty.

And when he was woken, it wasn't just a single *Boom!* It was an entire volley—seemingly right in his ear-hole.

In my right ear-hole? That means it's our guys.

He was quickly afoot, trying to fit his helmet with his left hand while the right grabbed for binoculars. He had already set his length for what he reckoned was halfway to the island. He wasn't quite at the halfway line between the two fleets, somewhat closer to the flashes on his left—the Nip fleet. Some flashes were coming from beyond Savo Island.

So could they be trying to outflank our guys?

He reported that.

It was a pitch-black night. Yet lo and behold! He was just thinking how difficult things were to make out, when suddenly the sky was lit up with flares...

Must be twenty of them, all over the Nip fleet.

His mind was stunned. *So many! But at least our boys now have some idea of how the opposition is distributed.*

The light seemed to stay high for a long time.

Then movement out the corner of his left eye grabbed his attention.

He swung his binoculars left. Then grabbed for his radio with his left hand while his right let down the binoculars to punch the 'All Points' button.

"Two ships landing troops west of Ruaniu, maybe even closer to Vilu."

"Repeat please," he heard from somewhere.

"Two ships landing troops west of Ruaniu, maybe even closer to Vilu."

"Got it, Berry," said an American voice. "Can you count the landing craft?"

"Can you get another flare over it?"

"Good as done. Call when you get a reading." And the line went dead.

The flashing lights and booms of big guns were deafening. He hadn't yet seen as many flashes from his right, but then most of the Allied fleet would likely be around the Point Cruz headland that limited his vision east.

But I can report every hit on the Nips.

He realised he was likely the closest man on the whole of Guadalcanal to this action.

Apart from those Nips heading for the beach up there—behind the action.

Then came flares in that area—a string of them, giving him a view of the coast for quite a way west of Ruaniu village.

"Two destroyers. Twelve to fifteen landing craft on their 'in' journey."

"Thanks, Berry."

Wow. This means the only road to the entire west of the island is cut. Our only access beyond that landing point is by sea. If we want to get troops west of the Nips, it'll have to be a landing, same as the Nips are doing now.

Guadalcanal didn't even have a road encircling the island. In the entire south, there was none. The only road west from Honiara finished on the west coast.

Even at that, it's not an all-weather road. So if we've to invade behind them from the coast, it can only be from the south! And we can't do that while outnumbered in The Slot. Protecting Honiara and the field is our only hope.

So it seemed that all that could be done before daylight was lambaste the Japanese troops now landing in the west, from the air with flares.

He knew that apart from coastal fishing villages, the western end of the island was uninhabited—impenetrable jungle with few rivers—so had no permanent fresh water.

And, seemingly, the enemy knows it too! So they'll likely work their way east—towards the Nips I ran up against. And me!

Yet he also knew that could not happen quickly. He was in far less danger from them, for the time being, than from the Jap cruisers shelling the shoreline...

But then his heart skipped another beat... *Bloody hell. If the Nips get even a half-mile advantage on our fleet, they could start landing troops right here!*

Then there was a sudden, massive explosion right before his eyes—so bright it momentarily lit up the sky, yet long enough for him to see it was a huge heavy cruiser, closest vessel to him, that had taken a direct hit, dead amid-ships. He saw debris and even bodies of men catapulted into the air—then, apart from spreading fire on the ship, only blackness all about.

He reported it.

But our lads now have a glowing target to aim at!

He had no idea, of course, by how many ships the Allies were outnumbered. He knew they must be, for rumour in the mess last time he was in Honiara was that the Japs had eight aircraft carriers still operating in the Pacific.

With most of them likely here in the south!

For the next several hours, the battle raged. He saw red glows on his right, as having seen many other direct hits to the Nips.

So our boys aren't having it all their own way.

And that was to be all he could know until either someone called him, or until daylight.

Then the barrages will start again, no doubt.

But meanwhile, all seemed like a truce had been called.

Twenty-nine

The dawn of 12 October found Beresford already awake, eyes straining through the first rays, counting ships. Last night there had seemed a dozen or more, yet daylight showed the Japanese had six, two heavy cruisers and four destroyers.

One of the heavy cruisers he'd last night seen hit was in dire trouble, listing heavily to starboard. The other and a destroyer were picking up survivors. He could now see three destroyers to the west where the landing had taken place, one burning and settling low by the stern, one picking up men floating on debris and the third despatching troops off by landing craft.

Did I sleep through something? That is exactly the spot where I reported the landing.

He had heard nothing, yet action had obviously taken place there.

Could I have heard it and thought I was dreaming?

He snatched at his radio, again pressing the 'All Points' button.

"Three Nip destroyers off the west coast, one foundering by the look of it, one picking up flotsam and one landing troops. Three landing craft heading for the beach, another loading and one returning from the beach."

"Thanks, Berry. Could you please repeat for others joining late? I'm taking action."

Berry repeated his message.

"BB says thanks," was his only reply.

He hadn't known *Hornet* had arrived.

Must have been them hit the destroyer I reported landing troops last night—the one now sinking?

He saw dive-bombers with torpedoes arrive from the west before he heard them. The scene was a long way off. The bombers went straight for the destroyer landing the troops, while following fighters strafed both the beach and the landing craft in transit. That part of it was a turkey-shoot—and maybe the scene on the beach also, although he couldn't sight that clearly because of the distance and because it was all still in shadow. It was only 05:38.

And there's not yet an enemy plane in the sky.

His radio beeped. It was Andy.

"G'don ya, mate," he opened with. "You are the only eyes up that end. I heard BB's answer. What's happening now?"

"I timed BB stings' arrival, mate. Just sixteen minutes after my report."

"Probably already primed and pilots on standby. What's happening now?"

"A turkey shoot on the landing craft, and, I think, the beach. There's a Jap heavy cruiser right in front of me, starting to settle. Her escort destroyer has skippies picking up the crew."

'Skippies' was the name for the motorised runabouts troop-carrying destroyers kept for just that purpose. They were also targets for strafing.

"The damaged 'big fellow', according to pundits here, is the heavy cruiser *Furutaka*. Are you saying she's a gonner?"

"I'm saying she is listing badly, is down by the stern and her crew is abandoning ship. She's at least out of the fight, and you can pass that on. Tell them to save their torpedoes and bombs for the other one. I can't read Japanese so I've no idea of its name or number."

He heard a chuckle as Andy signed off.

And even as he checked his battery, he heard the roar of aircraft taking off from Henderson—a loud roar.

They've either got the tarmac filled and packed ready enough for the big boys, or that's the test case.

Only one plane took off, and by the time Beresford could see it, it was already banking to fly east...

Either with casualties to Espiritu Santo or coming back to land again.

PBYs weren't used in battles because they were so slow. They were good low-level bombers and had exceptionally long range, yet were sitting ducks against fighters. Usually, once a battle was over, they were used as 'ambulances' for serious injury patients. B17s were too valuable as bombers to be wasted on such trips yet were used in emergencies.

He wondered if the strip was open again for the big boys, or if the Catalina had taken off from the harbour.

Almost before he finished such pondering, his ears were again assailed as the remaining Jap heavy cruiser's guns opened. It seemed in the direction of the airport.

And I guess any tick of the clock we shall have heavy bombers from Rabaul joining the fray again. And heavy bombers are always accompanied by fighter escorts, so there could be fireworks again, especially with BB close.

He watched as the *Hornet*'s torpedo bombers braved strong fire from their targets to swoop low and send off their missiles. A destroyer picking up survivors from landing craft that had been sunk was hit amidships. Both ends of the ship seemed to lurch as if already severed through its midsection, and a huge pall of flame and smoke burst skyward. Beresford, eyes glued to his binoculars, was amazed when, as the smoke cleared, twisted metal chunks and other debris were still falling. The ship was clearly split in two. He just couldn't believe that the stern half was already rolling over as if being turned by a giant invisible hand. The larger forward half settled at seemingly a more comfortable lie when a torpedo from the third plane in the attack struck that. The blast was less impressive, yet the bow seemed to leap up in surprise before the whole thing began sinking backward. He could suddenly see that the hull had burst opened to reveal hundreds of men being thrown into the water—dead or alive, some of both. Then quite suddenly that entire forward section was no more. She disappeared within a minute, along with all the troops still trying to get out.

And there must have been many, for it was obviously a troop transport, and from the first explosion it was but a matter of minutes before the second.

The stern half took only a little longer to submerge, with again, hundreds of men in uniform, obviously all ready to disembark, jumping for their lives. He tried to imagine the panic.

What could there have been? A thousand men crammed in there? Two thousand?

He had no idea how much space there was in a destroyer, how many it could carry, yet it was the vessel both sides persistently used for invasions.

Later in the day he received news that airmen had reported it was the destroyer *Fubuki*.

Likely it left Rabaul two days ago at daybreak, to arrive here before midnight last night. A forty to fifty-hour journey. So there must have been space enough for every man to sleep. So am I being too optimistic in saying a thousand?

Yet he couldn't get out of his mind the sight, in every part of that ship he had opportunity to see, of a solid mass of helpless men.

And how many would have been killed in that first massive explosion?

Yet when his mind then did a flashback to Townsville and Lt. Commander Feldt's tale of beheadings and crucifixions of even coast-watchers, his anxiety softened.

He could see only a fraction of what was going on. During the morning, two more Japanese destroyers arrived.

Laden with troops no doubt.

He reported it.

His mind again flipped to how many men the Allies might have on the island.

Andy said the 164th had brought ten thousand from Noumea, yet that sounds a lot. Yet then he later said we had five destroyers here in the fight, so if my one thousand is a measure, that makes his ten thousand possible.

It was a hectic day. By dark, he had seen the damaged heavy cruiser *Furutaka* slip beneath the waves. Then there had been the torpedoed troop carrier. About midday he reported a destroyer sunk after a dive-bombing off Savo Island, then another during mid-afternoon, all for the loss of three aircraft.

Whew, what a day! By the time of Andy's call, Beresford had remembered that he'd skipped lunch in all the excitement. *And I didn't have my mango and banana breakfast until after the* Fubuki *finally sank.*

But he'd remembered to light his little kerosene stove and shield it from view outside before dark. Andy had called to tell him that only one US ship had blown up—but that was by design. She was so damaged by gunfire that, come morning, it was decided she be stripped and scuttled. Heavy cruiser *Salt Lake City* received some damage, as did the light cruisers *Boise* and *Helena* and destroyer *Farenholt*.

"Seriously? Many deaths?"

"They're not saying, mate. They seldom give out that sort of news."

"What about BB?"

"Not a word, but her planes are flying, so she can't be in too bad a shape. Any activity your end?"

"Not since last report. The heavy cruiser seems to be limping—either that or they're fiddling with her steering. She could have rudder trouble—like the *Bismarck*?"

"Report it anyway, mate. If she's sick, it might be worth trying a PT attack. I got your report on the two destroyers damaged—they gel with the air-boys' report."

They wished each other a peaceful night's sleep, and after reporting the limping cruiser Beresford turned to decide what delight he would cook.

Or should I just dream about chocolate éclairs and piles of whipped cream?

~ * ~

He awoke to find the dawn already broken and the only craft in sight native canoes. Fishermen were casting nets.

There wasn't a cloud, and everything gave promise of a balmy day. It seemed the world had decided on a day off from war. He trained his gaze along the west coast but could see nothing. He climbed atop the crest of the little hillside his hide was on and even climbed a tree to better see over coconut palms that lined beaches. Because the tide was low, he saw some of the hull of the *Fubuki*. He was surprised—it had seemed from his hide that it had sunk in reasonably deep water. It was the forward half he could see. The stern had been a little further into The Slot. Yet nothing disturbed the ocean. It was just as if yesterday had never happened.

I bet it's a different sight over on Henderson Field.

The hours of shelling that not only preceded the start of the battle, but continued pretty much all the way through it, must have left some dreadful aftermath.

Yet with them losing a heavy cruiser and three destroyers, apart from the huge loss of life of their army when that destroyer went down and the turkey shoot of the beaches and landing craft against our sole destroyer, must have our lads giving a few cheers.

He returned to his post and wrote a letter home, giving them, without names and numbers, of course, a bird's eye view of yesterday's battle.

Thirty

It was nearly a week later.

Andy's estimated ten thousand troops arriving from Noumea had turned out to be three thousand, and Beresford's one or two thousand aboard the *Fubuki* was quoted by the marines back in the 'Dog on the Tuckerbox' as more like "up to five hundred." The two friends agreed to leave their estimates in future to what they could count on fingers.

The day after that great twenty-hour battle, despite the languid morning Beresford had woken up to, Henderson Field had been attacked from both sea and air. And on the next day. And the next. Meanwhile, with the Allied fleet retired for major repairs, Japanese cruisers bombarded the Field with non-stop shelling for an entire week. As an airfield or even a serviceable workshop, it was a shambles of useless real estate. And eighty aircraft had been destroyed.

Beresford couldn't count how many games of patience he had played during the idle days. He had even filled some hours trying to break his record of building card houses, yet the bure let in too much wind for that game.

Already the whisper was out that Vice Admiral Bill Halsey had been appointed the new Commander South Pacific Area. Bill, or

"Bull" Halsey as he was more popularly known in navy circles, had an excellent record of action against the Japanese—had even commanded *Enterprise* in the great Doolittle raid on Tokyo.

"Well, we certainly need some fresh blood upstairs," was the general cry around marine ranks.

"Why did they have to leave it so late?" asked others.

It certainly sounds like none will miss Vice Admiral Ghormley.

Yet the change made an indelible mark in the morale of all.

"At least it shows they haven't forsaken us," said others, an understatement after the pounding the island had taken over the last week.

Beresford was recalled from his duty for the time being. "Until we can sort out just where the Japanese are, in the interior."

During the week since the Battle of Savo Island, it was thought that so many Japanese had landed while Henderson Field was under such attack that their entire situation was extremely dangerous. At the moment they had no navy, no army and no air force.

"We're sitting ducks, should the Nips decide to charge out of the jungle."

It was common sense to realise that with now no airport, Honiara itself, with its harbour, was an obvious target.

Andy whispered to Beresford that he would not be surprised if the Yanks weren't already wiring it for destruction, before pulling out.

"What, and just handing Australia to the enemy, on a platter? Wasn't this their reason for taking a stand here in the first place? I remember hearing expressions like 'absolutely essential' and 'vitally important' and 'losing this would simply open the door to the whole Pacific'. Now they're thinking of quitting?"

"Well that's the word wot I'm gettin' from marines, mate."

"But we won that last battle. Decisively!"

"Yes, but we don't have any navy left. At least any they're prepared to send us. Every ship we had has limped off to lick wounds, and here's the Japs replied with a whole new bloody fleet to shell us nearly off the bloody map. And now we don't even have the airfield that was so bloody essential. A guess is that the bloody Nips are out there now, laying bloody mines so we can't get anything in to help us escape. And they've got an army just a bloody mile away. Or closer!"

Things were grim.

~ * ~

Washington DC

Leo Ferguson sat facing Teri and Randi Edwards, his fingers fiddling nervously with a fountain-pen from his elaborate desk set.

"I'm as sad as you are about this, ladies, but the evidence is indisputable. Jerry was my favourite agent, the cleverest—as indicated by the fact that for so long we never suspected him—but also cleverest in the legitimate work he did for us, and the most far-sighted. He could see around all sides of the box at once. He was simply the best."

"Indisputable?" Teri questioned. "I simply cannot believe it. We both knew him so well. I've believed for years that I could read his mind well. He was the perfect husband!"

"And the perfect spy, Mrs. Edwards. He's admitted it. Even given us pointers to accomplices. The holidays he took you on, the reasons he had his home office so safely barricaded from you, was not only because of material confidential to the FBI but material he was despatching to a Japanese agent in Sydney."

Then Randi spoke up. "We didn't know he had any contacts in Australia, even with his business. Or work for you. He never let that slip."

"As I said, Miss, he was both clever and professional. He had us all as hoodwinked. When we were given a hint that he might be a double agent, I scoffed loudest. But regulations said we had to pass the hint on to our bloodhounds, and they cracked it. I say again, he's confessed. He knows there is no going back to any life he's had up until now."

"Can we see him?"

He sighed deeply, his fingers still fiddling. "No. That is regulations."

"What will happen to him now?"

"He's still being interrogated. With this drawn-out campaign on Guadalcanal, we need to know what other information he could have about the area."

"I remember him taking me on one of his ships to Guadalcanal when I was about twelve or thirteen. A reward for my good school grades, he told me. Could he have been a spy for Japan even then?"

He shrugged. "Highly likely, but how can we now put faith in anything he tells us? We have to believe that anything is possible."

He could see that Jerry's family was still in shock, and he must tread warily. He didn't have to take notes; he knew that not only was everything being recorded, but that the entire interview was under surveillance by secreted cameras.

"On that trip, for instance, Miss, did you meet any of the people he had business with? Or social friends he wanted to look up? Not only in Honiara, but in any of the other ports you visited? Suva, Lautoka for instance? Or in Tonga? Or Apia?"

Randi looked blank. "All my thoughts were taken up in sightseeing and studying the natives for my school reports. I gave no mind, back then, to anything my father said or did."

"Back then, you say? Does that mean that more recently, you may have? Or you, Mrs. Edwards?" he said, turning to Teri. "Are you able to list every name Jerry may have given you during those years and up until now?"

Teri's eyes rolled. "There must have been hundreds. He was always reeling off names. Knowing people in the trade was his business right through the islands. Although I can see why it must be important to you now. But would h... a spy use real names? Especially a clever spy as you claim."

He noted that she even hesitated in referring to him as a spy for a nation like Japan—a situation he understood.

I can imagine how my own family would react if, out of the blue, someone accused me.

"You still haven't told me if, when his"—she paused, not even wanting to say the word—"interrogation, is done with. Will we be able to see him then?"

"Mrs. Edwards, that is a question I cannot answer. Everything that happens to him now is out of my hands. I have a black mark hanging over my competence, of course. Since his admission, he is no longer one of my agents. I am not sure if he is a prisoner of the US Marshall's office or even held under the US Treasons Act. As far as his personal rights are concerned, I am unclear, and it is not my prerogative to enquire. I hate to put it coldly, but I would think him, until further notice, a *persona-non-gratis*."

"What do we do? Do you recommend we wait here? Or with family in California? Or should we return to Pago Pago?"

"It could be quite a while, ladies. Even until the end of the war. If he is to be arraigned, it may well have to wait until we have access to Japanese records."

"That could be years!"

"It could indeed, I am sad to have to say. I consider your best options are California or Pago Pago. But Jerry, I'm afraid, you cannot have access to."

As they stepped from the building, Teri grasped her daughter's hand:

"Do you have the feeling that we too, could be considered accomplices? That quite apart from the fact that we can never return to the family life we had, we have to instead face a future of knowing we are being watched at every moment?"

~ * ~

On the afternoon of 23 October, the Japanese army came from the jungle to attack Henderson Field. The fact that a landing strip for light aircraft had been laid during the previous week renewed enemy interest. They had crept from their western end of the island, eastward through heavy jungle by the foot of the mountains. Natives from the area, cued to report whatever such Japanese manoeuvres were afoot, brought the news to Honiara. So marines were in place and able to drive the enemy back into the jungle. Yet the Japs persisted, and for three days a bloody battle raged. Losses on both sides were heavy.

From the sea, a Japanese light cruiser began shelling Henderson Field again, but it was severely damaged by dive-bombers and forced to retire.

Beresford had been despatched east to set up a hide near the island's eastern tip. It was a lonely area, a long way from even Henderson Field, let alone Honiara, yet gave him excellent sight of whatever was approaching the southern entrance of The Slot from the Coral Sea in the south, or the Pacific Ocean at large in the east. There was not even a road so far, yet native fishing villages abounded.

If there were a compensation for being now so remote from friends, it was two-fold—one that Kaoka Bay was indeed a Pacific paradise, beaches of glaringly white sand, coconut trees and other palms in abundance, and everywhere a blaze of floral colours. The other was that, because of its remoteness, he was asked to choose a native companion, insurance against Beresford falling ill or any problem with his radio. He of course approached Lobo, who jumped at the chance. His life had become far from 'normal' in that with his village now under Japanese occupation he did not risk going there. Any local who spent time elsewhere was interrogated under torture. He had been living in the town doing odd translating jobs for the Americans.

Now his language ability would help Beresford communicate with locals in his new locale.

They had been dropped off there by a PT Boat. He still had his walkie-talkie and could communicate with Andy and base. Andy's new hide was Vanuagobu, about halfway from Henderson Field to Beresford's new abode. It was where the road east finished.

What Beresford would not this time witness was the last battle of aircraft carriers in the Solomons campaign. It took place to the north of the Santa Cruz groups of small islands two hundred and fifty miles east, though an outlying province of the Solomons.

The Americans realised that there had to be a do-or-die battle against stronger forces, or Guadalcanal and all that depended on it would be lost. Vice Admiral Halsey also knew his future career would be measured by the outcome, despite having been installed to achieve what seemed impossible.

The Japanese light cruiser *Yura* was leading four destroyers down The Slot from their Shortland base, the very northern islands of The Slot, to link up with a 'new' Japanese fleet sailing from the north to make an all-out assault on Guadalcanal. Coast-watchers reported it, and five Dauntless dive-bombers attacked her, damaging her enough that she left the destroyers and turned to limp back home. The bombers returned to Henderson to refuel and next day renewed the attack to leave her so crippled that her crew scuttled her.

The destroyers then met up with the approaching fleet of four carriers, *Shokaku, Zuikaku, Junyo* and *Zuiho;* four battleships, *Hiei, Kirishima, Kongo* and *Haruna;* nine cruisers; twenty-eight destroyers; eleven submarines and seven support ships—troop transports, oilers and armaments.

Halsey's fleet, totalling only half that number, was racing from various ports. The *SS President Coolidge* was the first casualty. An ocean liner converted to troop carrier, she was departing Espiritu Santo in the New Hebrides, loaded with troops and supplies when she struck a mine on leaving the harbour; the troops had time to disembark, yet all their supplies went down with the ship. The cruiser *St. Louis* was racing from Alaska yet doubted she could be in time to help. The carrier *Hornet* hovered north of the coming battle site, waiting for the carrier *Enterprise*, Halsey's old command. She had been under repair at Pearl Harbour from damage at Midway and now raced to meet up with *Hornet*. The battleship *South Dakota*, also after repairs, was only ten miles behind *Enterprise*. Light cruisers *San Diego* and *San Juan* and fourteen destroyers made up the complement.

Catalina surveillance aircraft sighted the Japanese force at noon on 25 October, and *Hornet* left her waiting to intercept it. Early next morning when the American fleet was within striking range, a Japanese scout plane spotted it. It was to be an unusual battle—almost a totally aerial one. Dive-bombers and torpedo bombers from *Enterprise* attacked the carrier *Zuiho* while *Hornet's* aircraft severely damaged both the carrier *Shokaku* and cruiser *Chikuma*. Fighter planes from either side attacked dive-bombers of the other. *Hornet,* still hampered by the damages received in the last Guadalcanal battle, received so many hits that she was a burning wreck. She finally succumbed to several torpedoes. The battleship *South Dakota* was credited with downing twenty-six enemy planes. A further fifty-one were credited to other ships and Allied aircraft.

Enterprise also took a battering, yet she still managed to take aboard all *Hornet's* surviving aircraft. The destroyer *Porter*, picking up downed pilots, took a torpedo, thought to be from a submarine, and sank. Her sister-ship *Shaw* was able to take off her crew and all ditched men.

Come sundown, the American fleet limped towards Noumea. The light cruiser *San Juan* was so badly damaged, having taken a bomb through the fantail, she required more extensive repairs than could be gained there and so continued on for Sydney. It had been a costly battle, yet had so severely weakened the Japanese Guadalcanal invasion fleet, particularly its two carriers and their aircraft and crews, that the Allies were again given time to reinforce Guadalcanal.

Thirty-one

Beresford was summing up. The only two good pieces of news coming over the airwaves were of the Australians in New Guinea retaking the Kokoda airfield, depriving the Japs of one of the airports they'd been using to bomb Australia's north, and the second in Egypt. Britain's General Montgomery, or 'Monty' as he was popularly known, had been placed in charge of the entire African campaign. He defeated Rommel at El Alamein, only seventy miles from Alexandria and two hundred from the Suez Canal. He had not only stopped the Nazi's whirlwind advance on Cairo and the Canal, but had them retreating.

The sad news was that the Allies now had no carriers in service in the entire Pacific. *Lexington* had been sunk in the Battle of the Coral Sea, *Yorktown* at Midway, *Wasp* torpedoed by a submarine and *Hornet* at Santa Cruz. Both remaining carriers were now laid up being repaired. And the bravery of *Hornet* going into action whilst still limping was a loud bell ringing in all ears—the charge of the Light Brigade at Balaclava?

However within days of hearing the sad tale of the Santa Cruz battle, there was tragic yet not unexpected news for especially Lobo. General Vandergrift of the US Army on Guadalcanal had gradually been given additional troops by transports such as the ill-fated *President Coolidge* and was now informed that the 152nd Infantry was in transit from jungle-training in Noumea. So he was feeling more confident. His immediate plan was to push Japanese forces on the island, intent on capturing Henderson Field, back beyond the nine-mile range of their artillery. For some weeks it had been, day-by-day, pounding the coastal airport from every jungle point they had been able to control.

One such point was Lobo's family village, Kokumbona. It had already changed hands several times, so had been the centre of hand-to-hand fighting rather than bombardment, yet which caused many native deaths. The people were loyal to the Allies and for that reason treated harshly by the Japanese when in their possession—from torture for information to rape of the young women, even girls as young as ten or twelve.

Now word was leaked through, as was common in all the islands, of the latest action—and the latest was the Americans were attacking the Japs in that very village. The news had travelled via walkie-talkie, and Lobo's distress was severe. He worried for his family, yet was frustrated at it being two weeks away by foot through jungle with no roads, much of which was in Japanese hands. Time was of the essence as to whether his family, even his aged grandfather, had been able to flee into the jungle. If not, the fighting would likely be over anyway by the time he could get there.

"What you are trying to say, I think, dear friend," Beresford stated as a question, "is that there are too many 'ifs', too many unknowns, for you to even try going?"

"Yes, friend Berry. I am like you say. But I worry much."

Simply seeing the lad, one pretty much his own age or even a year or two younger, in such distress, was a telling tale of how unfair this war was to those who had no knowledge of far-flung empires at war, who could not even understand why they were fighting over islands that had no riches like gold or diamonds. Turning their simple lives absolutely inside out when they could not understand the reasons was a terrible dilemma.

And Beresford, confined with him in such isolation, felt as helpless in easing his distress.

These people have, for generations, been victims of international greed. Before the end of the nineteenth century the Germans landed on these shores to subjugate the people in the name of Empire Building, set about twisting their very culture by converting them to Christianity and forcing western culture on them. Was 'saving' them from cannibalism simply tossing them out of their boiling cauldrons into the fire? And after what we had been calling The Great War, now surely but World War One, the British moved in to tell them that what the German laws had imposed on them was all wrong—that now they must submit to British law. And now here is Japan trying to do the same, torturing and raping them in the process!

Yet even if he could get this outlook over the language hurdle to Lobo, it wasn't going to help him. Lobo's concern was only today's problem: what was happening to his family this very minute! And Beresford had no answer for that.

~ * ~

As quickly as the US was landing troops in Honiara and along the southeast coast, the Japanese were landing troops east of the airfield, on Koli Point. Now Andy informed them that US troops were landing further east still.

"I've got Nips landing troops ten miles bloody west of me and now three US cruisers landing what must be twenty thousand men in Aola Bay, ten miles east. This is it, I reckon, and it's gonna bloody blow up. The Nips between me and the airport will surely now push to link up with their mates camped under the mountain, them what've been batterin' Henderson from the south. We hold the far west and the centre of the island, with the Nips in that sandwich at Kokumbona. They've got the near east with Honiara in a sandwich, and now we got troops landin' in the far east, to put that lot of Japs and me in a bloody sandwich. If ya painted the Jap troops red, and the US troops white, mate, the entire island would look like a bloody barber's pole."

And all transports unloading troops were under air attack.

It certainly does seem like the final attempt to bust the nexus is pretty close. And there will be so many 'front lines' that it's going to be a massacre. So much of it will be in thick jungle with no roads, that tanks and mass movement of troops is impossible. It will all be hand-to-hand stuff, all right.

What neither Beresford nor Andy were in a position to know was that the damaged *Enterprise* was steaming north from Noumea, repair welders still aboard trying to complete damaged sections even as she bore towards further battle.

Andy was back on the line to 'All Points'.

"Five American cruisers supported by eight destroyers steamin' into Sealark Channel, right off Koli Point. Nip bombers attackin' them—I count thirteen. Over."

This was only some fifteen miles east of where the Savo Battle had taken place, and within the hour there was bedlam. The US force was suddenly faced with two Japanese battleships and nine destroyers. It was a massacre for the Americans. Cruisers *Atlanta* and *Juneau,* carrying troops to be landed, were sunk, as were five destroyers, against Japan's loss of two destroyers. Many troops in full battle gear, and their supplies, went down with their ships—on both sides.

Next day, 14 November, the enemy fleet separated into three divisions: the bombardment group pummelling the airport, the cruiser *Nagara* and six destroyers, and the third, a cruiser *Sendai* and three destroyers. At night, *USS Washington* began firing on the *Nagara,* and *South Dakota* attacked *Sendai*. Both initial salvos began fires on their respective targets. Enemy destroyers joined the fray, searchlights picking out both Allied ships, which quickly became targets for the Jap cruisers. *South Dakota,* under fire from three enemy vessels, suffered considerable damage, including the loss of both radar and radio. Her batteries managed to kill the searchlights, but she was so helpless she had no option but to withdraw and head for the Noumea dockyards. All three US destroyers were sunk. *Washington,* having sunk the Japanese battleship *Kirishima,* also retired. A Japanese destroyer was so badly damaged, she was scuttled.

In the second of the three areas of battle, *Enterprise* was so damaged that all her planes landed at Henderson and she also retired. In that scuttle, Japan lost her battleship *Hiei* and two destroyers, four others beaching themselves so troops could land, having sacrificed their equipment.

All-in-all in the two days of battle, Japan lost seven of its eleven troop carriers as well as nine destroyer-transports—a devastating reversal of fortunes in the naval battles.

~ * ~

Good news continued to arrive from the other side of the world, which helped ease some of Beresford's anxiety. Rommel continued to retreat as Tobruk was retaken by the Australian army, the Soviet army had turned the German advances along the entire Russian fronts to retreat, and with the Allies taking command of Mediterranean waters, the Vichy French scuttled the entire French Fleet in Toulon Harbour rather than surrender it to the Allies.

Winston Churchill at this stage of the European war declared:

This is not the end, it is not even the beginning of the end. But it is, perhaps, the end of the beginning.

In New Guinea the Australians continued advancing along the Kokoda Trail and westwards along the coast, to retake the town of Gona. There, for instance, it seemed the Japanese were in full retreat.

When the end of November came, Beresford was no longer having to placate Lobo. He realised that right now, with so much of the entire island in separate 'baskets' of combative control, it was simply impossible for them, even through the 'All Points' voice on the coast-watcher circuit, to get news of Kokumbona. He was resigned to being but another of the thousands of millions around the world who must languish in the don't-know situation for at least some part of the world war.

By mid-December, there was considerable land fighting going on with the Americans seeming to be a smidge ahead in terms of territory gained, yet well ahead on the count of heads. Nobody was saying, of course, what the death and injury toll figures were, except that enemy losses were 'several-fold that of our own'.

"Yet how much truth can we put into such statistics, Andy?" Beresford asked when the two were together again. "The mere fact they qualify nothing is sure indication that it's all propaganda."

"I think true," Lobo interjected. "My people carry dead and sick. They bring all American, dead to bury, sick to make better. They kill Japan man sick, then burn all dead. They say many-many more Japan man. They cannot count number, but know in heads," he said, tapping his temple.

And that was difficult for Beresford to argue with.

The three Australians were part of a group of coast-watchers and four natives attached to some, as was Lobo to Beresford. It had been quite a battle having the American 'manager' of the 'Dog on the Tuckerbox' to even allow them into the bar, let alone have them served a beer.

"No niggers in my diner," he had said with a decided southern accent. He was answered with not even a word from Dougie Kennedy, captain of the coast-watchers. Instead, the elbow of his left arm came up just at the right speed to knock the guy's chin high enough for his right uppercut to lift the bloke two feet off the floor before he crumbled into a heap where his feet had been.

Dougie didn't say a word until turning to the barman. "Four beers for our helpers too, please, mate."

Only when back at the table did his face break into a grin. "Bloody little poofter likely got this job because he was too scared to get into jungle greens," was the only comment he made.

The following month was to prove that Lobo's countrymen had been right.

The fighting was intense on both sides. The Japanese had no doubt had it as blandly pointed out to them that holding Guadalcanal was vital to holding the Solomon Islands, which was in turn vital in Winning the War. It was well recognised by the Japanese that with America's vast population and already extended manufacturing capacity, the longer the war went on, the better chance of the United States overcoming Japanese resources. So neither side was prepared to give an inch.

One resource that proved a decided advantage to the Americans was their first use of the flame-thrower in WW2. It not only reduced the enemy's ability to hide, but was an absolute morale-buster. And desperate to win, the Americans could not afford to be gentlemanly in a war already declared brutal by the treatment of prisoners by Japanese troops in Southeast Asia and the Philippines. It was a dog-eat-dog war—*and may the dog with the biggest fangs win.*

The 164th Marine Corps proved its reputation, and through a number of areas including the Point Cruz (Kokumbona) battle, their offensive continued across the entire island—not only effectively, but swiftly. It had had to be!

It was so quick that before Japan could assemble another fleet, it had no troops left on Guadalcanal, to support. The last significant battle on the island was the conquest of the Japanese last-ditch-stand on Mount Austen.

In the first week of January 1943, US-B17s began daily bombing of Rabaul, just north of the Solomons, Japan's major airport and shipyard in the South Pacific. It was the first sign to all, particularly those who had fought so hard on sea and land and in the air for Guadalcanal, that the Pacific War was fast turning a corner.

On 7 January, American, Australian and New Zealand bombers and Catalinas attacked a Japanese convoy landing stores and troops at Lae in New Guinea, decimating it.

With Rabaul airport at least temporarily out of action, Allied air forces were having a heyday attacking Japanese installations throughout the rest of the Solomon Islands, New Britain and New Guinea, sinking every Japanese ship caught at sea. Or in port.

The importance of having at last won out in holding Guadalcanal was already vividly evident.

Thirty-two

What now?

Andy and Dougie, with nothing to go back to in Australia and already with heady experience in coast-watching, had been won over in going to New Britain where, despite wherever in the entire archipelago they were assigned, they would be behind enemy lines.

"Devilish dangerous, mate," Andy prevailed on Beresford, "and we need every bloke we can get. Winnin' Rabaul off the Nips is surely the next target. Come on, mate—be in it?"

But Beresford wanted time to think. It was Forward Vision time.

"I do have a family at home, mate. And you can never imagine what the not knowing is like. It's a year since I've had any word from them, so I don't know if they're dead or alive. Or if my home's still standing. Or if they're living on charity. All jolly difficult!

"My pater is old—still alive when last I heard, but a year in England in these times might just have been too much for him. And brother Thomas is in the navy, and I now realize how dangerous a life that is, so neither do I know if he is still alive or not. I've a yen to go back to Fiji and check my mail—at least see what it says."

They were in their Honiara 'office', 'The Dog on the Tuckerbox', which now welcomed Melanesians with open arms, despite few had money. Yet suddenly many Yanks, too, had come to realize how helpful the locals had been to them and were pretty free with shouts. Or now brought them as guests. In fact last thing Dougie and his boys did before leaving the bar for their last time was donate a 'Tip Box' for the management to keep on the bar for native charity. They christened it with a brand new Aussie £5 note to start it going. Beresford's share had been thirty shillings, but he didn't begrudge a penny of it.

It was the old story of 'who you know', and he was given introduction by Andy to the chief controller of flight operations at Henderson.

"It was this bloke, Clive," Andy said in introducing him, "wot give the warnin' of the Nip fleet sweepin' on Honiara, wot saved the bloody town. Can you get him to Fiji?"

"We've got PBYs back and forward sort of every day. When you want to go, buddy?"

Beresford felt swept off his feet. "Eh, um, Friday?"

He'd had a lightning look through the days ahead, and this was Tuesday. All he'd had to consider then was what he needed to do before leaving.

Clive picked a clipboard up from his desk and walked to a blackboard. "Yep. Be here by 5 p.m. It's a night flight. Safer than day, buddy. You got much gear?"

Another lightning sweep. "A valise and satchel."

"Not a problem. Still waiting to hear if our set-down that flight will be Lautoka or Suva. Where you headed?"

"Lautoka, Clive."

"Okay. If I find it's Suva, you want to wait for a Lautoka flight?"

Beresford shrugged. "Why should I worry about time? Is there a war on or something?"

The three had a laugh. Beresford wrote down his address for Clive.

"If you hear nothin', buddy, be here at 17:00 hours Friday."

~ * ~

Lautoka had changed little.

He felt he'd been away twenty years. He'd certainly lived an eventful life in the interim, and it just seemed that long. First thing he did was take an Indian rickshaw to Noble Mills Pty. Ltd.

It was closed up.

It was coming up breakfast time, so he went to the Isa Lei and could smell the aroma of fresh bacon even before opening the door.

"*Mbula*," he was greeted.

"*Mbula*," he replied. He was the first patron so chose the table Josh had invariably used, propped his gear against the wall and asked for coffee, fried yam, bacon and egg, iced coconut juice and a turtle-breast soup starter.

Only the coconut-juice had he had in abundance in the Solomons, but there never 'iced'. This was the twist that made being back in Fiji exciting.

He picked up the *Fiji Times*, flown in from Suva yesterday so was still the latest news he could expect. The front page comprised two major articles—one covered a murder of an Indian merchant in Suva. *The motive could be racial,* said the caption to the photograph...

Ho hum! Nothing's changed. I wonder if they keep this caption set for every second edition?

The other headline was in a smaller type-font: *Guadalcanal Island free at last.*

I guess they waited a few days in case the Japs retook it.

It was the way he had felt about things there. It seemed that every time a victory of any sort was celebrated, within days it was usually totally driven from mind by a new catastrophe—the decimation of a fleet or Henderson Field shattered again.

Oh, I simply do hope that it doesn't now regress. If there is a God, and I really do have to wonder after what I've experienced, I pray that this turning point has really been achieved and that people can at least have a hope of restoring something of their lives. Anything would be welcome, I am sure. I have seen so many men utterly devoid of hope and sanctity—utterly destroyed as a useful being—turned almost into madness.

Even 'bush' hospitals he'd seen set up in the jungle after skirmishes flashed through his mind again now—simply more experiences that would forever haunt him.

I have all my faculty and all my limbs and all my essential organs. How many men must now go through the rest of their lives without at least some of these? How can they never feel they've been cheated by some power, political, spiritual or ethereal? There will be more change in man after all this than in anything geographical or cultural.

He ploughed through his breakfast not without sense of taste or enjoyment, but with most of his concentration still on what might become of the future's world.

The future's world rather than the world's future?

His own choice of thought now had him wondering where one met the other.

~ * ~

There was a pile of mail at the post office.

He asked if they knew what had happened to Noble Mill or Josh Noble.

He was taken to the manager's office, and Beresford was conscious of the manner in which Mr. Adams clasped his hand in greeting.

A Masonic clasp. His father had explained it to him years ago. "It is the greeting of one who belongs to a society of men instructed on values in life..." was about all he could remember, other than that his father had added, "Maybe in later life, Beresford, you may be considered eligible to join its selective ranks."

So he had, since then, always believed that if it enclosed his father in its philosophies, those belonging to it must be fellows of at least some worthy merit.

"I was—maybe even still am—an employee of Josh Noble," he explained. "I was his representative in Honiara when the Japs marched in and have been there ever since. Do you know his whereabouts?"

"I do not, young man. However I may be able to get close. I know Josh Noble well and am aware he approached the British Consul about what he could do in the war. He joined the Fijian British Army Corp and was shipped to India. The British there were trying to beat their way back into Burma. I've heard nothing since a note from him after arrival, telling me he'd been promoted to lieutenant."

He asked Beresford's background and was given a brief resume.

"And I see you clasp a handful of mail?"

"Yes. I had left instruction that mail for me from home should be held. And I congratulate your staff that it has been. I am anxious to read every word."

"I can understand that. Are you seeking employment, now returned?"

Beresford smiled.

All the times I fretted about not being able to get a job, and then wondering if I could keep it, and now I'm being hunted?

The very irony of it amused him.

"I certainly don't think I'll be seeking a job. I expect to still have a balance in my bank account and shall see to that after reading my mail. I was previously living at the Tanoa Guest House and found it admirably comfortable. I intend checking there."

"Ah! You are well advised. If unsuccessful, come back to me and I shall have other options. Also, young Branson, I am available if I can be of any other service to you."

For the first time in a year, he had met an Englishman who spoke like those he knew at home and presented as someone he could trust. So he felt happy at the thought that so quickly he had found someone to turn to if in trouble.

He found Tanoa Guest House remembered him and was pleased to see him back.

He had bought a bottle of wine en-route and now, at 10 a.m., poured himself a glass and began opening his mail.

Thirty-three

His mail took two hours to work through, much of it waiting for tears to dry so he could continue. His parents were both well although desperately worried about both sons. Some of the letters were written within days of each other because their news gave sketchy details of the terrible battles in the waters of Guadalcanal and they every day waited for the postman.

These were written, of course, before I sent my last to them...

Nor had they received mail from Thomas. They realised that him being on active naval service, it could be a month or more before being able to post mail, and the news of how many ships had been lost had them near frantic with worry on Thomas' behalf also.

"What also hasn't helped our concerns," his mother had written, "is that all over England, many mail-exchanges have been hit by bombs and both incoming and outgoing mail destroyed. In these cases, of course, there is no way of knowing if our mail has been part of it."

As soon as I finish here, I'm going back to the post office to see if I can telephone home. If they say "No," I shall see Mr. Adams. He did offer to help.

"The house was slightly damaged in the only air-raid of the district," his father had written. The Germans had been making spasmodic raids on all railway lines in the country, and a stray bomb had for some unknown reason come their way, but the damage was not severe.

He found it interesting that whilst every letter had been opened, there were no cutouts by censors.

But both always pay careful attention to what they write. That surely puts the censor in a good frame of mind.

He had understood that censors sometimes even deleted news that could prove demoralising, yet wondered if that might be the case only when addressed to a serving soldier, sailor or airman?

Those letters having to be addressed through the services' particular mail centres means the censors are under orders from HQ in every case, so are likely more strict.

Yet his parents being left in such wonder for such long periods he found highly distressing. It was that which kept tears springing to his eyes. There was also a letter for him from Josh Noble, telling exactly what Mr. Adams had told him.

And a picture-postcard of Tahiti's golden beaches, its message brief yet telling him much...

> *Dearest friend,*
> *I am off for holidays, please wish me luck.*
> *Pascal*

Smiling, he looked at the date. 14 March 1941.

So he waited five long months before hearing from Francoise and Gaston.

He wondered where they might now be, and in what capacity? Playing hide-and-seek in occupied France seemed such a long way from anything he'd experienced.

Yet I guess if one had to start looking for similarities, some spring to mind. Certainly to be so close to having friends at one hand and enemies the other is pertinent.

I wonder if any of the three ever took up my invitation to visit Folly Drift? But even if not, I still hope they are feeling fulfilled in their dangerous work, and keeping safe.

When finished his readings, he showered and shaved, making him feel much more his positive self, and returned to the post office.

"Sorry, sir," he was told. "The British Isles is one of the areas accepting calls only from people with a coded authority."

He asked to see Mr. Adams and was shown in.

"I'm sorry, lad," he answered, "but the information my clerk gave you is correct. Telephone lines in Britain are in such chaos that only official calls can be made. Even life or death. International calls to Britain go through a vetting desk, and vetting is simple. Only essential war-service calls can be even tried for connection. And I have no authorities in that area."

Disappointed but understanding, he returned to Tanoa, hung a Do Not Disturb sign on his door and had a couple of hours' sleep to make up for what he had missed last night.

~ * ~

He showered again, then called at his bank to retrieve some petty cash from his savings account, surprised at how much it had appreciated with salary from Noble Mills having been paid right up until he quit to join the coast-watchers.

Then he returned to Isa Lei for a late lunch.

And a shock greeted him.

He was walking towards the table at which he'd breakfasted, only to see it was occupied. The shock was that the occupants were Teri and Randi Edwards. Teri was signalling for the waitress to bring their check.

He began to veer away.

Those two I have only the fondest memories for. Yet doubt still lingers as to whether they were part of Jerry's deception. The last thing I want is Jerry finding out where I am. I simply cannot afford running into that family.

But Teri had seen him—and been as startled.

"Berry! Berry Branson!"

By now his back was to them, and he half froze. Half in that he was trying to quickly make up his mind whether to quit and run or turn and face them.

But do I want to forever feel bugged wondering if those two were part of Jerry duping me?

He had indeed enjoyed their company and sense of fellowship... *But then so did I with Jerry!*

"Berry!" he heard again from behind, although this time it was Randi's voice.

And Randi was very much not only a good sport but a good sort!

He turned slowly. Both were by now on their feet.

He waited for them to open the conversation—even anxious to see what, them having called his attention so spontaneously, would be their attitude.

Hail fellow well met, as our entire few days together had been? Do they intend to simply carry that on? Tell me either that Jerry is here too or will be disappointed that he isn't?

'Chicanery' was the word that flashed in his mind about Jerry in Apia, and he now wondered if this were also pertinent in the minds of Teri and Randi.

He showed no glee in seeing them, simply surprise as well as wonder.

"Berry, fancy seeing you here?" came from Teri.

"And you look no different other than even more suntanned," came from Randi.

Not a skerrick of change in their attitude, despite, if they were in the chicanery, I would expect they would know about his visit to me. But are they again simply being clever about it? Yet they could have simply got up and walked out, careful in case I should see them.

"Neither do you two look different—except maybe that you have lost some suntan."

He then simply waited. He wanted them to lead.

And they did.

"Come sit a minute," Teri said as she returned to her seat. "You must have so much to tell us. What's it been? A year? More?"

Randi also sat down again. Both continued with broad smiles.

"Two years."

The waitress came with their check. It was the same girl who had served him breakfast.

"*Mbula*," she greeted him again.

"And *mbula* to you, again," he told her with a smile.

"I was also here for breakfast," he explained to the Americans.

Teri would not take the check from the girl. She instead said, "I'll have more coffee," then turned questioningly to Randi, "You too?"

Then to Berry, she asked, "You here for lunch, then? Why don't you order, but have coffee with us while you wait?"

So he smiled for the first time, but just a little.

"Yes, why not?" He asked for a menu, and Teri ordered three coffees.

Well this is going to be interesting. Will they carry on the old charade, or will it be a different approach?

"Are you living here now?" Randi asked

"No. I arrived just this morning."

I'm telling them nothing they don't ask for. At least until I've a measure of their intentions."

"Oh, where from?"

"Guadalcanal."

Both looked shocked.

"But that's a real hot-spot. Surely it's dangerous there?" Randi asked.

"It's pretty dangerous everywhere in these parts."

"We just arrived this morning too. We're having a holiday, sort of in transit," Teri said.

"A holiday in Lautoka? From Pago Pago?"

Randi answered. "We've been back in the States for a while. California. We've had the Pago Pago house closed up and are just returning. We had to come via Fiji, so booked a few days on Beachcomber Island. We take tomorrow's ferry."

He recalled that Beachcomber Island, just off the coast from Lautoka, was a featured holiday paradise.

"Wouldn't be many tourists these days, I would have thought."

"They say Fiji is safe enough right now," Teri proffered.

Beresford knew the Allies were using Fiji as a jungle-training ground for rookie troops, but that was classified information.

"Probably."

Randi leaned an arm across the table and put a hand on Beresford's arm.

His mind flashed back to the several all-but intimate touches and loose cuddles they'd had during their Papeete-Pago passage. *Those that every time sent tingles through me.*

But now she had a frown on her forehead.

"You don't seem your old self, Berry. You were always bubbling. Or that's how we remember you. We've often thought of you and wondered what you might be doing."

"Yes," said Teri, "we have indeed. And Randi is right, you do seem taciturn. And you haven't even asked after Jerry, I note?" She ended that comment as if a question.

He thought quickly on how much he should declare.

"No, that's right. I haven't. So how is Jerry?"

The women looked at each other. "He's okay. He's tied up with war things at the moment. In the States."

"It's you we are interested in," Randi hastened to add. "Are you well? Or have troubles? This war thing is affecting everybody."

Beresford's coconut curry arrived, and conversation stopped as it was served.

"Can I have more coffee, please?" Teri asked.

Well, they certainly aren't wanting to rush away.

"I guess it's just the tension I've been under in Guadalcanal. But it will pass."

Now! he could hear Ego shouting at him. *Now's the time. Tell them and see how they react!*

"In fact I saw Jerry just after our journey together. In Apia. But maybe he didn't mention that."

He could tell in the instant that the utter surprise on both faces was genuine.

"Wh…what? When?" Teri asked.

"A week or ten days I think it was, after you farewelled me. He didn't tell you?"

Again, genuine surprise.

Had it not been surprise, surely one of them would have at least slightly frowned, or glanced at the other, for instance, but none of those four things happened.

So he was beginning to believe they were not in on Jerry's deceit.

"An accidental meeting? In Apia?" Randi asked. "He went off in one of his ships some days after you left, but that was part of his normal routine. But he said nothing to us about having seen you."

"Oh well, I guess it's not important."

"It just might be," Teri said almost impatiently. "Please tell us how you met, and what you talked about?"

"Oh, he was just interested in a letter he had given me to post in Apia—something about the address in Sydney."

"In Sydney?"

Now they looked at each other, yet in undisguised surprise. And shrugged shoulders at each other.

"It was just addressed to a GPO box number. He needed to know if I recalled the number or had written it down. Is that significant information to either of you?"

Again they exchanged questioning looks before both shook heads.

Teri then put a hand on Beresford's arm and stared straight at his eyes. "What are your plans for the next few days?"

Now he sat back, startled. *Bloody hell. Have I triggered a nerve in all this? Another trip to Pago Pago or something?*

"I've no plans. I'm on a sort of holiday too. I'm thinking of trying to get a passage home to England."

Although if this seems likely to give me some lead on the 'why' of all that ha-hoo with Jerry, it might be worth sacrificing a few days.

It had remained a nagging question in his mind, and he rued the possibility of it continuing for the rest of his life.

"Why don't you come to Beachcomber with us?"

Thirty-four

Bloody hell, what's a man to make of this? The last trip I took with these people was a ball—a great blast in fact, one to remember the rest of one's life. Yet look at its aftermath! The greatest mystery my mind has ever had to agonise over.

"Why?"

Teri held up her left palm and struck its thumb with her right forefinger. "One—your strange attitude needs explaining."

She then struck the palm's forefinger. "Two—our curiosity on this message to Sydney needs explaining."

Then the palm's second finger. "Three—some of Jerry's 'business dealings' we find vitally interesting."

Then the ring finger. "Four—maybe there's a connection here."

Then the little finger. "Five—my brain, and I'm sure Randi's, is flying around in circles at hearing what you've just told us, when we are desperately seeking answers to a second life our darling may have led.

"So," she continued, "do any of those things inspire curiosity in your mind? When we all three of us might be able to clear some of those questions and doubts? You know something we don't, and we sure as God now know things about Jerry that you don't—yet we cannot understand those things. Please come with us tomorrow and see if we can scrub any of these bloodsucking leeches off our brains?"

Beresford had been conscious of Randi's hand being back his arm once Teri had released her grip and that Randi's pressure had increased at every one of her mother's reasons being spelled out. It was now vice-like, and the blood had stopped flowing.

With his other hand he released her grip but kept holding the hand, gently.

He wanted to go with them for more than one reason.

"Will they have accommodation for me? And what is the tariff?"

"They are short on bookings because of the war, so prices are rock bottom. We'll pay for you anyway."

Oh in one sense this all sounds so much like leaving Papeete—when they gave me twenty dollars even though I was hired on a 'passage for keep and labour' basis.

He looked at Randi while asking, "Do I have to work my passage for this one?"

Both girls roared laughing.

"That's more like the Berry we remember."

~ * ~

He returned to Tanoa, his mind giddy with questions.

They give the impression they know something about 'unusual things' Jerry was involved in, yet also aver they 'now' know things about him they didn't know then. All that adds up to me likely getting an answer to my big question. And they've obviously got many of their own questions unanswered. And they're close together in their searching. And Jerry's not 'close' any more, it seems, but it looks like if I open up, they will.

And the thought of being with Randi again has me more than just a little excited.

His body went through a few little shivers just thinking around them being close again, especially in a totally laid-back, tropical beach atmosphere.

Even if it is in the middle of the rainy season, typhoons and all. Whatever, it will be a big 'hooray' situation after a year in Guadalcanal!

Having at last received his mail from home, despite his parents' obvious dejection with life in the circumstance, he at least knew they were well—*well at least alive!*

He there and then sat down and penned a long letter, assuring them he was now out of danger, was in Fiji and had their letters, the last dated December 1942.

I am tossing around the thought of trying to get home. At least here where you've been sending mail, I have access to my bank account. And yes, dear Pater, I have the wherewithal for a return journey. However after my gruelling experiences in the last place, I am now off for a few days rest at a delightful little island, with friends of old.

I also think much on brother Thomas and wish him the very best of luck.

I tried to telephone you this morning on arrival but find that only approved callers may phone into the entire UK. So if I am able to leave for home, I've no way of advising you. In fact I would more than likely be faster than the mail.

My love to you all...

~ * ~

It was so much like a summer day when he met the Edwards girls at the Beachcomber terminal, that all three remarked on it.

"If this will last for the next three," Randi announced, "I shan't care if even a typhoon then blasts its way here."

Yesterday he had left his laundry at the desk, then shopped for suitable clothes for Beachcomber, bought a new razor and eau-de-cologne, swim-togs and towel, then dined in at Tanoa and had an early night.

All kept conversation on the trip over, more than an hour, confined to small talk of weather, how great it felt leaving the pressure war inflicted on everybody even if just for a few days and on the dolphins that played around the covered ferry. Neither dolphins nor passengers seemed to care that the outboard belched lots of smoke, proof that with gasoline rationed, power-kerosene was added at something like two to one.

He couldn't but feel strange looking out over ocean that he wasn't scanning it through binoculars, looking for wisps of smoke or tiny shadows on the horizon. And his mind also wondered how many thousands of gallons of high-grade gasoline had gone down with all the ships and aircraft during the several battles around Guadalcanal.

He didn't speak of the war, however, only to say what a good feeling it was to be having this holiday. He also kept to himself how glad he was that he was out of the isolation coast-watchers lived in, the scratch food they lived on and the questionable water he so often had to drink.

But even the sight of little Beachcomber Island was a balm to those memories. It was tiny, one a body could walk around in a morning, yet the quintessence of what the mind conjured up in the expression *island paradise*. It nestled quite lonely on the blue ocean—not too much other land in sight, fringed with glistening white sand and overhung for its entire perimeter with coconut palms. Only here and there could one see parts of *bures*—cabins of woven leaf walls and thatched roofs visible through a jungle of hibiscus trees, and rambling bougainvillea in a kaleidoscope of colours.

The island was owned by the hotel—the common areas rustic in the extreme. Guest 'rooms' were the several *bures* dotted here and there, each sheltered in the privacy of its own patch of floral jungle.

On checking in at the desk, the hotel 'foyer' being a room with but two walls, they discovered they were the only guests. They took two *bures* side-by-side adjacent to the 'foyer', which doubled as a lounge, bar and reading room. The 'dining room' had no walls at all, and guests were invited, if they chose, to help the staff in the rustic kitchen.

Much of it reminded Beresford of the villages on Guadalcanal.

So life there was really laid back—a real little escape from the dreadful reality of the churning world so close in the west.

At lunch they continued to yet avoid the 'Jerry' subject that all realised was the very purpose of all three being together.

And the food proved as delightful as the atmosphere promised.

"On Sunday, when we get day-trippers from Lautoka and Nadi," said the manageress, the lady from the desk and the owner's wife, "we have the full *lovo*, a hog roasted in the traditional earth oven. But I'm sorry we cannot do that for you—it needs numbers of people."

"Well, we might just think on staying that extra day to take that in," said Teri. "Do you have need to spend Sunday back in Lautoka, Berry?"

"I shall need to check my appointment diary."

Again the girls laughed loudly, and their host left them to help prepare the next course.

"It's what our people in Hawaii call the *luau*. I can certainly recommend it," said Teri. "But isn't it hard to imagine that only a hundred years ago, all the people here were cannibals? Fiji and all the islands west, including New Guinea?"

"I think it likely that some far-flung little islands could still be," he answered. "I was reading not so long ago that even just before this war started, isolated islands were still being discovered on which the natives had never seen a white man."

"Some might now, then, have just seen yellow ones for the first time. And good luck to the locals if they found them tasty, is all I can say to that."

He couldn't help but shiver at the utter brittleness of Teri's tone.

It sounded even hateful!

He wondered what had sparked it.

"But let's try and leave the war out of it for the next three days," she then added. "Or four."

And all agreed.

"And," Berry quipped, "how about even an embargo on radio in the lounge, at least while we are the only guests?"

"Yes," cried Randi in full voice. "Please let me be the one to advise our host."

They agreed on that too.

Thirty-five

Teri carefully kept the embargo on 'talking Jerry' alive through the afternoon, dinner and evening. Yet they covered seemingly, every other topic.

Berry remained patient. He knew the answer to the question that had plagued him for two years would unfold.

Last thing I want is to jump into it before Teri is ready. She obviously has her programme sorted, and if she doesn't get to do it her way, she just might clamp up on things. She desperately wants to grill me on it, or I wouldn't be here.

He had learned on Guadalcanal that impatience had no influence on what was already in the system. One simply had to go along with what others had planned, yet all ended up told, even if the format were different. So he would wait.

Randi made sure that wherever they could sit in a cluster, like at table, or in a threesome on the beach, she was always sitting next to Berry. Never, he began to realise, was Teri in the middle.

Randi actually waits, I've now noted, until her mother sits, and I sit. Then she comes next to me, never to her mother.

He didn't mind, of course. And if he didn't ease an inch towards her so their arms touched, she would. So it quickly became ritual that they touch. Both obviously wanted it.

And surely Teri has noticed. She is not only an astute woman, but a mother. And isn't a mother always as well chaperone when her daughter is in a 'touch' mode with a man? Especially one who's been confined in a war zone for two years?

So he was conscious of the fact that Teri condoned it.

At least so far. If they've discussed it, Teri must have given the nod. If they haven't, she's still giving the nod. But there's surely a limit.

Another quiver ran through him as his mind romanced around the limit mark.

There was a dress code in the hotel. Being barefoot was the practice for all at all times, although at dinner in the sand under palm-trees, all lights being pressure-lamps, both girls wore smart cocktail-style dresses, brief, form-fitting and almost risqué. And no jewellery—at least on Randi. Her mother wore a throater of small pearls.

"Oh," he exclaimed as they arrived for dinner. "I feel quite honoured."

He hinted a bow, and both girls dropped a diminutive curtsy. And all had a giggle.

He felt comfortable in the normal informal wear for men throughout the country, the traditional Fijian *sulu*, a calf-length plain cotton wrap-around and a hang-loose short-sleeved shirt. He'd got used to such wear when living in Lautoka.

With so few guests, the menu was short—two options per course. Most island nations had a pretty similar sort of menu, although each with variations, and their hostess Natalie, a white Fijian born to British parents, had made cooking her hobby.

"I have help, of course. Alex and I try to give as many of the local people as we can jobs of one kind or another, but we have to watch costs. And with so many imported products no longer available, we've pretty much reverted to dishes with only traditional ingredients. And all are easily prepared."

She was interested that the girls lived in Pago Pago and that Beresford had lived in Lautoka.

"Two years at the Tanoa Guest House," he said, "Assistant Manager of Noble Mills—"

"Oh, Alex and I know Josh Noble," she said. "He's gone off to war now, and we're back to grinding our own cassava."

"I didn't know you did that?" Randi asked in surprise, obviously expecting some amplification of it.

"You will recall I went from your place to Apia. I had reasons for wanting to leave there, which we can talk about tomorrow, so being only able to work in British protectorates, I came here, and Josh, who I met accidentally, offered me a job. I spent several months travelling Tonga, Cook Islands, back to Tahiti, etcetera. Then he transferred me to Honiara, wanting to expand his business to the New Hebrides and New Caledonia. Having some French helped swing getting that job, I'm sure. Working for any sort of living was as foreign to me as working my passage on a yacht."

At which the girls again giggled.

Teri explained to Natalie how they had met Beresford, and she thought it a great joke.

"Well, I had no money, and had to get a job. And I couldn't work in Tahiti."

"Well, where did you work when Josh closed the mill?"

"The Japs had come to Guadalcanal by then. A handful of Aussie guys without families decided to stay and do coast-watching. I joined them for five shillings a day and all the food I could scrounge from villagers. But Americans like Teri and Randi here, now having despatched the Japs, I'm out of work again. I came back hoping Josh might still be able to use me."

"Oh, the war," Natalie bemoaned. "Alex and I had a nice little business here, employing twenty people, what with landscaping, keeping up our veggie gardens, livestock for the table, fishermen, cooks and cleaners. Now we're down to four plus a few part-timers as needed, and hands-on ourselves. And not covering costs. So hopefully the war will be over soon."

"You make us feel guilty," said Teri with a shrug of shoulders. "We'll definitely stay through Sunday."

"Oh, I didn't mean it that way, I just—"

Teri waved a hand. "We're not staying for that reason. We had already decided."

Natalie then laughed. She turned to Beresford. "One of your choices for dessert tonight, young man, is baked cassava pudding—but it's not milled cassava, it's the raw stuff grated and baked with sweetened milk and honey."

"Oooh!" said both girls.

~ * ~

At breakfast, once orders were placed, Teri raised a finger. "Jerry," she announced in an almost defiant tone.

Randi looked at Berry and, with a smile on her face, winked.

Last night when the three decided it was time for bed, Berry had offered to see the girls home.

"In case there's an air raid," he said.

Once there, Teri held up a cautioning finger.

"I'll leave you two alone. You're probably beginning to think I'm a neurotic old witch," she said to Berry. "Well, I'm not quite," she added with a smile.

She turned to Randi. "I'll see you inside in five minutes, girl. Okay?"

"Okay, Mom." Randi flashed her a smile.

She spoke again as soon as her mother had gone. "That gives us time for a five-minute kiss." She reached her arms around his neck.

"I'm all for that. But you're going to have to teach me. Did you know you're the first white girl I've seen in nearly two years?"

"Well, let's start slowly, shall we?" She pulled him down to her level, not far, and he didn't resist.

He had learned a lot about kissing during those five minutes.

And now Teri had broken the aura.

He had noted how Teri had literally 'dragged' Randi by the hand, on arriving at breakfast, to sit next to her. The two were facing Berry on the opposite side of the bench table.

The "Jerry!" seemed to reverberate in the air for several seconds.

"Did you say you met Jerry accidentally in Apia, Berry? Or was I wrong in getting the vibe that he went expressly to see you?"

Teri was staring into his eyes. His flipped to Randi, who had both eyebrows raised, her eyes as intense as her mother's.

"He came to see me. In fact, he had had a friend approach me the night before."

He had every intention of telling the whole truth. He had, last night, agonised over changing his earlier decision, asking himself why he should let his goodnight to Randi influence him to change it. After taking to his bed, he decided that he did indeed want to pursue a friendship with her—a loving friendship.

So can I now be so brutal as to tell it just the way it happened? I still feel that truth is best, yet will my hatred of him show, to drive Randi from me?

They waited while he hesitated.

"I hesitate because I had made up my mind, when realising we were coming here together for the express purpose of getting the truth, that I would tell it as I saw it. Yet today even more than yesterday..." He turned again to Randi. "I fear losing your friendships. I know you will not like what I say. But nor do I want to lie to either of you."

Randi's foot searched with a toe until it found one of his. It told him he was safe to speak his mind.

Teri fired her second retort. "We want the truth, Berry. We are yet to tell you how our lives have been turned inside out since we last saw you. And all because we have so many doubts. Doubts about our husband and father, doubts about his accusers. Your truth can hopefully help us. The mere fact you harbour doubts means it is serious."

Their breakfasts arrived, and Berry had a few minutes to compose his thoughts.

She's right of course, but 'Jerry's accusers'? Whatever he is accused of must be serious, that they are now without him. And in such a quandary.

When the young native girl had served their breakfasts and poured their coffees, he swallowed and started.

"Several days after I left you, Jerry seeing me aboard his ship for Apia, I had found myself a job. On a Thursday night—and I remember it being a Thursday because Friday was payday, and although my pay would have been only for three days, I was thankful my pockets were empty—I was mugged."

"Mugged?" Both girls were startled.

No doubt wondering what this has to do with Jerry.

"Chloroformed. I remember the ether smell. And it was a big man who came at me from behind. It was dark because I had worked late. I remember nothing after that until the next day."

He felt Randi's toe press more meaningfully.

"When I came to, I was lying on a concrete floor in a corrugated iron shed—old, because most of the iron was rusted. It had many holes—I could see daylight through them. My hands were tied behind my back."

Both girls were rigid, waiting.

"I was hungry, thirsty, had pissed myself and shit my trousers."

"Ah," came from both girls, but he didn't see why he should curb either language or detail.

They wanted the truth, so will get the facts.

"I don't know how long I was there, I know only that every bone in my body was aching from that concrete floor and the blood flow into my hands was being slowed down by whatever my wrists were tied with."

He could see that Teri, anyway, was getting impatient.

She wants to hear only about Jerry. Well, I want her to hear what Jerry subjected me to.

His utter hate for Jerry was being rekindled in his mind, and he wanted it to show.

"Eventually I heard the door being opened. The great Polynesian oaf who had drugged me and kicked me until ribs broke, or so it seemed, came in with another man.

"Jerry," I yelled. "I know I yelled it, for I was so glad that help had come—instinct told me it was my rescue. But the plain truth quickly unfolded. The man I had trusted and come to see as a friend to admire moved not a finger to help me. He put his kerchief to his nose because of the stench of me. And the sneer he made will haunt my memory for the rest of my life."

The girls were now looking at him as if in some sort of awe. Certainly wonder.

Yes, I know one is his wife and this one, with half her foot now resting on mine, is his daughter. But neither fact can change the story.

"I'll cut it short but tell only the truths. Jerry Edwards felt nowt for me other than that I might have information he wanted. He wanted to know if I remembered the GPO box number in Sydney that that letter was addressed to. And I simply didn't know it. I had been given a letter from a friend who asked me to post it for him and gave me an English shilling to post it insured. He persisted and persisted, expecting that I would remember the post office box number. I told him I never even looked at it. 'Did you write in down?' he asked. And I told him 'No'. He grilled me and grilled until it came to threats. Never will I forget the threat he made on my life."

And at that, both girls threw up their hands. *Are they disbelieving me? Simply refusing to believe their Jerry would be like this?*

But Teri dispelled that by simply asking, "What was his threat?"

Randi's foot was now working a massage on his.

"I asked him what was so important about me knowing that number, and he said, '*Whether you remember it or not, might just have a bearing on whether you live or not. That is what is important in this little tête-à-tête. So tell me!*'

"I eventually convinced him that I didn't know it, and I genuinely believe that that is the only reason I am alive today. His entire demeanour, as that conversation went on, convinced me that he was paranoid over it."

"Then, how did you part?"

"I was again tied and returned to the shed. I heard a motorcar depart. That afternoon the great oaf alone came back into the shed, battered me into unconsciousness, and I was found next morning in a city laneway, still bruised and unconscious. This scar..." He rubbed a finger over the bone below his right eye. "...is a memento of that beating. I came to in hospital, some hours later."

There was silence for a long time.

Teri was sobbing into a handkerchief.

Randi reached across the table, holding out both hands in invitation. He accepted and looked her again, straight in the eyes, both full of tears. She squeezed his fingers on both hands. Her voice sounded almost like she was drunk. "My father did all this?"

"I only wish I hadn't ever had to tell you. But I swear that as much love and admiration I had had for your father when we were all together, I lost them—it was like discovering a living Jekyll and Hyde. I am sorry to tell this to you both. This was my main reason for not wanting to stay in Apia. The police were after the Polynesian thug who was a vassal of your father. I was the only one who could identify him. I simply wanted out so I could forget the whole awful episode."

During the next couple of days, the girls held nothing back in telling Beresford their experiences with the FBI. How it had taken many months of half believing, half doubting.

"All that at least explains how he had clout in French Polynesia, working out of the US Consulate, for instance."

"We knew him only as an FBI agent, Berry. Neither of us had a clue that he might be a double agent. Yet the Sydney contact gels with what the FBI had on him. There is no doubt whatever in their minds, Berry, that Jerry is guilty as charged. He is in close custody until after the war, should we win it, when the FBI has access to Japanese records. But we still have no reason why he would do such a thing."

The girls then told Berry they now believed that all the records he took from Papeete were likely all vetted in his locked office, and some probably photographed for the Japanese. It was several days before the US navy took the cartons for return to the States.

The three ended their Beachcomber holiday suntanned, stuffed with food and wine and with arms about each other.

Each expressed relief that they had been able to talk about Jerry and satisfy their own minds of doubt, even if not understanding the 'why' of it all.

Epilogue

After helping Teri and Randi ready their property in Pago Pago for sale whenever the war should finish, he returned with them to Santa Cruz in California. With Teri's blessing he took Randi home to meet his family, for by then they had, with Teri's blessing, become lovers. Any number of cargo vessels plied foodstuffs to Britain, and they risked passage on one.

"Surely fate could not be so unkind as to see us further victims of this dreadful war," had been their shared philosophy.

Both were joyously welcomed at *Folly Drift*, and he found his parents in good health. The only further damage to their property had been some windows broken when a V2 rocket landed in the local cricket pitch. Thomas was not home, and nor had they had word of him.

"Which is good news," his parents said. "Had he been killed, we would have received the dreaded telegram." So Beresford felt proud that they harboured their worry with such fortitude.

He let pass with much empathy the incoming news that the Japanese lost their entire convoy in a major battle north of the Solomon Islands; also that Yamamoto, Chief of the Imperial Japanese Navy, was shot down in flames over the Solomon Islands; and of American marines landing in Bougainville—the start of their relentless march northwards.

~ * ~

Beresford Branson's invitation to Francoise, Gaston and Pascal to visit his parents should they be successful in their quest in England had indeed been accepted. The three had visited and been thanked for their help to him, with heartfelt welcomes.

The three Frenchies had left him a message:

> *Dear friend,*
> *You asked us to let you know if successful in our quest.*
> *We indeed were, and soon depart to achieve our goals.*
> *We are desperately in need of help and plead your support.*
> *May we succeed in both those quests, and also in seeing you again.*
>
> *Much love,*
> *Francoise, Gaston, Pascal*
> *9th January 1943*

Author's Note

For readers of nationalities other than Australian, it will likely prove helpful if the strange name of the coast-watchers' 'office' in Honiara is explained.

The Dog on the Tuckerbox is an Australian icon—a tribute to the early pioneers' 'best friend'.

Try typing just that name into your favourite search engine.

Meet

Kev Richardson

Following a career in business management at international level, Kev attained a degree in journalism to spend ten years travelling the world writing articles for airline and travel magazines—so he's had many adventures to pepper his adventure tales.

A sixth-generation descendant from Australia's First Fleet with an obsessive interest in his country's founding, he discovered how the true history had, over several generations, been suppressed—the people were never to know! Years of fact-finding revealed all, and Kev writes fictions around the true history. His qualifications are extensive; he is a Past President of *The First Fleet Fellowship* and a Past Secretary of *The Descendants of Convicts Inc.* For his work during Australia's 1988 Bicentenary he was created Honorary Life Member of *The Regiment of Redcoat Descendants.* He has delivered papers on the subject in Australia, New Zealand, Great Britain and in his retired abode, Thailand.

He writes, apart from his country's convict history, adventure fiction with an Australian flavour, as well as biographies on significant people—including an exciting part of his own life. He recognises the increasing trend for digital reading so all works are published both as traditional paperbacks and the economical eBook.

Works From The Pen Of Kev Richardson

The Letitia Munro Series

Letitia Munro - A true tale of Australia's first white settlement. In witless ignorance, convicts transform the world's biggest prison into a land of free enterprise and pride.

To Plough Van Diemen's Land - Second of the Letitia Munro trilogy. Children of convicts spawn a new ethos. Learning from hard knocks, many convert empty pockets into acres of sheep. Taboos emerge in the nation's spawning culture.

The Terrible Truths - Third of the *Letitia Munro* trilogy, children and grandchildren are must hide the truths of their heritage as society values change. Australia emerges as a veritable beehive of mines as minerals of every description begin showering riches on the land.

The Brogan Series

Brogan - Life on Australia's desert edge. Brogan, born in the drifting sands of the far outback, exemplifies the blood-and-guts characteristics by which Aussies are recognised even today.

Brogan's Bust - Flying a courier service in Amazonian jungles where graft and corruption make mockery of the law, Brogan finds backstabbing among cartel middlemen can turn a hiccup into a stumble that generates into a fall, beginning a slide that snowballs into an avalanche.

Brogan's Bella - Isabella and Brogan are victims in a deadly hijack. A carefree journey becomes a nightmare of death and terror. A year of incarceration and intimidation finds them facing the cutting of their very throats for even knowing the truths behind the hijack.

Misadventure - Brogan is off on a spine-tingling adventure in South America. He and his Becky hadn't counted on FARC taking hostages, military coups and drug-smuggling. This tale will really keep you turning pages.

Brogan Abroad - Brogan is embroiled in three simultaneous adventures. He plans none yet finds each destines him to having his throat slit in some dark alley. *Yet what can a man do,* he laments, *when to accomplish one I must fail at another?*

A Family Series

Faith and Frenzy - Religion is shattered as families opt to support this or that faith in England's Civil Wars. Peace and Order are themselves ripped into frenzied shreds as faith in God is torn asunder.

Gerard Rawes - Gerard's life is transformed from rags to riches. In England's eighteenth century, the emerging industrial revolution catapults him out of his world of serfdom into London's elite.

An Epic Life - True tale of reaching across the world to fulfil dreams—a major achievement in the nineteenth century. Two couples whisk their very lives into a froth-and-bubble existence to create, on the far side of the world, a dynasty.

***A Welcome War* (*Finalist in the EPIC Awards 2011!*)**
- WW2 was the most welcome and alluring war of all time. A ten-year-old lad becomes influenced more by military strategy, political power, and bathos than by parents or mentors. "In learning about life, it beats schoolwork, hands down!"

Beresford Branson Series

Pacific Paradox - A British son is banished to the South Pacific to learn responsibility. Suffering hunger and kidnap, he is working in Guadalcanal when Japan invades.

***My Red Cross* (*First ever 10 Star Award from Conger Book Reviews !*)** - A Red Cross agent in France during German occupation faces intimidation, fear, love, hate and pleas for help. He is trying to be Father Christmas, Jesus Christ and everybody's parent, yet has little to give but hope.

***A German Stirring* (*Second 10 Star Award!*)** - Deprivation in occupied Germany immediately after WW2 seems greater than that in most occupied countries during the war. Are the Allied victors guilty as charged, of major malpractices?

Beresford at Bay - At the end of World war II, the *Allied Control Council* is given leave to decide on the rebuilding of Germany. Political infighting however, makes headway difficult as the Big 3 trip and stumble over each other's feet. Beresford looks to a future of his choosing.

Independent Romance Novels

A Home for Old Ladies - The love story of a couple renewing life for a derelict home for old ladies—their inspiration, satisfying the ghosts of its former denizens—a true labour of love by lovers.

Summy Lu - The gripping tale of the ingenuity of one woman who survived in a time when war's influence was tearing families apart.

Turtle Island - Ever been pampered by a little luxury? The world's most exotic picturesque island attracts not only the rich and famous but all who can afford being spoiled rotten!

Independent Adventure Novels

What If? *Had Hitler not invaded Russia, WW II would have changed the entire globe!* - With an unready Britain prime for invasion, why force the colossus Russia to change sides? Opening a second front was Hitler's undoing.

***A Soul Forsaken* (*EPIC Award Winner– Finalist, 2016*)** - Abandoned by his own country, a victim of an antiquated law faces a hopeless future—even denied self-respect. A 'Boy Scout' sets out to relieve the distressed fellow's dilemma.

Connor's Cabal - A journalist's assignment in Thailand creates bedlam when his young tour-guide is kidnapped. Despite a four day deadline to avoid a death threat, even the police refuse action!

**Shadows** - A tremendously exciting tale of the French Resistance during the German Occupation in World War II. Featuring every sense, it grabs you to strike fear, love, hate, terror and glee into all Resistants every day in their lives as they plot to upset Occupation demands.

A must read for every soul with a spunky beat in their heart.

Soul of Australia Series

**Gurrewa** - The story of Australia's white settlement. It empties the vacuum cleaner with which modern Australians are at last cleaning under the carpet where for generations, the dust of truth was swept.

**Son of Gurrewa** - The sorry hand of fate most time visits only hardship on a developing community, yet occasionally, some pawns in the game of life find Lady Luck lends a hand. The odds for Adam fall a little each way.

**Dreamtime Drift** - Australian Aborigines find their very ethnicity being torn asunder again, as the city of Brisbane is founded as a Convict Prison for Second Offenders.

Memoir

**Positive Paradox** - A farewell life story of one turned author in his sixtieth year, every one of his twenty-six WingsePress novels earning Five-Star awards and even more, from recognized reviewers.

Letter to Our Readers

Enjoy this book?

You can make a difference

As an independent publisher, Wings ePress, Inc. does not have the financial clout of the large New York Publishers. We can't afford large magazine spreads or subway posters to tell people about our quality books.

But, we do have something much more effective and powerful than ads. We have a large base of loyal readers.

Honest Reviews help bring the attention of new readers to our books.

If you enjoyed this book, we would appreciate it if you would spend a few minutes posting a review on the site where you purchased this book or on the Wings ePress, Inc. webpages at: https://wingsepress. com/